OUT FOR BLOOD

OUT FOR BLOOD

BLOOD VICE BOOK EIGHT

ANGELA ROQUET

VIOLENT SIREN PRESS

OUT FOR BLOOD

Copyright © 2020 by Angela Roquet

All rights reserved.

This is a work of fiction. Names, characters, places, and incidents either are the product of the author's imagination or are used fictitiously. Any resemblance to actual events or locales or persons, living or dead, is entirely coincidental.

The scanning, uploading, and distribution of this book via the internet or any other means without the permission of the author is illegal and punishable by law. Please purchase only authorized printed or electronic editions and do not participate in or encourage electronic piracy of copyrighted materials. Your support of the author's rights is appreciated.

Cover Design by Rebecca Frank of Bewitching Book Covers

Edited by Chelle Olson of Literally Addicted to Detail

www.angelaroquet.com

ISBN: 978-1-951603-03-8

For Paul and Xavier,

who make my world go round.

Chapter One

At some point in nearly every girl's youth, she fantasizes about being a princess. She dresses up as Cinderella for Halloween or has a royal-themed birthday party. She beams at pet names like *Daddy's little princess*. Competes in pageants or campaigns for a homecoming crown in high school.

Sure, it's a tired cliché. But that doesn't seem to matter to millions of girls the world over. The animated princess movies keep rolling out, and the costumes and tiaras continue to sell. If they knew what being a princess was really like, it would reduce most of them to tears. If they knew what being a *vampire* princess was like, they'd run screaming.

Vampire princess. Before my rude initiation into undead society, the only place I would have found such a title acceptable was on the package of a cheap, all-in-one costume kit. The kind that filled the seasonal aisles of grocery stores around Halloween. I never expected the title to apply to *me*, or that it would weigh so heavily on my heart.

I stood as still as a gargoyle in the Blood Authority Training Center—BATC—war room, doing my best to pay attention to Dante's discussion with the Blood Vice generals and council representatives seated around the massive table. Ursula had excused herself hours ago. I was beginning to regret not slipping out with her, but I was too invested now. Too curious and equally terrified.

Dante sat at the head of the table. I had a perfect view of him from my corner behind Ursula's empty seat. Even as the new unofficial Princess of House Lilith, I didn't feel right about inserting myself between centuries-old vampires to discuss war. A vampling's input would mean nothing to them. *Less* than nothing.

Tonight, I was here to listen and learn. To be an extra pair of eyes and ears for Ursula. Eventually, my sire would want to be brought up to speed, and she'd appreciate the quick and dirty version of the truth over the curated notes that Dante was likely to sugarcoat.

We had far more questions than answers, and after Kassandra's betrayal, it was hard not to suspect that our enemies had infiltrated the Vampiric High Council, as well. What other households had the Free Blooders wormed their way into?

I tried to hide my cynicism behind a bored façade and studied those present in the war room—the BATC sergeants presiding over the three training programs. Kai Natani, the base's academic director. Four members of the council— Lord Carter, Lord McCoy, Lady Peyroux, and Lord Sorano. Dr. Marquis, the dean of Renfield Academy. Only two faces at the table were unfamiliar to me.

Lord Starling had sent his eldest scion, Ambrose, to the meeting in his place. He reminded me of Sonja with his wild curls and dark, piercing eyes that absorbed everything. Ambrose was older than his late niece by at least a few centuries, but his youthful face made me place his time of death somewhere around his twentieth birthday. The morsel of dry humor in his expression was also reminiscent of Sonja, though he remained silent throughout the meeting. I hadn't made up my mind yet whether I trusted him.

Vampiric family trees weren't much different from mortal ones—they all had their fair share of bad apples and nuts.

The second unfamiliar face sat to Dante's left. Notah Álvarez, alpha of the largest pack in St. Louis, and the American Alpha Association's Midwest representative. I'd never met the man before, but Mandy had helped find his daughter last year after the girl was abducted and buried alive.

Notah was twice Dante's size, with long, dark hair and proud features that spoke to his Mexican and Navajo heritage. He wore a necklace of animal teeth and turquoise over his suede dress shirt.

"The Moreau Pack has always been outliers," he said, addressing the council's concerns regarding which werewolves could be trusted to assist Blood Vice. "When Marcel began attending alpha conferences, I knew he was up to no good."

"And yet, you did nothing," Lord McCoy interjected. I couldn't decide if the statement was more question or accusation. Notah didn't seem to take offense. Everyone had mostly moved beyond the blame game and were now well into brainstorming counterattack strategies.

"I kept a careful eye on the Midwest packs Marcel attempted to endear himself to," Notah said. "The Raymores in Kansas City, and the Rosco Pack in Denver are among those I've maintained tabs on—although given Marcel's recent attacks, I fear he relies on covert agents to carry out the worst of his dirty work."

"Yes," Dante agreed. "His public associates are sloppy henchmen, serving only to distract from larger threats."

Sloppy or not, there was power in numbers. The firefight that had gone down at the Hearty Harem warehouse had proven that much. And the threat had felt plenty significant when the building caved in on top of Mandy and me. Still, I tried not to take Dante's words personally.

Lili and Alexander were dead. The attack that had claimed their immortal lives and destroyed the queen's manor in Evergreen was clearly the larger threat.

Dante had felt the prince's death the night of Laura's wedding, when he'd inherited the Eye of Blood. Then the captain of the Blood Vice division in Denver had called with the rest of the horrific news. What was left of the queen's blood harem and staff were crowded inside the BATC infirmary and spare barracks.

All the pride and prestige that had inflated my ego after uncovering Arnie Moreau's harem food service bomb scheme disappeared. Sucked straight out of my soul until only the bitter throb of failure remained. The evidence had been there, plain as day. And like every day since my death, I had missed it entirely.

Bart Haulette, the patsy Arnie had used to conduct his terrorist plans, had human roots in Denver but no pack ties. Yet he'd been making regular trips to the Mile High City, confirmed by his girlfriend who'd worked at the Nightfall Opera House.

Instead of another harem food service, Haulette had set up a housekeeping business in Denver under a stolen vampire identity. He'd established employment with the royal family months prior to the incident in St. Louis, and by the time the bomb at the queen's manor went off, Haulette's people were long gone, their base of operations vacated and bleached clean.

We had nothing. And this meeting was getting us nowhere.

Notah's brow creased. "However trivial a role the other packs play, Marcel's drafting methods are…concerning. He's distributing dangerous new drugs, and I have it on good authority that he was a catalyst to the Raymore alpha's death. It's how Marcel assumed de facto control over their pack—"

"That's hardly surprising," Lord Sorano said. "But we are not here to discuss retribution for a slain traitor."

Vanessa's grandsire looked down his bony nose at Notah as if he hated sharing the table with a werewolf even more than sharing the room with a vampling. Any time he spoke, my pulse quivered in my throat. He'd spared me a fleeting scowl upon his arrival but had avoided making eye contact since. I was glad for it.

"No, of course not." Notah ignored Lord Sorano's dour expression and directed his reply at Dante. "But it may be useful to know Marcel's intentions. You're familiar with Spero Heights?"

Dante nodded but then took notice of the confused faces scattered around the table. "A small, supernatural community in the Ozarks," he explained.

It was a bare-bones definition, but I imagined he wasn't eager to expose any more information about Spero Heights than absolutely necessary. The secretive nature of the town made it clear to me that they harbored fugitives. Dante was surely aware. It made me wonder what secrets he might have hidden there, as well.

Graham Pierce, the mayor of Spero Heights, was a former Blood Vice agent and a personal friend of the duke's. That was the only reason Roman and I had been granted safe passage for our investigation last year.

The town was protected not only by its near impassable mountain roads prone to flooding and landslides, but also by the creatures who inhabited the forest encircling the plateau the town had been built upon. The Eye of Blood had only given me a glimpse of them on the ride up. It had been more than enough. Especially after the resident poltergeist rolled out the welcome wagon.

"They are small in *numbers*, perhaps," Notah said with a cautious frown. "When Devin Raymore's pregnant mate sought asylum in Spero Heights, Marcel hired witches to assist him in retrieving her."

"Witches?" Sergeant Carmichael's nose crinkled. She and Notah were the only wolves in the war room—along with eight vampires and two half-sired humans—though being a fellow shifter didn't appear to earn the alpha any brownie points with her. "You expect us to squirm over a few magic dabblers?"

Notah opened his hands and laid them palms-up on the table. "I expect you to examine this information and consider the possibility that if Marcel is willing to work with witches, he might also be consorting with other shifters—or worse, the fay. We must exercise caution."

An involuntary shiver rocked my shoulders as I again thought of the forest creatures. It had been a feat to wrap my brain around vampires and werewolves and ghosts. I wasn't ready to graduate to witches and fairies and whatever the hell else was out there.

"We are not without our own wild cards." Dante's eyes flicked to me.

I could guess who he had in mind. But Dr. Delph, Spero Heights' psychic therapist, wasn't exactly what I would call a *wild* anything. He was more of a faded, dog-eared tarot card. If we brought someone like him into this battle, sure, he'd be able to read the enemy's mind—right before they bashed in his head.

"These witches killed Raymore's mate," Notah said. "Then they carved the pups from her belly." He paused at Carmichael's sharp intake of breath before continuing. "Word is, Spero Heights' new pack showed up to even the score. They're very loyal to those they offer refuge."

"And the pups?" Carmichael asked.

"Unaccounted for, though some suspect one of the Raymore deserters delivered them to Spero Heights for safekeeping. The pack has yet to announce a new leader," Notah added. "The Raymore namesake is nearly extinct, but Marcel has promised to help them…*reclaim* Devin's twin heirs in exchange for the pack's allegiance to the Free Blooders.

Whether they intend to groom one of the pups to become alpha or to tie up loose ends before assigning a new head family is still unclear."

At the mention of twins, I thought of Selena Chase and the pair of car seats I'd spotted in her truck. If I had babies in need of serious protection, I could think of no one better for the job than the she-wolf Roman and I had met in Spero Heights. She was fierce. Just recalling the acid in her gaze cued sweat to rise on the back of my neck.

Now *she* was a wild card. Not that Selena would give two shits about our cause. And I was certain she wouldn't abandon her post in Spero Heights or the babes under her care. If only Marcel had promised the Raymores that he'd tangle with her first instead of us. Maybe we'd be spared the trouble of dealing with him at all.

Lord Sorano cleared his throat, drawing the table's attention once again. "We should seek out these lost heirs to secure the Raymore Pack's loyalty."

"For shame, William." Lady Peyroux shook her head. "You would have us stoop to their level? We, the ambassadors of order and civility among our people?"

"What do you know of war, Louise?" Lord Sorano's gaze snapped to the dainty French vamp at the opposite end of the table. "Your toxic flowers notwithstanding, perhaps these unsavory endeavors are best left to those with the stomachs to carry them out."

"Tread carefully, my lord." Lady Peyroux's eyes narrowed. "Your empire relies upon my *toxic flowers*."

"I believe you have that backwards, fair lady."

"As backwards as your toupee?" she countered with a venomous smile that I rather admired.

"Enough." Dante ended the spat with a slash of his hand. "The pups will remain where they are—wherever that is. If Raymore loyalty is so easily shifted, it is not worth our time or energy. Besides, we have Marcel's brother."

After news of the attack in Evergreen reached the council representatives escorting Arnie Moreau to Denver, they'd gone straight to the Blood Authority Training Center hidden under the airport. It was the most secure location for a prisoner who could communicate telepathically with his sinister alpha brother.

The bat cave was also the safest place for House Lilith now that the Free Blooders had a taste for our blood. Regardless, being here made me feel like a coward. I was just thankful the council had been the ones to request the meeting venue. Apparently, being in close proximity to a member of the royal family right now wasn't considered good for one's health.

"We are back to the drawing board, then." Lord Sorano sighed and pinched the bridge of his nose.

As much as he unnerved me, I found his frustration relatable. I was ready to get out of here and do something useful. And if nothing constructive could be done, I was happy to take up space somewhere else. *Anywhere* else.

Dr. Marquis, the half-sired dean of Renfield Academy, folded his hands over the table. "If I may, Your Highness?" he asked Dante.

The new title of prince wasn't yet official, but everyone had adopted it anyway as if to win over Dante. Except for me. I could see how much the idea of taking his sire's place wounded him. The way the lines in his face deepened at every reminder.

"Yes, Dr. Marquis," Dante said, nodding his consent.

"Every werewolf at Renfield Academy has taken leave from training in order to aid in the St. Louis search," Dr. Marquis announced.

"Same for the werewolf cadets here on base," added Sergeant Carmichael. "They're assisting in the Denver sweep."

"So what?" Lord Sorano threw up his hands. "You expect us to sit and stay like good little dogs? You forget who you are dealing with."

"We will carry on as is expected of us," Dante said. "Beginning with the Imbolc celebration tomorrow night."

"Do you think that wise, Your Highness?" Lady Peyroux asked, a gentle note entering her voice.

I'd posed the same question to Dante before the meeting. His reply had not changed, but he delivered it with more conviction this time.

"We must present a strong front and not let our enemies take more from us than they already have."

"This attack *must* be countered," Lord Sorano insisted.

"And it will be." Dante pressed his lips together and drew in a long breath through his nose. "But as Lady Peyroux said, we are the ambassadors of order and civility. Our traditions and ceremonies are the cornerstones of that order. We will not sacrifice them on the altar of wrath."

But wrath boiled in all our veins, and no amount of pomp and circumstance could soothe it for long. I just prayed that the time Dante was buying would yield something useful that might point us in the right direction.

Chapter Two

When the meeting in the war room finally adjourned, I lingered, hoping to have a moment alone with Dante. I hadn't seen much of him over the past few nights—ever since we'd arrived in Denver, really. He came to bed right before dawn and was up and back to work as soon as the sun set.

I couldn't shake the feeling that there was more to his silent treatment than all the important people demanding his attention. Was this his way of grieving? Or did he blame me for what had happened to Alexander and Lili? Was I as useless in his eyes as I now felt? The fear settled like a chill in my bones.

"Could I have a word with you, Owen?" Dante said as I neared his end of the table. Our eyes met briefly, but then he looked away as if he hadn't seen the hurt in my gaze.

"Of course, Your Highness." Lord McCoy bowed before resting his hands on the back of Notah's vacated chair.

Dante's rejection felt more blatant each time he dismissed me. I hugged myself and hurried from the room, eager to find somewhere private to lick my wounds. Instead, I ran headlong into someone waiting in the hall.

"I'm so sorry—" I blurted before realizing who it was.

"Your Grace." Roman bowed, flashing his head of close-cropped, white hair. His tone was surprisingly earnest. Or, at least, it lacked the scathing resentment I'd expected. Still, I bristled in his presence.

As much as Dante had been avoiding me, I was sure I'd invested twice as much effort to evade my ex stationed at the bat cave.

"Agent Kni—*Sorano*," I replied, remembering that he had a new name now, too. Then I sidestepped around him and continued on my way.

I watched Roman turn in my peripheral, his stare following my movements down the corridor. The close quarters tightened the breath in my lungs, but something else in my chest relaxed as I realized that I didn't feel him in my blood. Not the way I had the last time our paths had crossed.

Our bond was fading. Maybe it was gone altogether.

"I owe you an apology, Jenna," Roman said before I reached the end of the hall.

I paused and considered the exit. For all my want of action and resolution, emotional rifts terrified me. Some things couldn't be solved with gunpowder and a badge. And those seemed to be the only tools I was any good with.

What would a princess do?

I'd been asking myself that question ever since Ursula had burdened me with the revelation that I was to ascend. *Me,* who couldn't hack it as a mortal detective nor as a Blood Vice agent. Yet I was somehow supposed to suck it up and play

Princess of the Damned now. It was time to dig deep and find more than I was sure I had to give.

My jaw clenched, but I turned around to face Roman. "Let's just chalk it up to the blood bond and move past it, shall we?" I said, offering him a strained smile that hurt my face with its insincerity.

"A blood bond is no excuse for the way I treated you." Roman swallowed, and his ice-blue eyes glazed over. The sight pulled a startled breath from me. I didn't know what to say to him, but if he started crying, this would get awkward. Well, *more* awkward than it already was. "I am truly sorry, Jenna."

"It's fine, really—"

"No." Roman shook his head. "No, it's not. You deserved better, and now you have it. I'm happy for you," he added at my skeptical frown.

"Thanks," I said, not sure how else to respond. "I'm…happy for you, too."

"I'm not courting Vanessa." His shoulders sagged. "I never was."

"I don't care what you want to call it." My tone shifted before I could rein in my annoyance. Apologies meant nothing if followed by lies. I paused to take a steadying breath before continuing. "Anyway, I was referring to your fully-sired status. You're a vampire now. Isn't that what you wanted?"

"It was." Roman's tormented features slipped under a blank mask as his focus migrated over my shoulder. "Thank you, Your Grace." He bowed stiffly, turned, and headed off down the hall.

I blinked after him, wondering what I'd said to change his demeanor. Then Lord Sorano's brittle laughter sent a jolt through me. I spun around and found him standing much too close. The invasion of my personal space sent me back a step.

"Still meddling in my household, vampling?" Lord Sorano inched closer, but I refused to give up any more ground. Ursula had schooled me well in the *refined* intimidation techniques the aged vampire lords and ladies liked to employ.

"I'd hardly call polite small talk meddling," I said, mindful of the way I worded my reply. If I lost my temper and uttered a direct insult, I didn't think it beneath him to challenge me to a blood duel. Current circumstances be damned.

"Vanessa briefed me on your and Roman's trip to Spero Heights." Lord Sorano's lips twisted into a knowing smirk as my face warmed at memories of the hotel room I'd defiled with his great-grandscion. The images flooded my mind against my will, permanently entwined with my one and only visit to the strange town.

"We were there to follow a lead on a case," I said, begging my inner sailor to keep things civil.

My last *official* assignment with Blood Vice had concluded with Ursula's capture, Roman's mortal death, and a house arrest sentence to be carried out at Dante's manor since he'd burned my home to the ground. More memories I did not care to revisit.

"I'm well aware of what you were *supposed* to be doing in that hellhole for degenerates," Lord Sorano said. He rolled his eyes and clasped his hands behind his back. "As I mentioned, I was briefed. What I'd like to know is if, while you were honeymooning with a blood servant pledged to my house, you happened to spy these twin babes the Midwest alpha spoke of?"

"No, I didn't." A frown tightened the corners of my mouth.

Lord Sorano pushed in closer until I had to crane my neck to maintain eye contact. "You do realize that lying to a member of the Vampiric High Council is a punishable crime, do you not, vampling?"

"Are you calling me a liar, Lord Sorano?"

"Simply ensuring that you're conscious of the severity of breaking our laws. Not all transgressions are as forgivable as you've been led to believe, no matter who you're…*friendly* with."

His ass was clearly chapped about Vanessa jumping the gun and forfeiting her house's right to legal retaliation—by making and then withdrawing her demand for a blood duel—over my so-called theft of Roman's blood. That Roman was half-sired made the misdeed that much more serious.

I still had my head and my freedom, which meant I'd gotten off easy. And everyone thought it was because I'd been shacking up with the duke. I hadn't been at the time, but now that I was, the rumor had graduated to common knowledge. Which chapped *my* ass.

Regardless, Lord Sorano would have to work harder than that to provoke an outburst from me. I ground my teeth and held firm to my neutral expression. Giving his hairline a pointed look seemed to help, too.

"Careful, my lord. If we spend much more time chitchatting, people might start to think *you're* friendly with me."

He snorted at the innuendo. "Then I shall get to the point. There was mention of a man you interviewed—Benjamin Macaulay—noted as Selena Chase's childcare provider in your case file." Sharp eye teeth peeked from between his parted lips. They were extended ever so slightly, but I wasn't sure if that was their natural state or if he was getting off on harassing me.

"There were no children in Macaulay's store when we questioned him," I said evenly. "And none present when we spoke with Chase. So, as I said before, no, I didn't see any pups. Not that it matters. Even if Raymore's twins *are* in Spero Heights, Dante said they're to remain there."

"For now." Lord Sorano tilted his chin and straightened the folds of his jacket. "But if your new prince does not retaliate in a timely manner, the council will be forced to reexamine the many options he's vetoed. Every passing moment of inaction makes us appear weaker and bolsters our enemies."

"Why tell me this?" I finally snapped. "I'm just a vampling—as you so frequently like to remind me."

"While that is true, and I have found your behavior *beyond* insulting to my house…" Lord Sorano's entire face seemed to pucker as if he couldn't believe what he was about to confess. "Perhaps a little vampling impulsiveness is precisely what we need right now."

Was that a compliment? I couldn't decide. The council rarely had anything nice to say where I was concerned. It was also entirely possible that the flattery was just a bit of extra rope to hang myself with. Before the shock had time to dissipate, Lord Sorano stalked off, leaving me speechless and alone in the dark hallway—alone except for Vanessa lurking around the corner.

House Sorano really had it in for me tonight.

"Trying to catch flies, Your Grace?" she asked at my slack-jawed expression.

There was the scathing resentment I'd been counting on.

Vanessa folded her arms and leaned against the doorframe of the exit, blocking my escape. I gave her black fatigues a once-over. The look was a far cry from the designer suits she'd sported as captain of Blood Vice's St. Louis field office. A ragged braid hung over one shoulder, and her face was clean of makeup. It made her look ten years younger, which was why I supposed she'd caked it on out among the humans.

"Are you spying on *me* or Daddy Long Fangs?" I asked.

"My scion, actually." Vanessa's unpolished pout twisted into a sneer. "I knew it was only a matter of time before he sought you out."

I shrugged. "So long as you know Roman approached me and not the other way around."

"No, of course not. I'm amazed you even remember his name after such a *regal* rebound."

"There was nothing to rebound from, Vanessa."

"Like I care," she hissed and pushed off the concrete wall to scowl down at me from her full height.

For not caring, she sure was salty.

"It was an honest mistake. The lifeblood bond was…intense." I sucked in my bottom lip and tried to ignore the images that Lord Sorano had forced to the surface of my mind once already tonight. "I was a sireless vampling, and Roman was only human," I said. "Neither of us were equipped to resist the bond. But it's over now."

"Oh, naïve little green fang."

"No." I locked my gaze on hers and steeled my voice. "The bond has run its course. There's no trace of Roman left in my blood. When I see him…I feel nothing."

Something I took for relief crept into Vanessa's expression, but it was gone too soon to be certain, washed away by sadness. And then her tough-as-coffin-nails glare was back in place.

"The blood bond may be broken"—her voice dropped to a lethal whisper, and she stepped in closer—"but you and I both know that's not what afflicts my scion." Vanessa's pupils dilated, eating away at the vibrant green irises that gave her an otherworldly appearance no matter how she was dressed or made up. It caused my breath to catch in my throat.

Just when I thought she might haul off and sucker punch me, Vanessa turned on her heels and marched off, her bootsteps echoing down the long hall.

Chapter Three

After surviving the rapid-fire encounters with House Sorano, I could have used a stiff drink. Since being undead meant I was permanently on that wagon—unless I could find a donor willing to tie one on for me—I instead decided to further test my luck by braving a visit to the senior werewolf barracks.

While the BATC's primary goal was to train field agents for Blood Vice, they also housed a small army of their own for catastrophic emergencies like the one we were currently in the middle of. In addition, they safeguarded the extensive collection of vampiric texts and private records kept on base.

Those who lived at the bat cave full time were separated into three groups, same as the cadets: vampires, werewolves, and humans. The segregation wasn't meant to foster ill will between species. It was merely for convenience. The vampires required a harem and kept odd hours. Most of the humans were half-sired and pledged to a noble household—a dream that could be obliterated with nothing more than an accidental scratch from a werewolf. The humans and wolves shared a cafeteria but kept to themselves for the most part.

The senior werewolf barracks also housed a few holding cells for moon fever, a condition triggered when a werewolf cadet was pushed too hard or went stir-crazy and shifted involuntarily. The forced nature of the shift tended to scramble their brains, sending them on a Wolfman-esque rampage unless they could be contained in time.

The cellblock was sectioned off from the rest of the building. It had a single exterior door flanked by two guards. A third sentry waited inside, slouched in a folding chair at the far end of a long hall, reading a tattered paperback.

Six steel doors were spaced between wide panes of thick, one-way glass. The windows were all dark save for the one I found Mandy propped against, elbows resting on the high sill. She wore her catsuit guard uniform but had forgone the red cape in favor of a cropped leather jacket.

Ursula had been too distracted by recent events to bother micromanaging my wardrobe, so I'd gotten away with my business casual attire—mostly dark slacks and blazers that fit well over my firearms. With my hair swept back in a low ponytail, I looked every bit the detective I'd been just before my death.

Mandy's pained scowl was laser-focused on the occupant of the cell in front of her.

"Thought I might find you here," I said.

She grunted in reply but didn't glance up. She'd hardly taken her eyes off Arnie Moreau since we'd arrived at the bat cave. I, on the other hand, couldn't stand the sight of him. My guts tightened as I turned my stare to the window.

Arnie sat in the middle of the floor, stuffing handfuls of

some noodle and hamburger casserole into his mouth. A silver collar encircled his neck. The thick chain attached to it was anchored to the back wall of his cell.

Arnie's meals were laced with a drug meant to keep him from shifting, but the collar was an extra failsafe. If he tried to shift, it would put him in a chokehold that rendered him unconscious. If he managed to break the collar, a sensor in the restraint would cue the room to fill with wolfsbane gas. It wouldn't kill him, but he'd be out of commission for several hours.

He wasn't going anywhere. We had him. So why did it feel like he'd won?

"They get anything new out of him yet?" I asked Mandy.

"No." The skin between her eyebrows puckered, and a soft growl stirred in her throat. "If they'd just give me five minutes alone with the bastard…"

"Preaching to the choir, sis."

I wanted to hurt Arnie just as badly as Mandy did, but from the looks of it, the BATC interrogators had already done quite a number on him. Purple bruises dotted his chest and jawline, and though he'd been in custody for less than a week, I could count his ribs.

The reduced sustenance had slowed his supernaturally fast healing. He looked pitiful, but I couldn't bring myself to feel sorry for him. Not when I thought of all the people he had killed. All those who might still die if we didn't break him soon.

There had been plenty of times I'd wanted to take the law into my own hands as a patrol officer. To inflict violence on the mortal monsters I'd once thought were the worst the world had to offer. In my opinion, serial killers and pedophiles didn't deserve humane treatment. But I'd played by the book and let the legal system deliver their sanctioned version of justice instead.

During my training at the bat cave, I'd balked at the more extreme punishments for breaking laws outlined in the Blood Decree. Some of the rules didn't sit well with me. Vampiric justice was certainly an acquired taste, but I found myself appreciating it more and more. I wanted to blame it on the bloodlust that had come with joining the ranks of the undead, but that was a cheap excuse.

This immortal life was not a right. It was a privilege. The vampires who had been *properly* turned understood that. I'd taken a little longer to come around, to appreciate that we had the potential to inflict so much more harm—not just on humans but also on our kind. On our entire species if we weren't *very* careful.

Arnie had tried to exact that kind of damage. He'd sacrificed his men as well as dozens of Blood Vice agents in his attempt to avoid capture. Before that, he'd raped and turned countless human girls against their will at the Scarlett Inn. I felt no remorse for the torture he'd endured while in custody. It would never be enough to balance his moral debt.

"How's the new queen bee holding up?" Mandy asked, her cold gaze still zeroed in on our prisoner. At my deep sigh, she added, "That well, huh?"

After a major upset, I'd grown accustomed to finding Ursula in a fevered outrage. Her particular brand of catharsis was destroying fine china and delicate baubles. Or at least, it had been.

"Ursula seems to be a little…catatonic lately."

"So, not smashing everything in sight then?"

"It's weird, right?" I folded my arms and shot a sideways glance at the viewing window.

Arnie had finished eating and was now *relieving* himself in a corner. His dark urine streamed toward the drain in the center of the room. Even though his back was to us and he couldn't see through the one-way glass, I diverted my gaze. Watching just felt too depraved.

I couldn't smell anything, but Mandy's nose crinkled, and the guard at the far end of the hallway stood, stretching his arms over his head.

"We'll hose him down after the meds have had time to take," he said.

I pressed my lips together and dipped my chin in response, thankful for my underwhelming sense of smell.

"Ursula holding her shit together is probably the only thing keeping Audrey from losing hers," Mandy said, picking right back up where our conversation had left off. "Levi is teetering on the edge of sanity, too."

"Well, that's just perfect." I threw up my hands. "If he does anything stupid, I'll be the one who gets blamed for it. I handpicked him from Renfield, and I'm already on thin ice with Dante—"

"*Chillax.*" Mandy groaned and finally looked at me. "Levi wants to see Audrey turned more than anyone. She'll be harder to kill and easier to protect that way. And what do you mean *on thin ice* with Dante? You're more popular than French fries right now. If not for you, the *entire* royal family would be toast."

I swallowed and tucked my hands under my armpits again. "Or if I'd dug a little deeper, maybe I would've uncovered the plot against Lili and Alexander, too."

"Shut it," Mandy snapped. "You've more than brought home the bacon for House Lilith, and it hasn't exactly been a piece of cake. Besides, Dante's the one with fingers in all the pies. I didn't see him trying to uncover Marcel's evil scheme. Did you?"

"That's five food references in under a minute." I gave

her a tight grin. "You should probably eat something before you take a bite out of the wrong diplomat."

"No shortage of those fuckers around here," Mandy grumbled under her breath, but she nodded at my suggestion and headed for the exit. I watched her go with a worried frown. Locked up or not, being this close to Arnie wasn't good for her psyche.

When I turned back to the window, my body jolted involuntarily.

Arnie stood right behind the glass, the chain on his collar pulled taut. His nostrils flared, and then his eyes locked on mine as he sucked in a long, slow breath. I couldn't hear him, but I read his lips easily enough.

You're next, sweetheart.

Chapter Four

An hour before sunrise, I went in search of Dante. I hadn't seen him since the meeting, but the war room was now dark. Our quarters in the guest barracks were empty, too. So was the narrow street out front—save for a few wolf recruits returning from the topside Denver hunt for Marcel and the Free Blooders.

The vampire cadets were likely hitting the harem one last time, and the human trainees would be in the showers soon, preparing for a very long day. So the sound of shots echoing from the range tunnel at the opposite end of the base piqued my curiosity.

I jogged through the deserted streets that saw only foot traffic and golf carts until I reached the south side of the compound. That's where I found Dante, standing at the mouth of the range tunnel with a pistol cupped in his hands. He'd rolled up the sleeves of his dress shirt but still wore the black suit vest he'd chosen for the conference. At the sound of my footsteps, he glanced over his shoulder and grimaced.

"Am I interrupting?" I asked, unable to keep the frustration out of my voice. If he blamed me for what had happened, I wished he'd just say so and get it over with. *Rip the bandage off, already.* Then at least I could assess the damage. I'd know where we stood.

"I have spent too long behind a desk," Dante said, ignoring my question. "I fear my aim will not inspire confidence."

He laid the pistol on a table as his target floated closer, carried along on one of the rails that ran the length of the tunnel. Half a dozen holes punctured the blank space around the silhouette. The rest of the shots were nothing to write home about, but they'd at least do some damage.

"You have an army of bodyguards who get paid to worry about their marksmanship," I said, offering him a weak smile. "Don't you have enough on your plate?"

"How is the House Sorano vampling's aim?" Dante asked, turning away to unhook the target. "Did he hit *his* mark after the meeting?"

"He only wanted to apologize." A dry laugh bubbled and then died in my throat as Dante faced me again. I didn't know what to make of his reaction. Flashes of shame and rage strained beneath the fragile mask he wore for the world—a mask I thought he had vowed to lay aside when with me.

"The blood bond is broken. Completely. I swear." I reached for Dante's arm, but he recoiled from me and crumpled the spent target into a tight ball.

"It is not *just* the blood bond." His jaw flexed furiously as he searched for his next words. "I've nearly lost you too many times—and I know that you are capable and can take care of yourself—but you are not invincible. However petty it may be, I hate that when you were most in need, it was *he* who saved your life."

"With human blood that he no longer possesses. Not bullets," I said, reaching for Dante again only to have him retreat to the table.

"And if our enemies rain fire down upon us again, whom would you trust to have your back?" he asked. When I didn't answer right away, he picked up the pistol and fumbled with the magazine release.

"Let the guards do what you pay them to—"

"I could employ a million guards, and it would not matter!" Dante dropped the gun onto the table and whirled around. He closed the distance between us and gripped my shoulders. "I hate feeling so useless, relying on everyone else to protect that which is most precious to me. Knowing that *he* is the far superior candidate for the job. Knowing that the only reason he is not at your side this very moment is because of my selfish desire and wrath. I saw an opportunity to cut him out of your life, and I took it without hesitation."

"Look," I said, hooking my hands over Dante's arms, "I was smitten with Roman over a blood bond. What you and I have is *au natural*. Doesn't that count for anything? Also, if we're getting retrospective here, I'm far more grudgy with you for setting my childhood home ablaze than you going all"—I twisted my head to one side and clicked my tongue—"on a rival suitor."

"Rival suitor?" A faint grin broke Dante's scowl. "Is my archaic language rubbing off, Your Grace?"

"I can think of something better you could be rubbing *on* right now," I said, my voice dropping suggestively. The idea that his bad mood had more to do with insecurity than disappointment kindled my libido. Besides, what better way to soothe his bruised ego and my wounded pride?

The smile I'd pulled from Dante softened, as did his grip on my arms. I thought I was losing him again until he surprised me with a frantic kiss.

"I want to give you my blood," he whispered, scanning the shadows around us.

It wasn't technically illegal, but it was a taboo practice that merited discretion. The only time it was considered appropriate for a vampire to drink another vampire's blood was during certain ceremonies, and it was never more than a drop or two, for symbolic purposes only. The Eye of Blood, possessed by orphaned members of House Lilith, made blood-sharing among us so much more…*complicated.*

"You don't have to do that." I shook my head and leaned in for another kiss, but Dante pulled away with a scowl.

"You have tasted Lili and Ursula. Why does the thought of my blood offend?"

"It doesn't *offend*. God, Dante." I sighed and dropped my forehead to his chest. "You have nothing to prove to me. There's no reason for me to go digging around in your past."

"I had hoped you might offer *your* blood by now," he countered.

My head jerked up. "Trust me, you do not want to break in your birthright on my final moments as a human. Can't you ask Ursula?"

Dante's eyes swelled with horror. "She hardly survived anointing you at the ceremony last year. I would not dream of adding to her current trauma by requesting something so intimate."

"What about my trauma?" I stuck out my bottom lip. Dante nipped at it playfully and released my arms so he could wrap his around my back, pulling me to him until our hips were flush.

"My dear, it was your steadfastness in the face of such trauma that drew me to you in the first place. Your confidence and resilience."

"Not my majestic elegance and beauty?"

"You *are* beautiful," Dante said, chastising my sarcasm. "But what impresses most is that it is not simply skin-deep."

My face warmed with the compliment, but before I could thank him, he kissed me again. It was the most affection he'd shown since Laura's wedding, but who could fault him? His sire had been murdered that same night.

Despite the painful incident with Kassandra, Dante had respected and loved Alexander. He'd called the prince his blood father, a name reserved for only the most beloved sires. Dante had spent fifty years as Alexander's vampling progeny, and from what I'd heard, he'd handled being replaced by his sibling scion with grace and humility.

Seeing how he was handling Alexander's death, I could believe it. But that didn't mean Dante was devoid of grief, or that I hadn't silently struggled this past week, trying to decide if it was sorrow or disappointment that had stolen him from me.

Confidence and resilience had not been on my side through that mess. Though it was Dante's emotions I was most concerned with now.

I could handle his grief. Insecurity, too, which Dante had done a better job of spelling out for me. Though I feared he was letting both emotions do the talking now.

"Share blood with me," he whispered again, grazing his lips against mine.

"Dante…"

"Just this once," he begged. "Before Imbolc. I want you to have the first taste of my immortality. I know that must sound—"

"Okay," I said, erasing his smug grin with a kiss. Dante

knew how to push my buttons all too well. Not that I would ever admit that to his face.

I didn't envy Audrey the way I had when she first landed on our doorstep. The Southern belle from Darkly Hall was scheduled to shed her mortal life at tomorrow night's Imbolc ceremony. She would then rise as Duchess of House Lilith. Dante's scion and blood daughter—*not* his blood bride.

It had taken a while to believe that wasn't her aim. Whether my doubt was thanks to the suspicious nature common of law enforcement agents or garden-variety jealousy was anyone's guess. But my visceral reaction to the thought of being *first* with Dante made it perfectly clear that I harbored my fair share of insecurity.

Maybe that was just the nature of love, and a hundred years from now, we'd still desperately crave heartfelt affirmations from one another. The thought didn't bother me as much as I expected it should. Though as Dante's fingers laced with mine, and he tugged me away from the range tunnel back toward the guest barracks, panic stabbed at my conscience.

It wasn't just my turbulent origins that made sharing blood with Dante a bad idea.

Ursula had taken a bite out of me during one of her less *regal* episodes. I couldn't be sure what all she'd witnessed through the Eye of Blood, but she'd been hysterical. Out of her mind. I was almost positive she'd missed Mandy's cameo during the invasive recap of my death.

Dante would not.

He'd recognize the dark-haired wolf in the shadows, and he'd put the pieces together. He'd know the truth that I'd kept from him.

The exiled Baron of House Lilith had not been anyone's favorite—well, maybe Scarlett's, but she was ashes in the wind now. Kassandra, too. The explosion at the queen's manor had seen to that, since their coffin-lock sentences were being carried out in the royal dungeon where the bomb had originated.

But regardless of how unlikable Ursula's late scion had been, if the council found out that Mandy had turned him into a midnight snack, we were fucked. Untangling that secret would no doubt reveal my true sire. The curtain would be ripped away, and it would be more than Mandy and I taking the fall. The council would launch an inquisition to uncover everyone involved. Roman, Laura, Collins—no one was safe.

Dante knew Raphael was my sire, but I'd kept Mandy's involvement to myself. Would the damning evidence my blood exposed spoil his first use of the gift he'd inherited from Alexander? Could he forgive me for not trusting him with the truth before now?

The BATC staff had done their best to accommodate the royal family on base, but only a certain level of comfort could be attained in a room with concrete walls. This was not a place for pleasure. That which went in was meant to be broken and molded into something new. Something harder.

I'd never considered myself a lover of fine things, but after a few nights at the bat cave, I found myself missing the silky sheets and plush pillows of our beds at home. The colorful canvases of skyscapes hanging in brightly lit halls. The fresh, earthy air enjoyed from the back patio under a star-speckled sky.

And, most of all, Dante's eager body pressed against mine.

I could get by without the other comforts for a little while longer, just not that last one. And it seemed I would have it again soon. Unless my confession spoiled the moment.

Dante removed the elastic from my ponytail. He raked his hands through my hair and pulled my face to his, his greedy mouth devouring mine. Tonight, his desire was vulnerable, fractured by grief and need. It unnerved me, but at the same time, I was relieved to not be the only one struggling with their demons. My misery wanted his company every bit as his wanted mine.

Exchanging blood wouldn't solve all our problems, but it would undoubtedly illuminate a few things that Dante and I needed help understanding about each other. I just hoped it wouldn't change the way he felt about me, or the way I felt about him, once all the cards were on the table.

I groped Dante's arms and shoulders, my fingers finally settling over the buttons of his suit vest. He took the cue and slipped his hands under my blazer, pushing the sleeves back to expose the twin Reaper TDs in my shoulder holster.

"I thought we had bodyguards on the payroll, Your Grace," Dante whispered. The tone of his voice was only half-teasing. "Ursula would not approve."

"Ursula doesn't get to undress me." I arched an eyebrow at him.

"Point taken." He finished tugging the blazer down my arms. I removed my guns and the holster while he made short work of his vest. When I went for the buttons on my blouse, Dante's hands closed over mine. "Please, let me."

I nodded and turned my attention to the buttons on his shirt instead. My fingers trembled, making the task more difficult than it should have been. The longer I waited to say what I needed to, the more my nerves twitched with indecision. It wasn't until we were both nude and Dante had pulled me onto the bed that I finally found a fragment of courage.

"Before I give you my blood, there's something you should know," I said, reclining away from him until he looked me in the eyes. I swallowed, struggling to find the right words.

Dante stroked my cheek with the back of his hand. "Whatever secrets the eye reveals, I swear to keep. You should know that by now."

When words still failed me, he placed a tender kiss to my lips. The embrace escalated quickly, and within seconds, I was beneath him, his blissful weight settling in all the right places. My legs parted and wrapped around his, toes curling over the swells of his calves.

Dante's mouth strayed from mine, and he worked his way down my neck, lining my collarbone with kisses. I waited for some hint of teeth against my flesh but was met each time with feather-soft lips and the heat of his steady breath. My heart leapt into my throat with conflicted anticipation.

"You are shaking, Jenna." He sounded confused.

"Of course I am." My voice was barely a whisper, slipping past the lump I couldn't seem to swallow. Dante went rigid and then tried to remove himself, but I locked my arms behind his back.

"Forgive me," he begged. "What a thoughtless idiot I am."

"No! It's... Just give me a minute." I tucked my face over his shoulder to hide my panic. The blood vision was already kicking in, which was never a great sign. The walls around us throbbed red in time with my racing pulse.

I'd been bitten before. By Rafael, Scarlett, and Ursula. Each time had been painful and without my consent. And yet, the harem donors and the patrons at Bleeders seemed to get off on it. Roman and Vin had both gotten off on it.

I wasn't so naïve that I didn't see the difference—but who could blame me for being a little fang-shy?

"Do you want to go first?" Dante nuzzled his face against my cheek, using his nose to push back a lock of my blond hair. His lips found my earlobe, but he was careful not to let his teeth even so much as graze my skin. "Maybe that would help."

"Maybe," I echoed, unsure if there was *anything* that could soothe my anxiety but willing to postpone it for a few minutes at the very least. "Where should I…?"

"Wherever you'd like," he said. "It will heal by dusk."

I admired the span of smooth flesh that ran from his jawline to his broad shoulder. If Dante had been human, the Eye of Blood would have shown me the veins throbbing beneath the surface. But the eye worked differently on vampires. It was another aspect of the gift, though it was useless in this moment, serving only to paint the concrete world around us red.

"Here?" I whispered against an enticing tendon in

Dante's neck. My tongue slipped out to sample the salt of his skin, and he shivered before nodding eagerly.

"Yes, that will do nicely," he said with the faintest lisp. If I bothered with more words, I was sure to stumble over them, as well. My fangs were already at half-mast.

I thought of Roman again and felt ashamed for it. He wasn't the only one I'd mixed blood and sex with in the past, but he was the only one I'd ever felt the irrational urge to give *my* blood to.

I understood the impulse had more to do with the blood bond than anything else, but that didn't stop guilt from assaulting me now for not feeling the desire to have a similar exchange with Dante. There were other factors at play too, though. For one, I wasn't starving myself anymore. The royal family was given blood pots three times a night. Which meant I was also out of practice with the fang-to-flesh action.

Dante stirred above me, twisting his head to one side as if to offer better access. My mouth hovered over the straining tendon in his neck. I swallowed, trying to summon saliva to my tongue, left dry by my hesitation.

This should have been easier than letting him bite me, but my anxiety couldn't seem to tell the difference. Maybe because I knew that biting him would seal my fate. How could I back out of giving him my blood after taking his?

Dante shifted again, and a new fear took hold of me. If this moment passed, would it be gone forever? Would I offend him so deeply that we could never come back from it?

Before I could change my mind, I latched on to Dante's neck. My lips formed a seal, and my fangs broke flesh, drawing a small gasp from him.

Blood gushed into my mouth. It was hot and bitter. Not at all what I was used to, but I swallowed twice before extracting my teeth and rolling my tongue over the twin wounds. They were already filling in, the skin knitting itself back together.

"Does it happen right away?" Dante asked, his voice layering over Alexander's and the familiar Imbolc anthem.

"With this blood, I anoint thee mine forevermore."

Yes, I wanted to answer Dante. But when my lips parted, it was *his* voice that spilled out, emerging from the time capsule his blood had unlocked.

"I am yours to command, sire."

The room I was in looked different from the one where Ursula's blood had taken me to reveal her final anointment by Morgan. There were fewer in attendance, and they were dressed in less finery—even Lili, though her ruby and onyx crown made up for it.

Those present looked either solemn or fearful. Dante had been turned right after the Civil War. The country was in mourning and recovering. Travel was complicated for the undead even now, but it had been much more challenging by horse and carriage, especially over long distances across volatile terrain. From Ursula's lessons, I knew that many vampires had headed west after the California Gold Rush, seeking out fresh territory where they could establish new lives and roll back the clock to disguise their immortality.

I somehow doubted that the lackluster attendance was to blame for the hollow ache settling in Dante's chest. It resonated through my heart now, the nostalgic pang of loss that I knew would never fully heal.

The Eye of Blood revealed *everything*. Every sound and smell, sensation and emotion. Just as I'd experienced Ursula's joy the night of her anointment, I felt the overwhelming swell of grief and agony in Dante. The complete lack of hope.

But he carried on, following the prince's lead throughout the ceremony.

Alexander turned Lili's dagger over to a servant and then opened his hand to me—dressed in Dante's memory—and helped me stand. "Come, dear Dante. We have only just begun."

As we exited the room, Alexander palmed my shoulder. I could tell in the pinched lines of his face that he was trying to contain his excitement, and I felt the strain in Dante's countenance as he tried to summon some scrap of enthusiasm for the prince's sake.

"The Gray Ghost. Bloody Bill." Alexander scoffed. "Wartime pet names are the only taste of immortality those men will ever know. Let this world forget the role you played in their liberty. Only then will you be free to shape the future from the shadows, as I have now done for a century and a half."

"As you wish, Your Highness." Dante's voice did not crack despite the despair churning his insides. He realized this was his death march. He welcomed it, and yet, his unconscious clung to whatever survival instincts had gotten him through the war.

Alexander led Dante down a dark hall and into a bedroom. A pair of oil lamps rested on a dresser, their twin flames painting the walls gold. Dante circled the bed, and a familiar armoire came into view. The trio of mirrors on the three doors were pristine, not foggy and tarnished as I recalled them.

Dante's reflection took me by surprise. He looked…older somehow. It was more than just the facial hair that encircled his mouth. He looked tired. Worn and defeated. Not at all the man I'd first met, but maybe closer to the one he'd become since the prince's death.

He opened the armoire door and then removed his belt

and coat, hanging them inside next to a sword in a shiny scabbard, and an ancient Colt six-shooter that looked as if it could've belonged to Yosemite Sam.

On the inside of the armoire door, dangling from a small hook, was a gold pocket watch. I felt its cold weight as Dante gripped it in his hand. Sorrow stabbed at my heart again, and my eyes burned with unshed tears.

"I know this is difficult, my scion." The prince squeezed Dante's shoulder. "The war is won, but you have lost so much. And now I ask more of you—*all* of you."

"I made an oath," Dante said, releasing the pocket watch and closing the armoire door. "What is left of my life is yours."

Dante's sullen reflection in the central mirror was now joined by Alexander's. They looked like a pair of drama masks, the prince playing comedy to Dante's tragedy. Both struggling to mute their overwhelming emotions, and both failing miserably.

"Yes, your life is now mine," Alexander said, his free hand taking Dante's other shoulder. "But your death shall be your own."

The prince's fangs sank into the curve of Dante's neck, and crestfallen as Dante was, I felt an exhilarating tug in the pit of his stomach. It wasn't necessarily…*erotic*, but there was a definite thrill to the act.

I'd thought Ursula's reaction to Morgan—and Lili's reaction to Lilith—had been the result of more intimate relations, but maybe it was just how humans experienced being fed on when they weren't terrified out of their minds or being ravaged to death.

Dante enjoyed the roil of pheromones and the sensation of his blood being sucked from the vein. And he hated himself for it. For feeling any sliver of bliss. I recognized the shameful sweep of nausea that followed. I'd experienced it plenty after my mother's death, as though happiness were suddenly off-limits. Something shameful and taboo.

Alexander's eager gulping echoed in my head, and Dante's eyelids grew heavy. Soon, their reflections began to fade in the armoire mirror. And then I found myself back in the base guest barracks, pressed between Dante and the wool blanket over our bed, the sharp taste of his blood lingering on my tongue.

Chapter Five

"Are you…here?" Dante asked, worry turning up the inner corners of his eyebrows.

"Yes." I blinked a few times as my pupils adjusted to the darkness now that the lamp-lit peep show was over.

"What did you see?" Dante rolled off me and onto his side, propping his elbow on a pillow. He cradled his head in his hand and waited for my answer, eyes wide and anxious.

"From the moment you last tasted the prince's blood to the moment he drained yours," I said.

"How does it work?"

I blinked up at him. "What do you mean?"

"I mean, how do you watch the scene unfold? Are you an invisible phantom, following from room to room?"

"Dante…it's *your* blood." I couldn't believe that the queen had never detailed the gift to him. Of course, I supposed she hadn't expected so many deaths in her house to license the family legacy this soon. "I watched everything through your eyes," I said, placing a hand over Dante's chest. "I *felt* everything, too. The suffering in your heart. The prince's fangs in your flesh."

At that, he blushed and looked down. "I see."

"You mentioned an oath you made to the prince."

"Yes." Dante frowned, but I could tell he'd expected me

to have questions. It seemed an obvious reaction to sharing blood with someone who possessed the eye. "I met Alexander in December of 1863, at a holiday party hosted by my soon-to-be in-laws. I'd been granted a short furlough after my promotion to general. Taking leave from the war was a rare privilege, so the celebration also served as an engagement party."

"And how did your future in-laws know the Prince of House Lilith?" I asked.

Dante's eyes unfocused, and he was silent for a moment before answering. "I was unaware at the time, but they were a prestigious blood family."

"You mean they shipped their children off to one of those blood charm schools?" I made a face, but I was pretty sure Dante already knew how I felt about the practice.

I had to admit, the blood finishing schools weren't *all* terrible. Audrey and Levi never had anything but good things to say about Darkly Hall and Renfield Academy. But Bathory House had made my skin crawl.

"Not exactly," Dante said with a small grin. "They oversaw a finishing school of their own. Of course, it had been presented as an elite boarding school to explain their wealth. In truth, the students were mostly orphans."

"So, donate your blood or enjoy being homeless?" I sighed and rolled my eyes.

"None of the girls were ever forced to surrender their blood or to remain at the school."

"I've heard the argument before, but I don't care for it now any more than I did then."

"Is that so?" A patient smile curled the corners of Dante's mouth. "And what if I told you that the finishing schools were put into place as a means to reduce the number of underaged donors?" My eyebrows shot up, and Dante went on. "Their blood is sweeter, but drinking from young donors can be dangerous to their health. In centuries past, there were…accidents. The schools are not just for educating donors on harem etiquette or ensuring innocuous familial ties. They are intended to create a pool of highly sought-after donors who can be regulated in such a way to ensure their safety and wellbeing."

"Why?" I asked, ever the skeptic. "I've met plenty of vampires who think humans are nothing more than cattle for slaughter."

"As have I." Dante grimaced. "It is a horribly prejudiced stance, especially considering we were all human to begin with. But, even the most bigoted vampires are beholden to the Blood Decree. Laws regarding the treatment the humans we depend upon are crucial to our survival. Humans outnumber vampires roughly one-to-three thousand in this country. We cannot afford to disrupt the fragile alliance we have with the few who are aware of us. The blood finishing schools are beneficial in that regard."

"I can agree with that much." I nodded, appreciating the points he'd offered. "Okay. So, your in-laws ran one of these schools, and the prince…was a patron?"

"Alexander was their most generous benefactor. He attended all their gatherings and often put on theatrical acts with costumes and swordplay for the children. It was actually my reputation with a sword that first caught his interest when Jane's father told him of our engagement."

"Jane?" It was the first time I'd heard him say his late wife's name.

"Yes." He sighed and gave me a gentle smile. "Looking back on it now, we hardly had the chance to know one another, and yet…she took my name and mothered my only son. When the two of them died, it felt as though my world had ended." Dante paused, and his eyes glazed over, but he quickly cleared his throat and went on.

"Jane's father sang my praises to Alexander. Most men of that era preferred rifles and muskets. Swords had become little more than a fashionable accessory. I was one of the few who knew what to do with one."

"Stab with the pointy end?" I offered with a lopsided smile. Dante snorted and danced his fingers up my ribcage until I squealed. "Continue," I ordered, swatting away his hand.

"Very well." His laughter tapered, and he grew solemn again. "News of my talent spread, and when Alexander and I met at the party, he made a proposal of his own. He offered to half-sire me."

"But…didn't that entail him following you into battle so you could be anointed regularly?"

"He sent me back to Virginia with three vials of his blood. Enough to last a month before he visited my camp to re-stake his claim, invoking his theater skills to impersonate a fellow Union general."

"I suppose fighting in the war on either side would have been a challenge—at least for the daytime battles," I said.

Dante nodded. "Though, half-sired men served on both sides. The Vampiric High Council allowed the conflict of interest with a treaty that deemed all half-sireds who died in the war to be beheaded or burned to ash. The few who survived were assimilated into harems or turned as official scions."

If my fuzzy memory from high school history class was correct, over half a million lives were lost in the Civil War. I chewed my bottom lip, wondering if I would have accepted the prince's vampy offer with those odds. "Sounds like quite a gamble."

The peak of Dante's shoulder curled over me as he leaned in to steal a kiss. "Yes, but it greatly increased my chances of surviving most mortal wounds and diseases—both widespread at the time. In return, I was to serve in Alexander's blood harem after the war ended. I could remain living with Jane and our children. But once our children were grown and Jane had…expired, I belonged to him."

I pressed my hand over Dante's heart, not knowing what to say. *I'm sorry* just seemed too trite and insincere. Part of me understood that had things gone differently, we likely wouldn't be where we were now. If Jane had lived to a ripe old age, the prince might have skipped over Dante and made another his firstborn scion. He might not have sired Dante at all.

Plenty of the queen's servants and servants in the noble houses were stalemate half-sireds. They'd pledged themselves to the vampires with the understanding that they would never be fully turned. It wasn't as raw of a deal as it had initially sounded. They experienced immortality and an extra boost of strength and healing mojo but still enjoyed daylight and *real* food. All in exchange for doing some minor household tasks and giving up an occasional sip of blood.

I'd read some book or another from Dante's library on the various arrangements. There were contracts in place—just like the one Roman had had with House Sorano and Blood

Vice—that detailed what would happen if a half-sired donor died.

If it was an optimistic and deceitful suicide, a death sentence was the usual solution. But if the death were accidental, the new vampling would often be passed off to a fanged employee of the household to mentor and train them in their new duties as a nocturnal servant. Very rarely were they adopted into the households they served as fully-fledged members themselves. It was frowned upon—like marrying a concubine, I supposed—but it did happen from time to time. Just not for the royal family. I was a first.

Dante slipped my hand off his chest and lifted it to kiss my knuckles. "When I rose as a vampire, I thought the pain would be less somehow. Not only did it persist, but my newfound bloodlust soon joined it. Feeding throughout my first few years was a vicious cycle of euphoria and shame."

"Dante." I sighed and cupped his cheek, wishing I had more comfort to offer.

"Save your pity." Dante shook his head then turned to kiss my open palm. "The country was rebuilding itself after a crippling blow. So, too, Alexander rebuilt me. He was there every step of the way, though I am certain he regretted his decision to sire me much of that first decade."

"Why *did* he choose you?" I asked. "It wasn't really just because he liked the way you handled your sword, was it?"

"Not entirely, no." Dante rolled his eyes at my crude double entendre. "While it is true that the royal family had traditionally sired artistic prodigies, I am not the only warrior in our household. Lilith, the first vampiric queen of the New World, found her second scion, Gabriella, on the battlefield during one of the Italian Wars of the Renaissance and was quite taken with her.

"Lili sired Alexander some decades before Gabriella perished in the American Revolution, and he too was fond of his blood aunt's fiery, devil-may-care nature. His swordplay was more for entertainment than combat, but she humored him with a duel from time to time. I think he hoped to find a replacement opponent in me."

Dante loosed a disheartened sigh, and his gaze slid away from mine to take in my bare stomach. He traced his fingers in a circle around my navel. It sent a pleasant tingle through my core, but I was too absorbed in his history to be deterred just yet.

"So, the prince chose you because you were a war hero?"

"That was the argument he presented to Lili." Dante snorted softly. "She didn't approve, which only solidified his decision. They had a private war of their own going on behind closed doors after she ejected him from her bed in favor of mortal lovers."

"Lili seemed to like you well enough when I first met her," I said.

Dante nodded. "Yes, but it took many years to gain her respect and trust." He leaned over to kiss the patch of skin he'd been fondling, drawing a small gasp from me. "How do you feel, my love? Still apprehensive about sharing your blood with me?"

A nervous laugh stole my breath. Playing twenty questions with him had taken the edge off my anxiety, but it still bubbled beneath the surface.

"Now that you know how involved the visions are, are you sure that *you're* still up for my blood?" I frowned, wondering if he fully understood what I'd said earlier about seeing through his eyes during the vision and feeling everything he had, both physically and emotionally. "I can appreciate your bond with Alexander and the up-close experience of your last night as a mortal, but there is nothing sacred or even humane about how I was turned. I wouldn't wish that on anyone—least of all you."

Dante's palm slid over my cheek, and I leaned into it, my gaze fixed on his liquid eyes. "If you endured it, so shall I. My marksmanship may be lacking, but I can be here for you in other ways. I can appreciate the experience of *your* last night as a mortal, too."

He sounded so desperate, it hurt my heart. I knew it

would hurt worse after he tasted me, but there was no dissuading him. It was time to get it over and done with. I swallowed and let his hand guide my chin over my shoulder, giving him the length of my neck.

"Please, make it quick," I begged, closing my eyes.

Dante brushed a feather-soft kiss to my jaw, and then another to the side of my throat before his mouth found the curve between my neck and shoulder. I sucked in a sharp breath, but when his fangs broke flesh, I felt nothing more than a light pinch.

Dante's tongue was hot, and the memory of it in other places made my blood quicken and burn in my veins. He rolled it across my skin in one long, languid stroke. Then his body went rigid above mine. I opened my eyes to find Dante's wide and dilated, staring right through me into the darkest recess of my mind. I gripped his arms, but I didn't bother calling his name. He wouldn't hear me.

Right now, I was sure the sound of Raphael's gluttonous chewing and slurping was thick in Dante's ears. He'd feel the blinding pain in my neck where Raphael had torn my flesh to the bone. The cold weight of the pistol in my useless hand. The damp, unforgiving concrete beneath me.

He'd see my partner, Will, just a few feet away, and feel the shame and remorse I'd been drowning in as Raphael finished me off. I didn't need a vision to recall the horror of that night in graphic detail.

Dante's jaw flexed, and a tendon in his neck twitched as his breath grew more labored. Sweat beaded across his brow, and then he panted out a relieved sigh before blinking down at me. The sympathy in his gaze was too much to bear.

"Jenna, I…" He blew out a flustered breath and ran his thumb over the spot he'd bitten on my neck. The exact same place Raphael had chosen. "I had no idea. I should have fed from your wrist or—"

"Save your pity," I echoed his earlier sentiment back at him and grinned, but his haunted stare refused to budge. "Are you…okay?"

"No. I don't believe I am. How are *you* okay?"

I tried to laugh, but a strangled sound escaped me. "Time heals all wounds, right? And for what time doesn't heal, there's vampire blood."

Dante kissed my shoulder and then laid his head on my chest as he burrowed closer. I could feel the swell of his ribcage against mine with each uneven breath he took. He looped his arm around my waist and slipped a leg over one of mine. If only I'd had someone to hold me like this after Raphael's *anointment.* I didn't know if Dante was trying to comfort me or himself at this point.

"You were so brave," he whispered. His breath sent goosebumps over my skin.

"I was stupid—rushing in like that when I'd been ordered to wait for backup."

"You could not have known what Raphael was. What he was capable of."

"But I could have listened to my partner," I said, my voice growing small as my throat tightened. "He might be alive if I had."

"And then you might not be here with me." Dante pulled me closer. "Your partner chose to follow you into that basement, and Raphael chose to end his life. Do not take so much credit for the actions of others. You are only one creature, however magnificent I may find you."

I snorted under my breath, trying my damnedest to see things the way he did and coming up short. Maybe I was just angry Will was gone, and with Raphael dead, I had no one better to beat up for it than myself.

"Speaking of creatures…" Dante said thoughtfully. "You shot Raphael quite a few times, but it seems to me that the anointment must have happened after Ms. Starsgard intervened."

"Maybe," I whispered, my voice squeezing past the heart that was suddenly lodged in my throat. "I don't think Ursula noticed that part when she bit me. She was too distracted and hysterical. And I haven't told anyone else that Mandy was there."

"Not even the House Sorano vampling?"

"No." As taken as I'd been with Roman, and as much as he had done to help me, I'd never fully trusted him. Not even after the blood bond. Not the way I trusted Dante.

"I will not speak a word of it to another soul," Dante said, his voice heavy with sleep. "I would not have before either, if you had told me."

"I know." I kissed his forehead and rested my cheek against his mound of dark curls as the approaching dawn tugged at my eyelids.

There were so many other things I'd intended to discuss with him tonight—important things, like our next move against the Free Blooders and Lord Sorano's implied threat against the Raymore twins in Spero Heights, and base security for the Imbolc celebration Dante was determined to host here.

But the sun waited for no one.

Dante's breath fell into rhythm with mine, growing shallower with each inhale. The chill of death crawled over my skin, but I took comfort in the bit of warmth where our bodies met. Then, as I felt the sun breach the horizon far above our concrete fortress, our harmonized breaths exhaled one last time.

Chapter Six

Unlike every other evening since we'd arrived at the bat cave, Dante lingered in bed a moment after nightfall reanimated us. Maybe it was the fact that we were tangled up in each other, arms and legs entwined just as they'd been when dawn had frozen us in limbo.

When Dante finally released me and rolled onto his back, I followed, draping my arm across his chest and slinging a leg over his waist. His chin was rough with stubble, but I kissed him anyway, ignoring the scent of my stale blood on his breath.

Dante moaned softly and slipped his hand under my thigh. "If only I could remain in bed with you all night."

"Can't you?" I whispered, squeezing him closer to me. Who needed the real world with all its ugly problems?

"I have three briefings and a dozen calls to make before the Imbolc celebration." His curt tone tore at my heart, but as I pulled away from him, he caught my arm and pressed a kiss to the bend of my elbow and then to my wrist. "Forgive me. I am anxious about tonight."

I nodded, silently accepting his apology. "I know it's tradition, but are you sure we should be celebrating Imbolc at a time like this?"

Dante's brow furrowed, and I could tell he'd grown tired

of the question. "With the losses our house has suffered, now, more than ever, we cannot afford to forfeit the opportunity to see it grow. It was Lili's last request of me to produce a scion, and I will honor her wish."

"Is there anything I can do to help?"

"Not at this moment, but perhaps soon." Dante exhaled a long sigh as I fingered a curl away from his forehead. "The captains from the St. Louis and Denver divisions are eager to assure me that they are doing everything possible, searching for Marcel and the Free Blooders around the clock. Agatha, mistress of Morgan's former estate in California, has requested a meeting to discuss the future of the household she maintains on House Lilith's behalf. Alexander's assistant perished in the Evergreen attack, as well. So, the late prince's estate in Texas is in disarray. I've sent Belinda to help, but there is only so much she can do without the proper clearance or the Lilosa name.

"Members of the council continue to call and offer their assistance—a ruse to feel for cracks in our foundation, no doubt. The especially bold house leaders have sent their most prestigious members to pledge themselves to our cause. Lord Starling was particularly clever in requesting that his scion Ambrose attend the council conclaves in his place."

"Why's that?"

"The House Starling heir has six psychology degrees."

Dante's head turned, offering me the full weight of his frown. "Ambrose studied under Wundt and Freud, and then adapted his own theories regarding vampire and werewolf psychology. Clearly, Bo expects that his scion will observe more than what we choose to reveal. If he gets you alone, do not let him charm you into answering invasive questions. I trust House Starling more than most, but House Lilith is not in a position to be handing out leverage to anyone."

"My lips are sealed—with a kiss." I nipped at his mouth, trying to lighten the mood, and earned a faint smile. Though it didn't last long.

"If you truly desire to help, then look after Ursula," Dante said. "She will need you tonight. We must put on a strong front for House Lilith. We are now three becoming four, and dwindling households are easy prey."

I nodded and looked away to hide my disappointment. I couldn't have cared less about schmoozing with all the nobles at Imbolc, but tonight was a big deal for Dante—and for Audrey. It would be Dante's first time making a scion, and Audrey's last night as a mortal. I was excited and nervous for them both. I supposed babysitting Ursula was the least I could do.

Dante slid off the bed and went to the small closet in the corner of the room. He found a charcoal three-piece suit and hung it on the back of the closet door before heading for the bathroom. I waited for the faucet to turn on before blowing out the breath I'd been holding and dropping my head back onto my pillow.

The only good thing about tonight was that once it was over, we could go home.

After Dante left, I showered and dressed, too. He was right. There was much to be done.

I left our room and headed down the hall to Ursula's door, pausing to smooth my hair and straighten my blouse before knocking.

Audrey answered, quickly latching on to my arm and staking me with her frantic doe eyes.

"Thank goodness," she said under her breath, then dragged me inside. She forced a cheery smile before turning to face the room. "Look who's come to join us?"

Ursula glanced up from a chaise lounge pressed against the far wall. The décor in her room was marginally fancier than the other guest quarters, explicitly designed with a regal liaison's comfort in mind. Of course, the BATC sergeants probably hadn't planned on the whole family staying over for an entire week. The rest of us got the semi-noble bunker special, with army-green wool blankets and wicker furnishings.

"Ethan will be here shortly," Audrey said.

"Ethan?" I echoed.

"Ethan Vionnet." Her hands clasped around my arm a little too tightly, the only sign of her frazzled nerves. "To dress us for Imbolc," she explained.

I looked to Ursula for confirmation, but she was busy staring off into space. Her red curls hadn't fared well in the humidity of the BATC, but it looked as though she'd finally taken Audrey up on her offer to braid her hair. Dante's pending scion's strawberry locks sported a matching French braid, but the similarities ended there.

Smudges of crusty mascara lined Ursula's eyes, but at least she'd changed out of her dress from the meeting the night before. A spot of blood stained the collar of her silk bathrobe. More had dried at the corners of her mouth, though the cup in her hand was mostly full. A tacky film gleamed on the surface of the liquid as if she'd been holding it for some time now.

When Ursula finally noticed me gawking at her, she nodded at a tea service set up on her night table. "Help yourself."

"Thank you, Your Highness." I crossed the room to fix myself a cup.

Everyone had fallen back on formalities since our arrival at the bat cave. It was in part to put on that strong face Dante was so adamant about. But more than that, none of us wanted to be the one who triggered Ursula's diva persona and caused it to resurface and begin her rampage anew. Ethan was looking like the most eligible candidate for that task, which explained Audrey's anxiety.

Looking the part had always been Ursula's forte and passion, and in the time I'd known her, she hadn't approved a single article of clothing on first glance. Designers and tailors were equally enamored with and terrified to work for her.

To be honest, I was ready for something to break her free of this depressing funk. Grieving was one thing, but the hollow expression that hadn't left her face since the news of Lili's and Alexander's deaths was beginning to wig me out.

We didn't have twenty years for her to go MIA like she had after Morgan. We needed her to be the queen the rest of the vampires expected. If she couldn't put on a good show tonight, Marcel and the Free Blooders wouldn't be the only ones we'd have to worry about attempting to overthrow House Lilith.

Dante was plenty capable of taking care of all the technical details behind the scenes, but Ursula was the one who had to wear the crown and wow the masses. She had to look as if she knew what she was doing. At the moment, I wasn't entirely sure she did.

As I finished my cup of blood, another knock sounded at the door. When Ursula didn't say anything, Audrey answered it again, revealing Ethan and three of his assistants in the narrow hallway, their arms laden with equipment and garment bags.

"*Bonsoir*," Ethan said timidly, bowing first to Ursula and then to Audrey and me. He ushered his people in ahead of him and directed them to set up a pair of mirrored folding walls before hooking the garment bags over them. Once they were done, he shooed them out of the room and set to work opening the bags, announcing whom each piece belonged to as he went.

The three gowns for Ursula, Audrey, and me were all a soft gray with glittery accents. Audrey's was the simplest design, with an empire waist and wide, sheer sleeves. It had an innocent quality to it, which seemed fitting for the occasion. Mine was more intricate—the sleeves, chest, and shoulders of the gown made of floral lace, the hem of the tulle skirt thick with glitter.

Ursula's gown looked like it belonged on an angel atop a Christmas tree. The off-the-shoulder dress was covered in a sparkling ivy pattern that spilled over the top layer of the full skirt. A second layer of metallic fabric, and a third of lighter gray tulle, peeked out from below.

"The silver is quietly regal," Ethan said, waving a hand at the lineup of dresses. "Though it is acceptable for mourning, without being as overbearing as white or black." He paused and glanced across the room at Ursula.

By this point, I'd expected her to cut him off and offer some improvement or another. To tell him the gowns were either too risqué or too modest. Kitschy or dull. Instead, she stared at the dress he'd made for her with a blank expression that suggested she wasn't seeing it at all.

"They're lovely, Ethan," I said, drawing his attention away in hopes of buying Ursula some extra time to get it together.

"*Merci beaucoup*. Would you like to try them on?" he asked. "Just to be sure no last-minute adjustments are needed."

"Why don't you go ahead?" I said to Audrey, who hadn't stopped ogling her dress since Ethan said it was hers.

"I'd love to." She clapped her hands and hurried behind the folding wall that displayed her gown.

Her excitement was a relief. During Lili's impromptu Midwinter visit, the queen had promised our pending duchess a family heirloom to wear for her final anointment. It had presumably gone up in flames along with whatever other House Lilith inheritance there was to be had at the queen's manor in Evergreen.

Ethan excused himself from the room, and I took the

opportunity to sit down on the chaise beside Ursula. She blinked at me as if she'd forgotten that she wasn't alone in the room.

"Would you like help getting into your gown?" I asked.

"I'm sure it fits," she said, her gaze sliding away from mine again. "Ethan knows my measurements by now."

I chewed my bottom lip, trying to figure out a tactful way to point out the obvious. "You haven't asked about the meeting."

Ursula's head lolled to one side, the indifference in her expression unwavering. "Dante has everything under control."

"So, you don't want to know what was discussed?"

"Maybe later."

I sighed and laced my fingers together in my lap. "I have a feeling I'm going to regret this, but someone has to ask. Are you going to be able to make it through tonight?"

Ursula's eyelids sagged, though she managed to meet my stare. "I will do my very best."

She'd said the same thing to Lili at the All Hallows' Eve ball last year when the late queen had asked Ursula what kind of queen she would be. Lili's doubtful reply resonated in my mind.

But will that be enough?

I wondered the same now.

Chapter Seven

Despite my pending princess status, Ethan had added a second set of hidden, split pockets to the skirt of my dress. It made reaching my thigh holsters so much easier than hiking up layers upon layers of tulle. I wondered if Ursula would put an end to my secret agent alterations once she regained her senses. Either way, I was glad to have access to my personal arsenal tonight.

The BATC was not an especially inviting venue for the Imbolc celebration. But with Lili's manor blown to bits and barely a week to re-plan everything, our options were limited. At least half of the vamps previously invited had canceled their RSVPs. Whether that was due to the drab new digs or safety concerns was the million-dollar question. The bat cave had one thing going for it, though—the crystal cave mouth that loomed over the pool at the far end of the base. The natural wonder was as beautiful as any backdrop for the occasion.

Kai had ordered the lights in all other sectors be shut off during the ball in an effort to confine guests to the open space around the pool. The setup was as much to ensure their safety as to defend the base from potential enemy spies recruited within the noble households.

Security up top and at the sub-level entrance had been tripled, and six additional guards were stationed inside the senior werewolf barracks where Arnie was being held. Dante had thought positioning them outside the building would be too obvious if the Free Blooders attempted a breakout during the party.

I was sure Mandy would be keeping Arnie company tonight, too. She'd already petitioned Dante to leave her behind to keep a closer eye on our sole prisoner, but the duke had refused her request. Leaving one of his own on base would insult the sergeants and cast doubt on their militia, which would not do. We were indebted to them for their hospitality. Besides, Dante knew how much I worried about Mandy in the field as it was.

Before the guests began to arrive, Murphy tracked me down outside the cafeteria where I'd accompanied Audrey and Levi for the future duchess's last mortal meal. The spread included catfish and fried green tomatoes, cornbread, and peach cobbler. Audrey's hair and makeup were done, but she'd held off on changing in case of spills. With as much food as she was shoveling into her mouth, I just hoped she wouldn't need a stick of butter to fit back into her gown.

"Lookin' sharp, Skye," Murphy said by way of greeting. I didn't mind his use of my mortal surname. I was proud of the woman who'd given it to me, and being called *Your Grace* a hundred times a night at the bat cave had me on the verge of madness.

Murphy dipped his head toward Audrey next, who covered her bulging mouth and blushed. I couldn't fault her for gorging. If I'd been given the chance to load up on my favorite foods before being turned, I would have been a blimp. Now, the thought of mortal food turned my stomach. I'd learned the hard way that it could do that *literally* if a vamp attempted to consume anything other than blood.

Murphy was already dressed for Imbolc, his usual plain suit upgraded to a tux with a silver-lined bowtie. All the House Lilith guards would be gussied up tonight. The idea was for them to blend in—to make up for the lack of guests, and so no one would be alarmed by the aggressive level of security Dante had insisted on.

"What've you got there?" I said, nodding at a wooden box tucked under Murphy's arm.

"Somethin' I was hoping you'd deliver to the queen-to-be," he said with a nervous grin before turning the box up and opening it for me to see inside.

Tucked within a nest of black velvet was a crown that rivaled Lili's. Twisted filaments of dark silver formed peaks and waves all around the band, the points decorated with diamonds and sapphires as blue as Ursula's eyes.

"What happened to Lili's crown?" I asked as Murphy

closed the box and handed it to me. "Was it damaged in the fire?"

"It was never recovered," he answered under his breath. "Only the ceremonial dagger."

"But a house fire don't get hot enough to melt jewelry most times," Levi said from Audrey's table. When Murphy glared at him, he gave us a sheepish grin and pointed to one ear. "Sorry, wolf hearing."

"There's a chance it was stolen or destroyed in the initial blast before the fire," Murphy said, turning back to me. "But, hey"—his face stretched into a tight smile, and he popped his fist to the side of my lacy shoulder—"we got bigger sharks to fry, don't we? Perk up. Gotta make all these stuffed shirts see who's in charge."

"In charge. Right." I pressed my lips together and folded my arms around the crown box.

Audrey was a pendulum between frozen, doe-eyed terror and ecstatic denial. Ursula had turned into a catatonic rag doll. Dante was drowning under the weight of running everything and grieving over the sire he'd lost before they'd had a chance to bury the hatchet. And me…

I was caught in the middle, unsure how to feel about anything right now. Murphy's awkward pep talk wouldn't change that.

"I'll take this to Ursula," I said, patting the top of the box.

I left Murphy with Audrey and Levi and headed back to the guest barracks. On my way through the building, I stole a glance inside the room I shared with Dante. I hadn't seen him since dusk, and midnight was fast approaching. Guests would start arriving any moment.

The tux Ethan had made for Dante hung on the closet door. The subtle, shiny pattern over the tailcoat matched the lace of my dress. A silver vest and matching ascot tie completed the look. Ethan had outdone himself. And Dante was cutting it close. It wasn't like him to be late to a soirée, certainly not one hosted by House Lilith.

I closed the door and continued to Ursula's room to see how her preparations were coming along. Luckily, Ethan had offered up his assistants to help with the future queen's hair and makeup. I had a hard enough time dolling myself up without looking like I belonged in the circus. With the elaborate dress, I'd gotten off easy tonight with some loose curls and red lip gloss.

A queen coronating herself, such as Ursula would be doing, required a little more pizazz.

I knocked lightly at her door and let myself in. Ethan's people were gone, and I found Ursula once again on the chaise, wearing the same blank expression. At least the makeup hid the circles under her eyes, and her hair had been de-frizzed and pinned up on top of her head, forming a bed of curls for the crown to sit on.

"Special delivery," I said, holding the box out to her.

Ursula turned her chin up at me. "Is it time?"

"Almost."

Her gaze slid away again, and I noticed the dagger abandoned in her lap, the folds of her dress weighed down by the heavy, metal sheath.

"Do you have a plan?" I asked.

Ursula swallowed and blinked a few times. "I will crown myself before naming Dante and you as the new prince and princess. Then I will give Dante the ceremonial dagger to anoint Audrey. I'll thank everyone for coming, invite them to dance and make merry, and retire for the evening."

"That's great, but I meant for after." I put the crown box on her night table and sat on the edge of the bed. In the tight space, our dresses nearly touched. "You're not just the queen now—you're the head of House Lilith. There are a lot of decisions to be made about our future."

"I told you, Dante will take care of—"

"Dante is taking care of *everything* on top of grieving the loss of his sire." My harsh tone drew her spin upright. "*You* are the queen. *You* are supposed to lead us."

"You want to know my plan?" she barked. "I'm going to get through tonight. Then I'm going to get through tomorrow night. I'll hire someone to remodel the Ladue manor to make it suitable for hosting these ridiculous parties demanded by the masses. And then, in a century or so, once you and Dante have a substantial little *brood* of vamplings, I'll take my forever rest—alone—and the two of you can take over all this nonsense. That's my fucking plan, Jenna. Does that work for you?"

"It's a start," I snapped right back at her.

It was a relief to hear her express any emotion, even if it was anger. At least she wasn't throwing things at me, which was fortunate, considering the dagger within easy reach.

"What about the Free Blooders?" I asked next. "Do you have any thoughts on what we should do about Marcel and his crusade to overthrow us and declare a free-for-all on the humans?"

"House Lilith has many enemies," Ursula said, her bottom lip crumpling with mild annoyance. "We always have, and we always will. I do not make a habit of wasting time on thwarting the half-baked agendas of terrorists. That is what Blood Vice is for, and as much as you think I'm dumping my duties on poor Dante, Blood Vice operations are his territory."

"Well…" I hitched an eyebrow at her. "You're the queen now."

"I heard you the first time," she said through clenched teeth.

"If you wanted to evenly distribute some of those household duties, you know I'm more than capable."

"You're suggesting I put *you* in charge of Blood Vice?" Ursula snorted. "You'd love that, wouldn't you?"

I shrugged. "Why not? I know a helluva lot more about Blood Vice than wind farms—or any other of House Lilith's business dealings."

"You're getting ahead of yourself, scion." She snatched the dagger out of her lap and handed it to me as she stood, shaking the wrinkles from her gown. "Imbolc first. Then we'll see about your reckless ambition."

"Yes, Your Majesty." I hid my grin until she gave me her back and headed for the door.

Poking the bear was rarely a good idea, but sometimes it was necessary to make sure the bear was still alive. I was glad to see this one was. Even happier to have survived the stunt without getting my head chewed off or a dagger through the chest.

A portable chain railing hung around the cave pool to keep guests from slipping in, and spotlights had been tucked inside the cave, hidden behind jutting rocks. Their light bounced off the purple and blue crystals of the domed ceiling and reflected across the water's surface, casting an enchanted glow around the makeshift dais that arched over the pool like a bridge from a fairytale.

There were under a hundred guests, all dressed in muted mourning colors to show their respect. Solemn or not, they all seemed wowed by the setup. A touch of arrogance steeled my nerves when I thought about how disappointed the snobs of the underworld would be once they heard what they'd missed out on.

Imbolc with House Lilith was exclusively celebrated by vampires and debuting scions set to be turned for the occasion. Presenting new blood spawn to the queen on this sacred night was a tradition—for the noble households, anyway—dating back some four hundred years, to when the royal family had set up camp in the New World.

I wondered if Roman had been looking forward to such an honor, rather than the botched chiropractic ending he'd received. I swallowed my guilt and scanned the filling compound, wondering who else had been scheduled to die tonight besides Audrey. With the royal family in mourning, all other Imbolc anointments had been postponed.

Sergeant Sorano, Vanessa's sire, hovered near the mouth of the lit street that led from the compound's entrance to the cave, shooting suspicious glances at the guests. I supposed Vanessa and Roman were working, either guarding Arnie or the tunnel entrance. It seemed they were the black sheep of their house. I was partly at fault for that, but there wasn't much I could do about it.

My eyes snagged on Dante as he slipped from the shadows that spilled between the barracks and the designated party space. He'd finally changed into his tux. Even worn to the bone, he held his chin high, the epitome of regal fortitude. The vintage style suited him, and pride swelled my heart as I remembered that he was mine. He admired me from across the room, pleasure warming his gaze, and then made his way toward the dais where Ursula, Audrey, and I waited.

Ursula had reclaimed the dagger, but the crown box was still in my possession. It gave my hands purpose, keeping me from wringing them like Audrey was doing every five seconds. I couldn't blame her. All eyes were on us, and not all of them were friendly.

"Thank you for joining us, cousin," Ursula quipped as Dante took his place between her and Audrey.

"You are very welcome, Your Majesty," he replied with a bow that was more for our guests than her. Whatever friction there was between us, we had to rein it in tonight. This moment would set the tone for the future of House Lilith.

Dante's gaze stretched over the crowd until he found Sergeant Sorano. She nodded at him, a silent signal that I assumed they'd planned in one of the meetings leading up to the celebration.

"All guests are present," Dante said to Ursula. "We can begin whenever you are ready."

A spark of panic lit Ursula's eyes. The murmur of the crowd tapered as if they had sensed the shift, like vultures swooping in for a closer look. The shift lent to her distress.

"Can you do it?" she asked Dante in a small voice.

"I cannot." He took her hand that held the dagger and relieved her of it before pressing a kiss to her knuckles. "But I will remain here by your side."

"As will I," I said.

"Me, too," Audrey whispered, not to be left out of our family pow-wow.

Ursula swallowed and lifted her chin as the room fell silent, anticipating her address. I held my breath, waiting as well, and hoping this wasn't all a big mistake.

"Good evening, noble allies of House Lilith," Ursula began, stepping forward to the edge of the dais. "I had not expected to take Lili's place for some time to come, but tragedy has befallen our family, and now we must honor those we have lost by doing our best to carry on their legacy. Forgive me for intruding upon this sacred holiday and during such a tumultuous time to crown myself as your new queen."

Dante held up Lili's dagger, letting it rest over his open palms. I followed his lead and flanked Ursula's opposite side, opening the wooden box as I did. Ursula took up the crown with trembling fingers. She placed it on top of her pinned curls, and a collective gasp echoed off the cave walls.

I couldn't decide if the sound held more disgust or awe. The look on Ursula's face suggested she wasn't quite sure either. Regardless, she took the dagger from Dante and lifted it over her head before laying it diagonally across her chest.

"Ursula, Queen of House Lilith, third sovereign of the New World," Dante announced.

"By the blood!" the crowd replied. Their collective voice was even more conflicted, ranging from relief to chagrin. As long as they behaved, I couldn't bring myself to care how they felt about my sire's new station. Or mine.

Ursula turned to me and placed her free hand on my shoulder. "As my scion, I name thee Jenna, Princess of House Lilith."

"By the blood!" everyone cheered again, the cacophony filled with more menace than I'd noted before.

Next, Ursula turned to Dante. "As my faithful cousin, I name thee Dante, Prince of House Lilith."

"By the blood!"

Ursula unsheathed the dagger and handed it to Dante. "And now we return to tradition and welcome our dear Audrey, Duchess of House Lilith, into the fold of night on this blessed Imbolc Eve."

Chapter Eight

Though I'd tasted Dante the night before, seeing the blood well on his fingertip, and Audrey's eager, pink lips open to receive it sent a pang of jealousy through me. I had to look away. The adoration in her gaze was too intense, even before Dante declared her his *forevermore*.

The ugly feelings knotting up my stomach only intensified once he led her away from the pool and back toward the guest barracks. Before the night was through, Dante would drink Audrey dry. He would then spend the day secluded in her room and rise with her at sunset before mentoring her through her first feeding—on *Levi*, her werewolf beau, I reminded myself, trying to take comfort in that fact.

Ursula finished her queenly duties, thanking everyone for attending and inviting them to enjoy the party as a string quartet set up in the glowing mouth of the cave behind us. Then she left the dais, descending on the side where Murphy and Lane waited to escort her back to her room. I made to follow, but Ursula turned suddenly, leaning into me until our foreheads nearly touched.

"You will stay and pretend to enjoy yourself," she said under her breath. She ran her hand down the length of my arm in a more amicable gesture that I assumed was for our ogling guests.

"What? Why?"

"*Someone* from House Lilith has to remain to play hostess." Ursula gave me a tight smile. "You want more responsibility? Prove you can handle it."

Well. That had come back to bite me in the ass a lot sooner than I'd expected.

"As you wish, Your Majesty," I said through clenched teeth. Then I swallowed my resentment and bowed.

Ursula left me at the foot of the dais. She cut a wide path around those gathered at the pool's edge, her chin held high, and eyes focused straight ahead. Murphy and Lane flanked her, their cold gazes clearing anyone in the queen's way.

I instantly regretted not begging Ursula to reconsider. A murmur bubbled up from the crowd, and as I turned to stare out at the guests, I couldn't help but notice the dark glances aimed in my direction.

These were more than just vampires. They were wealthy elitists from ancient, supernatural bloodlines. The idea of submitting to Ursula—whom many of them believed had murdered her sire, neglected her first two scions, and then abandoned her responsibilities to our kind—was hard enough to swallow. But submitting to an adopted vampling that the late queen had mostly assigned out of spite?

Yeah, that wasn't happening anytime soon.

The string quartet broke into a haunting melody, further

unnerving me. I wondered how difficult it would be to slip away and hide out with Mandy in the senior werewolf barracks until the party was over. I was even willing to face Arnie again. Anything over this.

"Your Highness." Ambrose Starling emerged from the crowd. He'd slicked back his curls, much like Dante did for formal events, and wore a black sherwani—a long, Indian dress coat—with silver embroidery.

The vampires nearest the dais parted as though he were contagious. A line had been drawn somewhere, and it was clear that no one was prepared to choose a side yet. Except maybe Ambrose.

"Would you honor me with your first dance as a princess?" he asked, folding one hand behind his back and extending the other to me as he bowed.

I automatically slipped my hand into his, too relieved to refuse. It wasn't until Ambrose's opposite hand settled on my waist that I recalled Dante's warning and questioned my rash judgment. The sly grin tugging at the corners of Ambrose's mouth didn't help.

"Your sire left before I had a chance to offer proper congratulations," he said.

"I'll be sure to pass along your kindness." I stole another glance at the guests as the music swelled, competing with the hushed gossip.

"Don't worry about them, Your Highness." Ambrose pulled me closer as I struggled to relax and let him lead me through the waltz. "A little envy is to be expected in your position."

"Envy?" I scoffed, unable to ignore the wrathful eyes that followed us. "I think you have your deadly sins confused."

Ambrose arched an eyebrow. "You are the new queen's scion and the prince's lover. All without being a trueborn of House Lilith. Who wouldn't be envious? You're the Little Orphan Annie of vampiric society."

"And somehow, the only lady of the house who isn't a redhead," I mused aloud.

Ambrose's smile softened. "Sonja said you had a sense of humor."

The confession caught me off guard, and I stumbled over the toe of his shoe. Ambrose's grip on me tightened, keeping me from falling on my face. He seamlessly curled my body inside the fold of one arm and then spun me out again, as if my error had been intentional and part of the dance.

"Sonja spoke to you about me?" I whispered as we edged farther around the pool to a spot that was less crowded.

"She said you were a riddle she couldn't quite solve." His gaze sharpened, scrutinizing me as if he wanted to pick up where his niece had left off. "How does a sireless vampling convince the Duke of House Lilith to permit her into the Blood Authority Training Program?"

Truth be told, there hadn't been much convincing. I'd assumed that Roman had just been trying to scare me off when he told me how slim my chances of being permitted were. But then Dante had hardly resisted at all. It wasn't until sometime later that I learned—through hazing from the other cadets—just how rare my circumstances were. That I'd become the duke's pet project.

The question of *how* lingered in Ambrose's gaze, and I realized it hadn't been rhetorical.

"I asked nicely." The answer was true enough.

His eyebrows rose in challenge. "Some might wonder *how* nicely."

"I helped to bring down the Scarlett Inn and then a serial killer who'd been targeting vamplings in St. Louis. How's that for nice?"

"Yes." Ambrose didn't sound surprised in the least. "And then you saved the queen from a would-be assassin and located the rogue duchess. You've been a busy little bat." Before I could reply, he added, "But the rewards you reaped went beyond training for Blood Vice, didn't they? You managed to escape the consequences of forging a lifeblood bond with a half-sired pledged to House Sorano—of all vampire families—and then acquired the second most regal sire in the country. Am I leaving anything out?"

"Why? Are you writing my biography?"

The music downshifted into a slower, melancholic tune, and I took the cue to disentangle myself from Ambrose. My palms were moist, though not from the energetic waltz. I tried to be subtle about drying them on the skirt of my dress. The scowl twisting at the corners of my mouth was harder to disguise.

"There's no need to be defensive, Your Highness." Ambrose gave me a disarmingly innocent smile, but he didn't offer his hand for another dance. "I do not mention all of this to offend. Quite the opposite, really. I admire you—your ability to survive and thrive against all odds."

"I got lucky," I admitted. But after everything that had happened recently, I wondered if my luck had run out.

"Once is lucky." Ambrose snorted. "Luck repeated as often as yours…"

"I somehow doubt those who have died because of me— Sonja included—would consider me a beacon of good fortune."

"The burden of Sonja's true death is not yours to bear," Ambrose said, placing a hand over his heart. "I imagine Cain Davis discovered that she was on to him."

"On to him?"

"Yes. She suspected House Hanson's half-sired from the first night of your training, when he attempted to dispose of you in this very pool." He nodded at the dark water I'd all but lost my mind in after Cain's so-called prank. If it hadn't been for my lifeblood bond with Roman, I might still be at the bottom of that pool, rotting away in a soggy coffin.

"She shared this theory with you?"

"During one of her calls home," Ambrose explained. "House Starling is more familiar with the mortals of noble households than most, given our medical experience, so Sonja was well aware that Davis had once managed Scarlett's harem. Like the serial killer you apprehended, she surmised that Davis, too, harbored a misguided allegiance to the exiled baroness."

"Why didn't she say anything to the sergeants on base?" I asked.

Ambrose cocked his head. "Vampling or not, by now, you must be aware of how well unsupported accusations go over against members of powerful households. Your training should have covered that, did it not?"

I ground my teeth. "Right. Of course."

How quickly I'd let my privilege as a member of House Lilith blind me to the flaws in our legal system. That would be one of the first things I tackled when—or *if*—Ursula appointed me to manage Blood Vice. High-society vamps couldn't keep getting away with crimes that signed death warrants for the rest. And they couldn't keep using their power and influence to enact steeper retribution on those who slighted them.

Plus, the blood duels had to stop—and not just because I'd almost found myself on the wrong end of one. They were barbaric and an entirely inaccurate way to determine if a party was guilty. Tradition be damned.

Ambrose watched me carefully, some mixture of curiosity and amusement in his gaze. "You seem so troubled, dear princess. Perhaps there is something I can help with?"

I willed the strain in my face to release and managed a smile that felt more like a grimace. "I already have a therapist, thank you. Besides, we leave tomorrow night."

"Did the queen not tell you?" Ambrose folded his hands behind his back and rocked onto his heels. "To be fair, it was only just decided tonight. I'll be accompanying Lili's surviving harem to St. Louis."

"Is that right?"

"As you well know, humans heal slowly. Someone has to oversee their physical recovery and tend to their emotional trauma. Fortunately, I excel in both fields."

"How convenient." My fake smile ached in my cheeks, and I was sure it was no longer fooling him—if it ever had. Ambrose grinned despite my obvious discomfort.

"I look forward to spending more time with you and, perhaps, solving the riddle that eluded my late niece," he said.

I didn't consider myself a complicated gal, but Ambrose looked at me as if he saw a thousand secrets waiting to be unearthed. There was really only one that I kept close to the vest, and I could count on one hand the number of people who knew the truth.

No way would I invite a second shrink to the party. I hadn't wanted the first one, but Dr. Delph was psychic. There was no time for peeling back layers with him—he cut right to the core of an issue and tackled it head-on. Of course, that gift was only useful in person. If I wanted his advice long distance, I had to put on my big-girl panties and spell out my troubles for him, something it looked like I'd be doing again. Real soon.

I had a feeling it was going to take a pro to help me survive Ambrose's scrutiny.

Chapter Nine

I was surprised to find one of Lili's former servants in Ursula's room the next evening, tucking clothes into a suitcase laid out on the bed. He was a handsome, middle-aged man with sandy hair, though after noting the light blue of his eyes, I wondered how long he'd been frozen in time. Two butterfly bandages stretched over his left eyebrow, and a gauze sleeve covered his right forearm.

Ursula lounged on the chaise sofa, her pale legs crossed and exposed through the folds of a black, silk bathrobe. Her crown had been put away, but her chin had a noticeable tilt, even if the life hadn't fully returned to her eyes. She was trying.

"Would you pour the princess some blood, Benson?" Ursula said before setting her teacup on its saucer so she could wave me over to join her.

I was glad to find her in better spirits, though mine were frayed thanks to the encounter with Ambrose the night before—and the cold bed I'd slept in by myself. I'd avoided lying down until the last second, busying myself with packing Dante's and my things. I was ready to be home.

"So," Ursula said after Benson had served me and returned to her luggage, "how was the ball?"

"Okay, I guess." I pressed my lips together and took a sip of blood, letting my gaze trail away.

After the awkward dance with Ambrose, I'd stuck around long enough to hobnob with the few relatively friendly faces I'd spotted in the crowd—Blair Hanson, Louise Peyroux, Kai Natani. Then I'd slipped away and spent the rest of the night with Mandy on top of a picnic table outside the base cafeteria, listening to her gripe about not having cell service in the bat cave. It was the farthest away she was willing to be from the senior werewolf barracks.

I couldn't help but wonder if Mandy had hoped the Free Blooders would attempt to break Arnie out during the party. It would have made things easier, I supposed. Taken all the legwork of finding them out of the equation. But I somehow doubted playing defense would get us very far in this battle.

Ursula watched me over the rim of her cup, and I realized she expected a *real* report this time. Genuine interest was a good sign, though I didn't have much else to offer.

"Uh… House Hanson is working on some fancy facial recognition software they plan to integrate with the Blood Vice bodycams—and whatever human law enforcement cameras they can gain access to. The database they're building not only includes all confirmed members of the Free Blooders, but their known associates and fellow pack members."

Ursula frowned. "Didn't you train with a Hanson scion? Was she the one wearing the knock-off Novak last night?"

"Yes, on both accounts. We also trained with Mic Novak. The two of them were close."

"Hmph." Her bloodstained lips curled with distaste.

Wilhelmina Novak had voted in favor of coffin-locking Ursula just over a year ago. It had been a vengeful move after Mic was falsely coffin-locked for Sonja's murder. Even after the real culprit had been uncovered, and her grandscion set free, Lady Novak was still bitter. She hadn't attended a royal ball since. I'd noticed Mic at one or two, though he'd been absent last night.

"What else did you learn?" Ursula asked, holding out her cup for Benson to refill.

"Only two houses were unaccounted for. Kai Natani confirmed that they weren't in any danger—just rude asshats who forgot to cancel their RSVPs."

Ursula bristled, but it wasn't until she shot a sideways glance at Benson that I understood her concern. "Do you require any assistance packing?" she asked.

"All done." I gave her an apologetic smile. "Dante's good, too."

"Benson, would you be a dear and see if the harem needs any help?" Ursula asked as he finished zipping the suitcase on her bed.

"Of course, Your Majesty." He bowed first to her and then to me, not a hint of animosity in his voice or demeanor. Once he'd left the room, I turned back to Ursula.

"He seems nice."

"He does, doesn't he?" A crease cut across her brow, and she sighed. "Clyde disappeared the day after we left for Denver."

"Clyde? One of the wolves Lili delivered after Midwinter?"

Ursula nodded. "Holland, his partner, waited to tell me until last night. I think he was hoping that Clyde was simply taking some time to mourn in private, but since he hasn't returned…"

"You think he might be involved with the Free Blooders? But Lili said they were some of her best."

"Then who better to recruit?"

She had a point. I didn't have to like it, but I certainly wouldn't have put it past Marcel after everything he'd already done. The Moreau alpha didn't play by any set of rules that I was aware of. He'd double-cross and blackmail anyone necessary to get what he wanted.

"Benson was previously half-sired by one of Lili's guards," Ursula said. "He's now in Lane's care."

"His eyes…"

They hadn't been as frosty as Roman's or Cain's, but I'd met enough half-sireds now to tell the difference between human blue and one-foot-in-the-grave blue. Ursula gave me a withering glare that suggested she was glad I'd waited to share my tactless observation until after Benson had left the room.

"He was in a coma for a few days, and no one could tell us when he'd last been anointed. As soon as he woke and consented, Lane fed him. He'd been with Lili for over a century. I imagine he will be quite useful in years to come—if he can be trusted."

"Do you have any reason to doubt his loyalty?"

"I doubt everyone's loyalty." She snorted and swished the blood in her cup before taking another drink. "Time will tell if he's a good fit for our house."

"Speaking of useful new additions to the household… Ambrose Starling informed me that he'd be tagging along, too."

"Someone will need to care for the new harem donors. Considering the severity of their injuries, Harold is just not equipped."

"But Ambrose Starling?" My nose wrinkled. "I'm a little surprised that Dante agreed to the arrangement after the warning he gave me."

"Dante didn't," Ursula said. "You were right. I put too much on his shoulders, too soon after his sire's death. Besides, Ambrose came to me."

"Yeah, he came to me, too." I folded my arms, trying to decide how much I should share. Ambrose didn't know anything damning enough to warrant upsetting Ursula. For now. "He asked to dance and instead grilled me while I tripped over his feet."

Ursula smirked. "The interrogation tango. Classic."

"He's too…smug. And curious." I huffed, earning a chuckle from my sire.

"If only he were a cat."

"Does Dante know we're bringing Ambrose home with us?" I asked.

As if on cue, a knock sounded at the door.

"He's about to," Ursula said as Dante and Audrey entered the room.

By human standards, the newly risen Duchess of House Lilith didn't look any different than she had the previous night. Maybe a little flushed in the cheeks as if she might have a fever or be excited, given the unnatural dilation of her pupils.

To those in the know, Audrey was the posterchild for a well-fed vampling. I'd witnessed similar symptoms in the faces of countless fanged patrons at Bleeders. Dante would make sure his scion never knew the devastating hunger I'd suffered my first few months as one of the undead. I couldn't even envy her for that—I was grappling with too much jealousy as it was.

"How's Levi?" I asked.

Audrey's fangs extended with a faint click. She gasped and covered her mouth with one hand as her face turned a darker shade of red.

"That good, huh?" I ignored Dante's wide-eyed glare and stood to refill my cup from the pot on Ursula's night table. I filled one for Audrey too, an apology for my rude remark. Her fangs retracted as I handed it to her.

Dante's scowl softened, and he pressed a kiss to my temple before facing Ursula.

"Mr. Murphy is escorting the extended harem to my private jet," he said. "They are scheduled to depart in twenty minutes. The loaner jet offered by House McCoy is on standby and ready when you are."

Ursula glanced down at her bathrobe. "I suppose I should change then. Jenna, princess, my dear scion…" Her gaze drew up to me, and a mischievous half-smile touched her lips. "Be a peach and fill in the prince and duchess on our new houseguest while I get dressed."

She was getting far too comfortable throwing me to the wolves. But I supposed if torturing me was what Ursula needed to get it together, then I'd just have to suck it up and take one for the team.

With everyone on high alert and the Free Blooders still at large, extra safety measures had been taken regarding our travel. Ambrose and Lili's surviving harem donors would fly directly to the smaller airport in downtown St. Louis where several of the guards who had remained behind would be waiting to transport them to the manor in Ladue. It was as much to scope out our route as it was a decoy.

Meanwhile, the royal fam and our personal guards would take the loaner jet to the Columbia airport, two hours west of St. Louis, and drive the rest of the way via more vehicles loaned by House McCoy. I didn't mind the extended commute if it meant avoiding Ambrose a little longer.

Dante had been every bit as furious as I'd expected about the news—that Ambrose was tagging along, *and* that I'd allowed him to corner me at the party. I was sure the only reason he didn't have more to say about it right this second was because he didn't want to undermine our new queen so soon after her coronation. That and all the eyeballs on us.

A royal family does not put their disagreements on public display. Such behavior is beneath us. The rule had sounded more genuine coming from Dante, though Ursula had included it in one of her scion lessons in the library. Not that my sire ever felt compelled to take her own advice. Her lessons were pure hypocrisy.

After buckling Audrey in, Dante headed to the front of the plane to sit beside Ursula. I wanted to be glad for the break from my sire and Dante's broody stare, but instead, I felt rebuffed. I was the princess, was I not? Why did I suddenly feel as though I'd been ditched at the kiddie table?

Mandy sat in the seat across the aisle from me, knees pulled up to her chest, gnawing a thumbnail down to the quick. Her cropped leather jacket looked more punk than assassin tonight, paired with ratty jeans and high-top sneakers. She clutched her cell phone in her free hand, not-so-patiently waiting for takeoff.

The flight attendant had ordered everyone to wait until we were airborne before firing up the electronics. Standard procedure, *blah, blah, blah*. But I was pretty sure the request had more to do with the bomb squad inspecting the plane. I'd spotted them as Murphy had ushered us up the airstairs.

The pretense was no doubt for Audrey. Dante had likely ordered the flight staff and guards to watch what they said around the new duchess. She'd been a delicate damsel as a mortal, and I was betting that death had stiffened everything but her upper lip.

I had a clear view of Audrey in her seat directly in front of Mandy's, and like Mandy, she held her cell phone at the ready, periodically glancing at the blank screen out of habit. I imagined she was eager to check in with her friends at Darkly Hall to tell them all about the big night.

I *still* didn't have a phone of my own. After everything that had happened, it just hadn't been a priority. And there wasn't exactly a convenient place to pick one up at the bat cave. Besides, anyone who knew that I was alive—or who I cared to be in contact with—knew how to get ahold of me through Mandy.

I warmed my hands between my knees and stole another glance over the seat in front of me and the top of Levi's head. There was an empty row in front of him and Audrey, but then Murphy and Lane filled the two seats behind the prince and queen.

The loaner jet was smaller than Dante's, but that had been part of the plan, too. Besides, extra guards didn't do us much good in the air, and there would be more waiting to pick us up in Columbia. Though the close quarters still weren't cozy enough for eavesdropping.

Ursula's muffled laughter trickled back to me. From Dante's grumbly mumble of a reply, I imagined the joke had been at his expense. I again strained to see over the seats and passengers that separated us and was rewarded when Dante's head rotated, and our eyes met.

I flinched at the irritation in his gaze. The look definitely had more behind it than my misstep with Ambrose.

Shit. What now?

"Cable first, then Laura. Okay?" Mandy said, drawing my attention as the plane began to move toward the runway.

"Cable won't have anything more to tell you than he told Dante an hour ago," I argued.

"You don't know that—plus, I want to be put on the search schedule as soon as we get back. No time to waste."

"You think you'll have better luck than all the other Cadaver Dogs in St. Louis?" I asked.

Mandy pressed a finger to the side of her nose. "Luck has nothing to do with it." Her teasing grin faltered as I peeked over the seats again. "He doesn't like the idea of you taking over Blood Vice," she whispered. "Which makes it sound like a swell plan to her royal majesty of dramaville."

I snorted softly. "Thanks for the recon."

"Sure thing, jellybean." Mandy moved the finger away from her nose and flicked her earlobe. She never passed up an opportunity to point out her superior senses.

Werewolves outclassed vampires in many ways, but what it all came down to in the end was raw power and longevity. Werewolf life expectancy was only slightly longer than humans. Vampires could live forever, and given adequate blood, we could survive almost anything—well, more than the average wolf could survive, anyway. And the longer we persisted, the more powerful we became. It was a sore spot for many wolves, and probably why the thought of joining the Free Blooders appealed to so many.

During my training, I'd read about the early alliances between vamps and wolves in America. Not all the wolves had agreed. The divide had weakened their position and resulted in a less-than-ideal arrangement that fast-tracked the vamps to the top of the pyramid. As back-stabby as the fanged crowd could be, they knew how to present a unified front when it counted.

Over time, the Vampiric High Council and House Lilith jumped on the progressive bandwagon and gave the wolves more rights and status. They could train to join Blood Vice. They could register their packs with the American Alpha Association and receive special benefits and protections through the terms of their alliance with the council.

For some wolves, it was too little, too late. For others, nothing short of the top of the food chain would suffice. As long as they had to answer to the *Vampiric* High Council, they couldn't fool themselves into believing they were equal or free.

For a wolf like Mandy, who was intimately, viscerally familiar with what freedom was and was not, joining Blood Vice was more than enough. It meant being able to free others who were trapped the way she'd once been. But for a power-hungry alpha like Marcel Moreau, it meant he couldn't just take a bite out of anyone he damn well pleased.

"Shit on toast." Mandy gritted her teeth and tucked her nose between her knees as the plane gained momentum.

"Just breathe," I said, as much to myself as to her, and inhaled stiffly through my nose.

The plane's tires bumped over a rough spot in the runway, and Mandy moaned. "Tell me when it's over."

I exhaled and leaned back in my seat as the nose of the plane angled upward. Soon, the blinking lights through my window disappeared, leaving only darkness.

"All clear," I said, patting Mandy's leg. She took a few long breaths before looking up again. A thin, yellow ring around her pupils glowed in the dim cabin light.

As Mandy's eyes returned to a more human hue, she shook her head and stuck a pinky in her ear. I felt my own ears pop and cringed. Soon after, the flight attendant announced that we could power on devices and move about the cabin.

"Come on," I grumbled at Mandy as she held her cell phone out of my reach. She dialed Cable's cell number one-handed and shoved her free palm up under my chin, turning my face away as I slapped at her arms.

Audrey and Levi both turned in their seats to gawk at us. Admittedly, it wasn't a very proper way for a princess to behave. It took another backward glance from Dante before I finally relented and let Mandy have her way.

I knew I didn't have to worry too much about Laura. Dante had arranged a wolf detail from the L.A. Blood Vice division to look after my pregnant sister and her husband. The Free Blooders were capable of anything, but they were scarce when it came to true confrontation. They played in the shadows, with spies and assassins and calculated attacks that allowed them to quickly disappear before the cavalry arrived. It was also the reason I suspected they hadn't attempted to free Arnie.

Mandy finished her call with Cable and dialed Laura next. She handed me the phone since her wolfy hearing allowed her to pick up on the conversation from across the aisle. After half an hour of my sister wailing about her honeymoon plans and how fat she was going to look in a bikini, I was relieved when an incoming call chirped over the line. Until I recognized the number.

Not that long ago, I'd considered Max Collins my best friend. He'd almost followed me all the way down this supernatural rabbit hole I'd crawled into. He even completed training at the bat cave with Mandy and me. But after my misstep with Roman that had nearly ended in a blood duel with Vanessa Sorano, Collins had had enough. He'd resigned from Blood Vice and my blood harem, and all but told me to forget his number. I didn't blame him.

Mandy swiped the phone out of my hand and sent the call to voicemail. She winced at my wide-eyed scowl, but we both knew better than to have this conversation in such a tight space—especially with another wolf right in front of us. When her phone chimed with a text notification, she turned the screen up for me to see, heading off another slap-fest.

911. We need to talk.

Mandy rolled her eyes and pecked out a quick reply.

This is really not a good time. If it's an emergency, maybe try the Blood Vice office.

Two seconds later, Collins chimed in again.

It's a Jenna emergency.

Mandy's jaw flexed as I snatched the phone from her and unbuckled my seatbelt. I punched in Collins' number as I headed for the tiny restroom at the rear of the plane, but I locked the door and turned on the faucet before hitting *dial.*

Chapter Ten

"Hey, kiddo," Collins answered on the first ring. I savored the warmth and familiarity in his voice for a second before spoiling it with my reply.

"It's me. What's going on?"

Collins sucked in a long breath. I could almost see his shoulders square on the other end of the line. "The doctor who stole Vin's *research* was murdered two nights ago. Vin's convinced it was a targeted hit. The guy was about to publish his findings in some medical journal."

Sweat tickled the back of my neck as I pressed the phone tighter to my ear. I didn't know what to say. What *could* I say?

"Vin took some time off work," Collins continued. "He thinks he might be next. Wouldn't even tell me where he was going. That's how freaked he is right now." After another long pause, he snapped, "You still there, Skye?"

"I'm here. I just… I can't really help without incriminating Vin or myself, you know?" I chewed my bottom lip, not realizing my fangs had slipped out until I tasted blood. I examined the damage in the narrow mirror above the sink, also noting that my vision had taken on a pink hue.

Nerves. The Eye of Blood made them hard to deny.

Collins sighed in my ear, a frustrated, annoyed breath that told me he was ready for this call to be over. "Just tell me you didn't hunt this guy down so I can scratch your name off my list."

"I'm a suspect?" I was too shocked to be offended. "Wait, why do you have a list? This sounds like a case Blood Vice would have taken over, and—are you a detective now? When did that happen?"

"I'm not a detective. Blood Vice did take over the case. My list is purely for Vin's peace of mind."

"Oh, and I'm a suspect?" I repeated, allowing myself to feel insulted this time. "Vin didn't even tell me the doctor's name."

"Yeah, but you and I both know the kinds of resources you have at your disposal," Collins said. "It wouldn't have been that difficult."

"Trust me, I have bigger bats to fry right now."

"Right now?" For just a second, I wondered if he would ask what was going on in my little underworld, but then he circled back to Vin. "Does that mean you eventually plan to tie up this loose end? I know your relationship with the doc didn't end on good terms, and he mentioned that you threatened to turn him in to the council."

"Yeah, if he tried to do any more experiments with vampire blood," I hissed under my breath. "Which I would have no way of knowing, would I? But, if you need a proper alibi, I've been in Denver at the bat cave for the past week. You can ask Mandy."

"I would have if she'd answered her phone," Collins said. "I also would've asked why your people have been so sloppy this past week. I've had to cover at *three* crime scenes until Blood Vice showed. I swear to God, if I hear one more 'must be a full moon' joke, I'm going to beat someone to death with a box of donuts."

"Idiots." I rolled my eyes. "Full moon's over two weeks out." Which reminded me that this month also featured a micromoon on the new moon—something for which Mandy and her wolfy colleagues often planned a special camping trip. Any vacation leave was certainly canceled by now.

"Most humans have no idea. Why would they?" Collins snorted. "The office is buzzing with gossip of other incidents where Blood Vice arrived late, too. That's how I found out about the doc's gory end, though I didn't know he was the research thief until Vin tracked me down to confirm how the guy had died."

"Blood Vice is stretched a little thin right now," I confessed. "Everyone is searching for Marcel Moreau. He's the leader of a new terrorist group. They call themselves the Free Blooders—"

"I don't wanna know," Collins cut in. "I left all that behind. Not my vampires, not my circus of the damned."

"Right." I sighed. "Of course."

He was human and could do that. I often wondered if I'd have done the same, given a choice. But it was harder to ignore a world after it made you one of its own.

"Tell Mandy to check in when she can," Collins said, then he ended the call without saying goodbye.

I'd pass on his message, but I'd also encourage Mandy to warn him about the Free Blooders. However much he wanted to leave this world behind, he needed to be prepared. Because if Marcel had his way, this damned circus would be everyone's problem.

I worried that Dante would question my lengthy trip to the plane's restroom—vampires had little use for them—but it turned out, he had his own disturbing news to deal with. After I handed Mandy's phone over and buckled my seatbelt, she leaned across the aisle to fill me in.

"Six bombs and counting," she whispered. "The Free Blooders are busy tonight. The Sorano Munitions plant in Alabama was hit. One of Peyroux's wolfsbane farms is on fire, too."

"What's that?" Audrey turned and blinked at us, pausing to open her mouth wide in a mock yawn. I felt the pressure building in my ears, too. We were descending. "Did you say something about a fire?" Audrey asked.

Levi reached across the aisle and squeezed her arm. "Are they being too nosy—noisy, Your Grace?" he asked, twisting in his seat to give Mandy a dirty look. "I got headphones in my bag if you'd like some music to listen to."

Audrey smiled and patted his hand where it rested on her arm. "I'm fine, sugar."

I gave Mandy a small nod, trying to show my appreciation without drawing any more alarm from the duchess. The wide, distant gaze Mandy used to return my look told me that she was still listening. I strained to hear too, but all I could make out was the muted timbre of Dante's replies to whoever was on the other end of his call.

Six bombs. And right after Imbolc. Marcel had waited until he knew the nobles loyal to House Lilith would be out in the open, traveling home from Denver, when receiving the news would unsettle them the most—as it was no doubt unnerving Dante now.

Security detail would have been lighter at Marcel's targets tonight too, the best guards having accompanied their masters to the celebration. And the fact that he'd crippled operations needed to combat him and his ilk hadn't escaped my attention either.

If Lord Sorano was desperate for action before, he'd

downright demand it now. I would bet he'd get the votes needed to veto Dante's protection order over the Raymore twins, too. If that happened, House Lilith's leadership would be called into question. This was the beginning of a drastic downward spiral.

We were between a tomb and a hard place. Right where Marcel wanted us.

"Apologies, Your Highness," the flight attendant interrupted Dante's call. A timid smile twitched at the corners of her mouth. "The captain has requested a private word with you."

"We are about to land. I will check in once we touch down," Dante said into his phone, loud enough for me to hear this time. Then he ended the call.

Turbulence rattled the plane as he stood, and he braced himself between his vacated seat and the cabin ceiling. The attendant almost face-planted, at the last second grabbing Murphy's beefy arm where it hung over the aisle.

"Whoa there, sister," he said, offering his hand to help her upright again.

"Is there a problem, captain?" Dante asked as he entered the cockpit and slipped into the co-pilot's seat. When I couldn't make out the pilot's hushed reply, I looked to Mandy once again.

"He can't reach McCoy's men on the ground," she rasped under her breath. The yellow ring had returned around her pupils, and the armrests squeaked in protest at her death grip. "Something's wrong."

"Is that the fire you were talking about?" Audrey pressed her forehead against her window. A soft light haloed her strawberry locks just before the night sky exploded, filling the cabin with a hellish glow.

The plane shuddered violently and tilted to one side. My face connected with the back of Levi's seat, and the holsters of my shoulder harness dug into my biceps. An armrest gouged my hip as I was flopped around like a ragdoll, barely held in place by my seatbelt.

"Is everyone all right?" Dante shouted over Audrey's shrill screams.

"What the devil was that?" Ursula demanded. "And would someone kindly shut her up?"

Smoke bloomed outside the plane's windows, and for a second, I couldn't tell which way was up or down. Even when the air began to clear, the world made no sense. Just a blur of flames and flashing emergency lights, slicing up the night.

I reached for Mandy, but she was secure, her body curled in an uptight ball, sneakers planted against the back of Audrey's seat. The duchess was having a harder time, though her screaming had subsided. She braced one arm against her window, fighting the pull of gravity and dissecting my view of the flaming pit that smoldered beneath us.

Levi reached across the aisle and clutched Audrey's free arm. "I've got you," he said.

The plane's wings slowly leveled, but my relief was stunted as a blaring alarm sounded from the cockpit.

"There's an airport in Fulton," Dante shouted over the noise.

"It's too far." The pilot pressed a button, silencing the alarm. "We have a fuel leak and an engine fire."

"Well we clearly cannot land here," Dante barked.

"There's plenty of flat farmland nearby," the pilot argued. "We should make use of it while we can, though it'll be dicey in the dark."

"There," Dante pointed.

My eyes followed, and I realized that his blood vision had kicked in. Mine had, too. It was hard to tell how much of the red haze was from the burning airport, and how much was thanks to the Eye of Blood. Either way, we were going down fast.

"*Fuuuuuck.*" A whine passed through Mandy's clenched teeth that were suddenly too big for her mouth.

"Hold it together, Starsgard," Levi shouted, his voice edged with gravel. "Save the shift for after the crash, case you need healin'."

"We're gonna crash?" Audrey cried.

"I meant *if* we crash," Levi amended. "Mighty unlikely," he added, unconvincingly.

Though the severe angle of the landscape through the plane's windows didn't leave much doubt to cling to at this point.

Chapter Eleven

I swallowed and tried to breathe through my nose. If I opened my mouth, I was sure I'd start screaming. Either that or my heart would pop straight up and out through my throat, my stomach right on its tail.

I was usually more collected in a crisis. Or at least, I was more prone to action. But there wasn't much use for that in a plane that was falling out of the sky.

"Brace for impact!" the captain shouted. Not that we were doing anything other than just that.

I gripped my armrests tighter and tried to hold myself in place. Each time the aircraft wobbled, my seatbelt rubbed against the throbbing ache in my hip. Mandy whimpered beside me, but before I could offer any encouraging words, the plane pulled up, and we touched down.

The landing lights washed over the empty field before us, illuminating the upturned earth responsible for our graceless, bone-rattling ride. With my blood vision in full effect, the beams appeared pink against the crimson-stained landscape. That we were in one piece seemed a promising sign. The pond up ahead was less so.

"Water!" Dante and Ursula shouted at the same time.

"What? Where?" The pilot stopped fiddling with the controls to squint into the distance. "Shit. Hold on!"

The screech of brakes grew sharper, and then our bumpy sprint ended as the nose of the plane plunged into the pond, splashing water over the windshield. The momentum threw me forward, and my seatbelt threatened to cut me in half. I couldn't unbuckle it fast enough.

"Are we alive?" Mandy croaked. Beyond the frazzled nerves, she seemed unscathed. Audrey and Levi, too. I scrambled toward the cockpit as the cabin lights flickered on.

"Jenna!" Ursula grabbed my arm as I passed her seat. "You're okay." She blew out a relieved sigh that warmed my heart, despite our current dilemma. Then Dante's arms were around me, squeezing the breath from my lungs.

"Is Audrey—?"

"She's fine," I answered, extinguishing his panic. There was plenty of that going around, as made evident by all the budding fangs.

Murphy groaned as he helped the flight attendant off his lap. He delicately adjusted his crotch, where I imagined the woman had landed none-too-gently during the turbulence caused by the airport explosion.

"Still no word from McCoy's men," the pilot announced. "They might not have survived that blast."

Audrey made a noise somewhere between a gag and a sob, the pilot earning a cold glare from Dante. Playing pretend seemed a little pointless, all things considered, but the duchess's first breakdown as a vampling was a pitiful sight. Muddy, mascara tears trailed down her cheeks and mixed with the twin rivers of blood leaking from her bottom lip. Her fangs were fully extended, eyes dilated, and nostrils flared. When she noticed me staring, she covered her mouth with one hand and loosed another sob.

Levi knelt in the aisle to unbuckle her and then pulled her into his arms. He smoothed her hair with one hand and made soft noises in her ear before retaking his seat, nestling Audrey in his lap. Any other time, I would have rolled my eyes. But if not for Levi, Dante would have swooped in to handle the coddling, and that wouldn't do. Not tonight.

"We can call in a Blood Vice transport," Dante said, turning to Murphy, who already had his phone out. His fingers worked swiftly over the screen.

"One step ahead of you, boss," Murphy said, then grimaced as he adjusted himself again. "Anyone hurt? Should we request a medical unit, too?"

"No. I think we got lucky," Dante answered, taking another look around the cabin.

"Did we?" Lane asked, watching Murphy check his groin a third time. "That's not what I'd call it."

"There's some good news," the pilot said, shuffling past us and toward the back of the plane. "The engine fire went out on its own. There's still a gas leak, though. Which means we should exit the aircraft to be safe. We didn't make it that far into the water. The luggage door at the rear should get us close to shore."

As the senior guards of House Lilith, Murphy and Lane followed the pilot first, leading the way ahead of the royal fam. Mandy and Levi slipped in behind us. They both looked ragged from fighting the shift through the plane's descent. Supernatural instincts were a bitch, and we were all eager to be on the ground.

The luggage door wasn't much more than a small panel covering a hole near the plane's floor. There were no airstairs either. The pilot pulled a lever on the panel and yanked it up and out of the way. My blood vision had faded, but the submerged landing lights made the pond water glow a murky green beneath us, offering a sliver of guidance in the pitch-black night.

Murphy exited first, sliding on his bottom and hunching his shoulders to squeeze through the opening. He hit the pond with a thunderous splash and swore.

"This water might as well be ice," he hollered. "And it's waist-deep. You want me to carry you, boss?"

"I should think not." Dante sniffed and straightened the lapels of his jacket. "You can carry me when I'm dead—*truly dead*—Mr. Murphy."

Ursula held up a finger in Dante's face as she wedged past him. "Enjoy your pride. I'm opting for comfort."

Lane went next, echoing Murphy's splash and colorful language. Then they both reached up to help Ursula out and into Murphy's arms. The pilot tossed Lane a flashlight. The guard clicked it on and aimed it at the shoreline before he and Murphy sloshed across the pond with Ursula.

"Don't worry, Your Grace," Levi said, rubbing Audrey's shoulders to soothe her teeth-chattering shivers. "I'll keep you warm and dry." He pressed a kiss to her knuckles before making for the exit.

Unlike Murphy and Lane, Levi squatted and turned his back to the doorway, leaving a hand on the bottom lip of the opening until he'd cleared it. He entered the water soundlessly, save for the shuddering inhale that followed. His eyes were rimmed with gold when he looked up, searching for Audrey.

Dante helped the pilot lower the duchess down to her wolfy guardian before turning to me.

"Shall I carry you?" he asked, as if he hadn't just thumbed his nose at Murphy for offering the same.

"'Cause I'm not gonna." Mandy snorted. "If that water's waist-deep on Murph, I'll be dogpaddling my way to shore."

"I'll make do," I said, ducking through the opening.

I tried to keep one hand on the plane as Levi had, but ended up slipping and landing on my back in the pond. The sharp cold clamped around me like a fist. I flailed my arms, struggling against my buttoned suit jacket and desperately trying to stand before too much moisture found its way into my holsters and firearms.

Dante and Mandy dropped to either side of me, splashing more freezing water into my face as they attempted to help. Mandy reached me first, though when she grabbed my arm, I almost lost what little footing I'd found in the silt at the bottom of the pond. As embarrassed as I was, I had to admire her for coming to my aid. She could barely keep her chin above the water's surface.

"Are you all right?" Dante asked, grasping my opposite elbow.

"I'm fine. Just a klutz," I said, glad it was too dark for everyone to see my burning cheeks and soggy ponytail. Dante waited a moment until he was certain I could stand on my own, and then turned to help the flight attendant down.

Headlights flashed across the body of the plane and the luggage door as the pilot squatted in the opening. He shielded his eyes with one hand and squinted through his fingers. I turned to find two SUVs in the distance, bouncing roughly over the field as they approached.

"Looks like McCoy's men made it out, after all," the pilot said, confusion furrowing his brow.

Dante sloshed after Mandy and me as we headed for the shoreline past the rear of the plane. It was a slow, cumbersome trudge, the muddy pond bottom sucking at my shoes with every step.

We hadn't made it far before the SUVs arrived, stopping with enough force to summon a dirt cloud up into the near-blinding high-beams. Several passenger doors flung open, but before I could get a look at the men, I was thrust face-first into the icy water.

"Get down!" Mandy hissed as I came up gulping for air. She pushed me under again before I had the breath to protest. Dante's elbow cracked me in the shoulder, and I realized Mandy had dunked him, as well. And just in time.

The sound of bullets punching through metal echoed above us. But it was the screaming that ripped at my heart and shot blind hot panic into every nerve ending.

Free Blooders.

Of course they'd found us. Six—no, seven bombs in a single night? How could one *not* have our name on it?

Mandy dragged Dante and me sideways, toward the shadows under the rear of the plane's fuselage. As soon as there was a break in the gunfire, she released us, then pushed off the pond's bottom and swam for shore. If she decided to shift, heaven help these bastards.

I sucked in a ragged, shivering breath and blinked the water from my eyes. The blood vision was back. I assumed for Dante too, considering how quickly his hand found mine.

"Hurry," he whispered, pulling me farther into the shadows that stretched past the tail of the plane. My muscles resisted, stiff from the cold, but a fire bubbling in my core kept me going. I stole a glance over my shoulder, my attention snagging on some small movement in the water.

The flight attendant lay face-up in the pond. Two messy, dark holes marring her white dress shirt. Above her, the pilot's legs dangled from the luggage door opening, blood dripping from the hem of his pants.

That had almost been us.

It could still be us.

The realization tightened my throat, and I had to fight for my next breath as Dante dragged me along. Once we reached the darker shadows behind the plane, he redirected me toward the shore again.

The water grew shallower, my clothes heavier, and the air colder. I shook free of Dante's hold and struggled to unbutton my jacket with numb fingers. I needed my pistols. If we were going to be gunned down by the Free Blooders, I'd be taking some of them with us. There was no way in hell I'd go gently, princess or not.

"I can see Audrey," Dante rasped, peeking around what little cover the plane's tail offered. "She's alive."

My jaw clenched as the gunfire resumed, and I gave up on my buttons, opting to rip the jacket open instead. I unholstered my pistols and shook the water from their barrels before joining Dante to assess the scene.

My heart sank as I took in the carnage. Audrey was indeed alive, though I wasn't sure the same could be said for Levi. He lay unmoving over the duchess. Blood stained the back of his gray sweater. Audrey squirmed and writhed beneath him, pinned to the ground. Not far from them, Ursula grunted as she rolled Lane onto his back. His eyes stared up at the night sky, as empty and unforgiving as the bullet hole carved into the center of his forehead.

I swallowed the bile rising in my throat and searched for the others, immediately recognizing Murphy's hulking silhouette. He aimed and fired twice, killing the nearest vehicle's headlights. Before he could squeeze off a third shot, a bullet caught him in the arm.

Mandy picked up where he'd left off, taking out another headlight before dancing a few rounds across the SUV's windshield until she lined one up between the open passenger door and frame. A gurgling scream let me know she'd hit her mark. Not to be outdone, Murphy extinguished the remaining headlight, and darkness settled across the field.

With the Eye of Blood, I could see straight through the vehicles' windshields to the remaining Free Blooders within. I didn't expect to recognize any of the men, but if I could get a decent look at one, I might be able to pick him out of the endless pool of suspected contacts Blood Vice had amassed.

One of the drivers reminded me of a past associate of Arnie's, a man I'd pet-named Mustache, with cringe-worthy facial hair and a sleeveless vest. February in the Midwest was freezing, but werewolves ran hot. Good thing, too. The fashion disaster revealed a half-sleeve tattoo that covered the man's biceps.

As if he realized he'd been made, he threw the SUV into drive and floored it, heading straight for Mandy. She stood closest to the water, the pond's eerie green glow streaking her damp hair and leather jacket.

I wanted to scream at her to move, but everything happened too fast. The SUV's grill connected with her chest, and she flew backward, landing hard in the water. The passenger door opened, and a man approached the pond, rifle in hand. Blood blossomed across his chest before I even realized I'd taken aim. More consciously, I shot through his open door at the exposed driver in the front seat. The man took a round in the neck and another in the back as he attempted to exit the vehicle.

"The queen!" Murphy fired at a man who'd slipped from the other SUV. His shots were too slow, but they were enough warning for Ursula. She ripped Lane's pistol from his hip holster and pointed it at the man.

The Free Blooder dropped and rolled out of her trajectory as she squeezed the trigger. The motion brought him alongside Audrey instead.

The duchess had finally crawled out from under Levi, though she remained at his side. There was blood on his sweater. Even more on his pants—one leg in particular. His slacks were shredded up to his thigh, and the visible flesh was no better off.

Audrey frantically tried to stop the bleeding. Her hands were covered in blood. It was smeared down the front of her coat and across her cheeks, likely from scrubbing at her relentless tears. *Or licking her fingers.* Vampling urges were hard to manage even when everything *was* going according to plan.

When the Free Blooder rolled into her, Audrey screamed and clawed at his eyes. The man was twice her size, but she fought for all she was worth as he yanked her up by the arm. Until he jabbed his pistol at the side of her head.

"Stay back!" he screamed, knocking the barrel against Audrey's temple as Murphy drew closer.

"Amos is bleeding out. We have to move!" The driver of the still-occupied SUV laid on the horn.

I took a careful step toward Ursula, both pistols aimed at the man holding Audrey. "You'll never make it out of here alive if you harm her."

The Free Blooder sneered at me. "Looks like she's my insurance policy then." He dragged Audrey backward toward the SUV.

"No, no, no," the duchess wailed, her dilated eyes darting from me to Murphy to Ursula to Levi's unconscious body. She covered her mouth with her stained fingers and moaned pitifully.

"Take me instead," Dante called. My gaze darted away from Audrey for a split-second, long enough to see that Dante had left the cover of the plane and now stood in the thin light surrounding the pond. "I am a far greater prize for your master, I assure you," he pleaded.

"And now we have you, too. Don't we?" The man snorted and gave Audrey a shake, rekindling her sobs. "We'll be in touch." He released Audrey's arm and knotted his hand in her hair before shoving her headfirst into the back seat of the SUV.

"Tires?" I whispered, dipping my pistols downward as the man climbed in after Audrey.

"No." Murphy gritted his teeth. "Won't do no good. They're armored. All of McCoy's are."

"We have to do *something*."

"There is nothing we *can* do," Dante said, clutching his hands in and out of fists at his sides. "But…they won't kill her." He made it sound like a question, then quickly answered it himself as if fearful that someone might offer up more doubt than he could bare. "No. Not if they intend to use her to blackmail me."

"We could follow them in the other SUV," I suggested, my voice straining against the tightness building in my chest.

"No." Dante's jaw flexed. "A car chase would only further endanger Audrey."

The SUV door slammed shut, and the vehicle began to back away. Our window of opportunity was closing. Panic hitched my breath, and my hands shook more from nerves than the cold. A few seconds later, the darkness eating the horizon swallowed the vehicle and any hope of saving Audrey.

Dante stumbled forward a step and dropped to his knees on the muddy bank. The green glow of the pond gave his skin a sickly hue.

"Call McCoy," he ordered, waving away the hand Murphy offered. "Get the GPS information for that SUV and relay it to Blood Vice. Pull all of our best agents off the Free Blooder search and refocus their efforts on recovering the duchess immediately."

"No." Ursula's sharp tone froze Murphy in place. He swallowed and gave Dante a pleading look as the queen chastised the prince. "You'd be giving them exactly what they want."

"I don't care." Dante's eyes were suddenly dangerous, his wide, inky pupils bleeding black all the way to his lashes. "The long game you wish to play is getting us nowhere, and now my scion has been taken."

Ursula took the hand I extended and let me pull her up onto her feet. Her white sweater dress was speckled with blood, though none of it appeared to be hers. She smoothed her hands down her stomach before turning back to Dante. "Suffering makes you reckless, cousin."

He lifted his chin. "Not all of us have the luxury of disappearing for a few decades when life serves up misery."

Ursula said nothing. Her gaze trailed away from his and settled on Lane, her assigned guard, who had given his life for his queen. I knelt beside him and brushed my hand over his face, closing his gaping eyes.

My mind slipped further into despair as I turned toward the pond. *Mandy.*

I rushed into the water, making it up to my knees before the sound of sloppy chewing drew my attention to the stretch of shore on the opposite side of the abandoned SUV. In the pool of light spilling from the open driver's side door, I found her—gnawing on the creep who had tried to dispose of her in a watery grave. I was sure the snack was more to speed healing than to celebrate revenge.

Mandy noticed me and grunted before shaking out her wet fur. She circled the SUV, taking slow, uneven steps, and then stopped beside Levi's still form. Her breath fogged the air as she ran her muzzle over his body, and then she loosed a howl that sent up the hairs on the back of my neck. Though the sound wasn't as bleak as I'd expected it to be.

When Levi groaned, I understood why.

Chapter Twelve

Blood Vice's idea of a medical unit made me feel like a prude. Maybe I was just spoiled from all the blood pot room service at home. Feeding fang-to-flesh with an audience felt too intimate. Luckily, I was not in desperate need of blood. Murphy, on the other hand, had a bullet wound to heal.

He sat across from Dante, Ursula, and me, shamelessly sucking on a paramedic's arm. Mandy was sandwiched in on his other side, shifted back into her human form and dressed in an oversized hoodie she'd taken off one of the dead Free Blooders. Her soaked clothes and shoes were in a garbage bag on her lap, which she propped her elbows on as she crammed another protein bar into her mouth. She'd swiped the whole box from the paramedics after refusing to let them look at her broken ribs. To be fair, Levi was in more desperate need of their attention.

Audrey's bodyguard *slash* donor-no-longer-in-waiting lay on a gurney between us. Before offering up her blood, the paramedic feeding Murphy had hooked Levi up to a morphine drip and removed a bullet from his shoulder. Her partner, a male werewolf who was now driving us back to St. Louis, had dug four more rounds from Levi's calf and lower thigh. He was in bad shape, but Harold and Ambrose had been contacted and were busy sterilizing a room in the basement to take over Levi's medical needs once we arrived—which would be any minute now, given the wailing sirens that parted the highway traffic ahead of us.

The ambulance looked kosher from the outside, if a little larger than standard. It was designed to contain a wounded werewolf in the event they became conscious enough to shift—something I was *really* hoping Levi would hold off on until we got home. As soon as he went furry, he'd want meat, and a lot of it. After half a dozen protein bars, I was sure Mandy was ready for something real to sink her teeth into, too. The dead Free Blooder's heart had been more of an appetizer, considering the calories she would need to heal her injuries.

A trembling sigh escaped the paramedic crammed in the back of the ambulance with us, and Murphy finally withdrew his fangs from the bend of her arm. He waited for the woman to press a piece of gauze over the twin punctures he'd left behind and then helped her apply a bandage.

It was all very polite. And impersonal. And I assumed quite possibly the first time he'd fed directly from a donor since Yoshiko.

Murphy's gaze snagged on mine, and I resumed staring at Mandy. Even with her flat-browed scowl, I was more comfortable looking at her than anyone else right now.

As soon as Levi had been loaded into the ambulance, Murphy received word that the SUV Audrey had been taken in was found abandoned and torched off I-70. The Free Blooders' trail was dead. And three more bombs had been reported, all affecting noble vamp households that supported the current hemoarchy. To make matters worse, Ursula had forbidden Dante from redirecting any additional Blood Vice resources to search for the duchess.

The agents were spread thin and working overtime as it was. Still, I couldn't help but sympathize with Dante. If the Free Blooders had taken him instead of Audrey, I would have been ready to move heaven and earth to get him back, too.

Though it had been a short conversation—thanks to the prying eyes of the paramedics—the tension between the queen and the prince simmered beneath the surface. They silently stewed, refusing to speak to each other or anyone else. And I was seated right between them. *Lucky me.*

Levi groaned, his back bowing over the gurney and his sweaty chest straining against the straps that held him in place. My shoulders squared as the paramedic checked his morphine drip. The woman mistook Ursula's sour expression for criticism, and her face flushed.

"I'm so sorry, Your Majesty. I wish there was something more I could do for him," she said, blinking stiffly as if struggling to maintain consciousness herself.

Murphy had taken a healthy pull from her vein. The bullet he'd caught had gone all the way through the meat of his biceps, so at least nothing had to be dug out. For now, he was wrapped and in a sling. A couple of blood pots, and he'd be operational again.

Unlike Lane.

My breath tightened in my throat, an unexpected reflex every time my thoughts drifted back to him. It didn't seem real. None of it did. The airport explosion. The plane going down. Levi fighting for his life. Audrey being abducted. Lane just…*gone.*

The ambulance slowed as we took an exit ramp off I-64. We'd be home soon. My stomach churned at the two-minute warning. As soon as Levi was handed off to our in-house medical staff, and the paramedics departed, Dante and Ursula would pick up where they'd left off.

I wanted to be nowhere near that shitstorm. I also knew I was the only one who had half a chance of surviving it and keeping the two of them from ripping each other to shreds. The task would have seemed less daunting had I anything even remotely helpful to bring to the conversation. But I didn't.

I was numb. Completely drained, both mentally and emotionally.

And I had no idea how or *if* we would get Audrey back.

Ursula was right. Dividing and depleting our resources was exactly what the Free Blooders wanted. It would be the cue that launched whatever their next move was. And it would be the final nail in House Lilith's coffin, practically an invitation for the council to overthrow us. Dante had to know that. But love was the killer of common sense, even among the most rational.

Ambrose met us in the driveway, immediately addressing the paramedics as they wheeled Levi's gurney out of the ambulance. "Let's get him downstairs. He'll need a blood transfusion and likely more pain meds before we can coax him into shifting."

For all my irritation at having Sonja's uncle as a house guest, I was relieved and grateful that I hadn't pushed harder for Ursula to rescind the invitation. He was all business when it counted, and it definitely counted right now.

Mandy trailed after Levi's gurney. A bullet hole torn in the back of her pillaged hoodie revealed a purple bruise creeping around her ribcage. More speckled her thin legs, and her toenails were caked with mud. Murphy followed her inside, his suit jacket draped over his good arm. They paused in the foyer as the rest of us joined them.

Dante and I were damp from our dip in the pond, but the heat in the ambulance had helped keep the chill at bay. Still, I looked forward to dry clothes. And some blood, if for nothing more than to calm my nerves. Ursula was dry, having been carried over the water, though the blood spatter across her white dress reminded me just how much worse the night could have been.

Audrey's abduction aside, our bodyguards had done a bang-up job. Especially considering the shape they were in now.

One of the house guards pulled the front doors closed behind me, sealing out the cold night and revealing Harold in his white jacket. He bowed to Ursula, his old hands shaking as he folded them against his chest. "Welcome home, Your Maj—"

"Save your fawning," she said and jerked her chin toward the basement stairwell where Ambrose directed the paramedics carrying Levi. "You're needed elsewhere."

"Of course, Your Majesty." Harold bowed again and then hurried after Ambrose.

Their voices trailed off, but the silence was soon interrupted by the clicking of tiny toenails. Sweet Pea, the teacup Pomeranian Dante had gifted Audrey for Midwinter, raced down the south-wing hallway.

Audrey had cried when she learned that no pets were

allowed at the bat cave, but a donor from the harem had volunteered to dog-sit while we were away.

Sweet Pea whimpered and pranced a circle around us until Mandy dropped her trash bag of clothes and scooped up the little beast, groaning as if she'd forgotten her injuries.

The lights and garlands Audrey had begged Dante to leave up through Imbolc hung from every wall and banister. They reflected off the glossy white surface of her piano in the corner. She'd played *Jingle Bells* a dozen times during Midwinter, begging Mandy to stop singing the Batman smells version. She'd also taught herself the song from the opening credits of *Henry's Courtroom* to impress Laura.

Audrey hadn't been with us for very long, but she'd left her mark. This was her home, and now it didn't feel like ours without her.

Sweet Pea whimpered and licked Mandy's chin as the girl sniffled, earning a tender look from Murphy. Their usual banter was ruthless, but the head of the royal guard was more of a bleeding heart than he'd ever admit. He cupped Mandy's shoulder with his bear-sized palm and nodded toward the south stairwell.

"Unless someone's changed Yosh's Saturday menu, the harem should have plenty of leftover offal chili," he said. "And I could use a shot or three of blood."

Mandy sniffled again but let Murphy lead her away. Bits of dried mud crumbled from her feet, creating a trail across the hardwood floor. With Belinda in Texas, I wondered who was coordinating the household duties—and managing the harem, for that matter. We were a very large family without our mother hen.

The paramedics emerged from the basement with an empty gurney in tow. They paused and bowed collectively to Ursula, Dante, and me. A radio on one of their hips buzzed, requesting assistance with a 10-91w—a werewolf bite—at a nightclub in St. Charles.

"Thank you both for your exceptional service tonight," Dante said, shooting a sideways glance at Ursula.

"Yes," the queen added. "We are most grateful."

"Thank you," I echoed, stepping aside as the guards opened the front doors for them.

We waited in the foyer, listening to the paramedics close up the ambulance outside and speed off to their next crisis. And then the unspoken truce ended.

Dante stalked into his office and snatched the handset from the phone on his desk. Ursula and I followed, though I remained a safe distance behind. My caution was rewarded when Ursula unplugged the cord attached to the phone's base, ending Dante's call before he could finish dialing. He turned suddenly and smashed the handset against the wall behind his chair.

I remained in the doorway, unable to muster the courage to enter the room. I could hardly bring myself to look at Dante. This felt all wrong. He was supposed to be the levelheaded one, taming Ursula when she came unhinged. Not the other way around.

The guards in the foyer traded uncomfortable glances. I assumed, like me, they wondered which side they'd take should things between the queen and prince escalate. For many of them, Dante had been signing their paychecks for decades. However, Ursula was now their queen. *Our* queen. And *my* sire.

"The council will judge our actions," Ursula stated calmly. "We will not give them reason to accuse us of abusing our power and position by redirecting resources toward a personal matter while we are at war."

"I will not stand by and do nothing." Dante pointed a finger in her face. His eyes had gone full black again, fangs budding beneath the curl of his upper lip. "You may be queen, but do not forget who paved the path for your reentry into this family and positioned you to inherit the keys to our kingdom."

Ursula swatted his hand away and plucked the cell phone from the breast pocket of his suit jacket. "I haven't forgotten, and I'm not telling you to do nothing," she snapped. "I'm only asking that you *think* your actions through first—as I have."

"Have you?" Dante scoffed. "Is that so?"

"*Yes.*" She bit off the word with so much venom that I jumped. "We will get Audrey back. Tonight. By the *only* means necessary." Dante didn't budge. There was a healthy amount of skepticism in the gaze he pierced her with, though the whites of his eyes had returned. As Ursula stared him down, some spark of understanding seemed to dawn on him.

"You mean we're going to—?"

"Yes." Ursula nodded.

"You know the way?"

"We have someone who does."

Dante ran a hand over his mouth and jaw, his gaze narrowing as he considered Ursula's plan—a scheme I was completely oblivious to. "Can Holland be trusted, though?" Dante asked. "I heard about Clyde's disappearance. They could be working together for the Free Blooders."

"Let me worry about that," Ursula said. "Do you want your scion back or not?"

Dante's brows drew together, but he nodded.

"Then go change. Both of you," Ursula added, tossing a glance over her shoulder at me. Then she looked down at the screen of Dante's phone and opened his contacts list. "Dress warm, wear sensible shoes, and meet me back here in thirty minutes. We have a road trip ahead of us. But first, I have some strings to pull."

She held the phone to her ear, giving Dante and I her back as she paced to the opposite side of the room. "Radu, darling," she purred. "Your queen has a little proposal for you."

I didn't stick around to pry for more details about Ursula's plan or to question her need for the black sheep of House Vlad. If it could conjure hope in Dante, that was good enough for me. Still, having no idea where we were going or what we were doing made preparing a stressful task.

I decided to leave my Reaper TDs and shoulder holster behind to dry out, but I did grab my Browning and tucked it down into a slip-on hip holster. The black sweater I chose hid it well. Jeans and combat boots completed my come-what-may ensemble.

My hair was gritty with half-dried pond water, but there wasn't time for a shower. I twisted it up into a messy bun at the nape of my neck and called it good. Then I chugged the pot of blood that had been delivered to my room and headed out.

Ursula hadn't mentioned guards, but there was no way I

could take off without letting Mandy know. I found her at the breakfast bar in the upstairs harem, shoveling spoonful after spoonful of chili into her mouth. Murphy sat on a stool beside her, slurping from an oversized coffee mug. He watched her with a concerned pinch between his brows as if he were confused about where all the food she devoured went once it passed her lips. Like there might be a black hole living in the pit of her stomach.

Sweet Pea lounged on the stool on Mandy's other side. She lifted her head and yipped softly at me as I neared them—half-greeting and half-warning.

"Ursula has some plan to get Audrey back," I blurted as I stole a glance at the watch on my wrist. "We leave in fifteen minutes."

"Wait, what?" Mandy said, cheeks bulging.

My shoulders hunched in an embarrassed shrug. "That's all I know. She told me to change and meet her back in Dante's office."

"Where are we going?" Murphy asked, pushing his stool back.

"Uh…*we?*" I glanced at the sling wrapped around his arm.

"There's no way I'm staying here." He stood and puffed out his chest, wincing slightly when his shoulder protested.

"Me either." Mandy swallowed and stood too, her jaw flexing from the effort. "I better go change." She grabbed a handful of beef jerky from a bucket on the counter and headed for the south stairwell. Sweet Pea hopped off the barstool and scampered after the girl, snagging a piece of fallen jerky along the way.

"*Uh…uh…*" I stammered, trying to find the right words to stop Mandy without hurting her feelings, but she was gone too soon.

Murphy touched his shoulder and winced again. "I probably got time for another cuppa, yeah?"

I blinked at him and gritted my teeth. "I really don't see Ursula or Dante being okay with the two of you coming along. Until you've healed, you're more liability than asset."

"Liability?" Murphy snorted. "I'm not head of the royal guard for nothin', *Your Highness*," he added before topping off his cup. He lifted it to his lips and proceeded to chug, still glaring at me over the rim.

"Great." I sighed and dragged my hands down my face. "I'm going back to Dante's office before I botch this plan any more than I already have."

Murphy grunted, and a line of blood leaked from the corner of his mouth. I took that as my cue to fuck off and made for the stairs.

Chapter Thirteen

When I made it back to the foyer, I found Ambrose waiting. He stood at the top of the basement steps, wiping his hands on a bloody towel that he quickly tucked into a pocket of his white doctor's coat upon noticing me. His professional attire made him more approachable than the finery he'd donned at the bat cave, though the tight smile that twitched up the corners of his mouth offered little comfort.

"How's Levi?" I asked, hugging myself.

"Stable," he answered before expounding. "We've begun the transfusion, but I doubt we'll make it through more than a unit or two before he's ready to shift. Two wolves from your security staff are hunting the property. A fresh kill will go a long way to help in his recovery. Once he shifts back, we'll resume the transfusion and see if he needs any temporary casting to support his leg as the bone completes its healing."

"Good." I sighed and nodded.

"Then he'll just have to stay off his feet for a few days," Ambrose added, the skin at the corners of his eyes creasing. "With the duchess missing, that might be…"

"Impossible?" I finished.

Ambrose pressed his lips together and offered me an apologetic smile.

First Dante, and now Levi. We needed Audrey. Without her, it was only a matter of time before House Lilith self-destructed. I sure hoped Ursula knew what she was doing.

"How are *you* holding up?" Ambrose's tone held as much curiosity as concern, and I was immediately reminded of his shady interrogation at Imbolc.

"Fine," I answered with a tight smile.

"Fine?" His eyebrows rose, creasing his brow. "You just survived an airplane crash, a member of your family was abducted, and one of your guards is in critical condition. And you're...*fine?*"

He didn't know about Lane, I realized. But I couldn't bring myself to tell him. I'd start crying, and then there would be no denying that I was on the verge of falling apart. Dante had already jumped off that cliff tonight. If I would be of any use in getting Audrey back, I needed to cling to this emotional deadlock for as long as possible.

"I'm doing as well as can be expected, all things considered," I finally amended.

Ambrose clicked his tongue. "Well, I hope you'll at least find some time to open up to that therapist you mentioned before."

"Right." I bit the inside of my cheek, wondering if that was yet another tidbit I should have kept to myself. These sneaky old vamps retained details like veteran detectives.

The doorbell echoed through the foyer. It set the hairs on the back of my neck to attention, and red flashed across my vision, a knee-jerk reaction when every surprise the evening had presented thus far had turned catastrophic.

"Good evening, Mr. Vlad," one of the door guards greeted Radu as he ushered the ancient vamp and his entourage inside.

For such short notice, I was surprised by their snazzy suits. Then again, it was Saturday and nearly midnight. They'd probably come straight from Bleeders. I recognized a few of the security techs from the club and noted the laptop bags and briefcases they carried. Then Zane, Radu's so-called scion, snagged my attention just before the blood vision had a chance to fade. For the first time since we'd met, he was crystal-clear in the Eye of Blood.

"Looks like someone's a real bat boy now," I said under my breath. Zane's eyes narrowed. Maybe he'd heard—though it could have been his natural reaction to me, given our hostile past.

"Your Highness, Dr. Starling," Radu greeted us, bowing slightly to me before offering Ambrose his hand.

"How's the blood business, Mr. Vlad?" Ambrose cracked one of his teasing grins. I'd found them suspect at first, after Dante's warning, but they were beginning to grow on me.

Either that or I was just more tolerant now that my friend's life was in his hands.

"Business is…"—Radu cocked his head from side to side—"*busy*. Between the increased traffic at the club and the renovations at the opera house, I can hardly catch my breath."

"Perhaps House Lilith can help with that," Ursula called from the mouth of the south wing as she joined us. She'd changed into a pair of black slacks and a matching turtleneck. Dante appeared a split-second later, emerging from the semi-circular hallway that wrapped around the backside of the office and led to his bedroom. He wore all black, as well. Our little trio looked fit to rob a bank.

"Your Majesty." Radu dipped into another bow before taking Ursula's hand in both of his. "Lovely as ever," he cooed before turning her arm over and pressing his thin lips to the inside of her wrist.

The gesture drew a scowl from Zane and a nose crinkle from me. Ursula handled it with more finesse, layering her other hand over his and twisting until they were in the double-handshake position, placid smile never leaving her face. Radu didn't resist the correction. I doubted he meant to offend Ursula. Having the queen of undead society visit his club was at least *part* of the reason his surviving establishment was thriving despite the threat the Free Blooders posed.

"As I'm sure you can guess, House Lilith will soon be undergoing some major renovations, as well," Ursula said, skipping over the usual niceties. "There is also a rather large household at the late prince's estate in Texas that will need to be reassigned. Employees—guards and donors—who will need to find new employment."

Radu's thick brows lifted with interest, but his eyes were sharp with reserve. "Good help is hard to find, but while the opera house is out of order, I already have too many employees living off the small stipend I can afford until they are back to work."

"I'm aware." Ursula touched Radu's shoulder and shot Dante a sideways glance before continuing. "I'm prepared to invest the selling price of the Texas estate into the opera house in exchange for you taking on these extra employees—once you've reopened, of course—*and* if you'll agree to loan us your security staff for the evening."

"Ah." Radu smirked. "You baited it nicely. But as you can see,"—Radu turned to glance back at the techs he'd brought with him—"I assumed you would eventually seek my more *sophisticated* services. Blood Vice is burning the stake at both ends, from dusk to dawn. It is not good for morale."

"This is not for Blood Vice. And it has less to do with tech than it does…muscle."

I coughed to hide an involuntary snort. *Muscle?* More like ruthless amorality. It was the most diplomatic thing I'd ever heard Ursula utter.

She offered Radu a pinched smile. "I'd like you to handle a personal matter for House Lilith. Audrey, our new duchess, has been taken by the Free Blooders. With everyone searching for Marcel Moreau, we cannot afford to redirect Blood Vice resources. But we *can* grant you access to their databases and files so you're prepared."

"Prepared for what, exactly?" Radu asked.

"To storm the castle, darling. What else?" Ursula was trying to make light of our dilemma, but the strain in her voice and the set of her shoulders gave her away. "Our head of security's office in the basement has been set up to accommodate you. We have another personal matter to attend to tonight—one that will hopefully yield the location of our dear duchess, unless your research should reveal her whereabouts first. Either way, as soon as we know where she is being held, I'm counting on you to retrieve her by any means necessary."

Radu tapped a finger to his dimpled chin. "*Any* means necessary?"

"Any and all," Dante echoed, offering his support of the queen's plan.

"And if we do not locate the duchess this night?" Radu inquired. Tying up his security staff indefinitely was not on the table, and he was wise to spell it out for us—even at the risk of insulting the queen.

Dante's chest swelled indignantly, but before he could bite the hand we were asking to feed us, Ursula cut him off. "One way or another, we'll have her location before dawn."

Radu frowned sympathetically. "If you were anyone but the queen, I'd consider your optimism naïve."

Ursula chewed her bottom lip, and her breath hitched with desperation. "If you find out where she's being held before we do, I'll throw in House Lilith's West Coast estate, as well."

Radu's eyes twinkled with the challenge. "Let's get to work then." He motioned his men toward the basement, waving both arms to hurry them along. Before following them downstairs, he turned and bowed in farewell. "May the best detectives win."

Ursula's panicked expression dropped as soon as he was out of sight. "Vlad always was a sucker for a game of chance."

Ambrose smirked as though he agreed, but then his demeanor fell neutral once again, likely for Dante's sake. The Prince of House Lilith was in no mood for games. His gaze hadn't shifted from Ursula. Whatever her plan was, it was clearly the only thing on his mind right now.

"I should go check on Mr. Bishop," Ambrose said, excusing himself before heading back downstairs.

There was no dissuading Murphy and Mandy from coming along. Ursula wasn't thrilled by my loose lips, but to be fair, she hadn't exactly said this was a top-secret mission. That she'd relented so easily, allowing wounded guards to accompany us, filled me with equal parts relief and frustration.

Of course, I'd heard her task Radu's team with the heavy lifting, but that only seemed to add to my confusion. How were we going to get Audrey back if we weren't actually *going* to get Audrey back?

Though our little field trip apparently didn't require fully functional bodyguards, I was a bit unnerved by Holland taking Lane's place as the queen's new guard, especially after hearing Dante's concerns. Donnie would have been my choice, but he'd been Lane's best friend, so he was busy helping our late guard's sire make funeral arrangements.

Just after midnight, the six of us piled into one of Dante's SUVs. Murphy wedged a flashing light bar between the dash and the windshield to keep the Hi-Pos and night travelers from slowing us down on our way to wherever the hell we were going. Soon, we were on I-64, heading east toward Illinois.

"So…would anyone care to fill me in?" I called from the back seat. Anxiety had finally gotten the best of me.

Mandy grumbled in agreement, a stick of beef jerky in each hand. The pouch of her hoodie bulged with more. Ursula sat in front of me, Dante next to her. And Holland drove, much to Murphy's displeasure. With his arm in a sling, all the head of the royal guard could do was scowl from the front passenger seat.

Ursula twisted sideways and rested her arm on the back of the bench between us. Her red hair lay in a braid over one shoulder. The black casualwear was quite a stretch from how formally she'd dressed while at the bat cave. It made her seem younger, I supposed. Like Vanessa Sorano in her fatigues.

"Do you want the long version or the short?" she asked.

"Short," Mandy said at the same time I answered, "Long."

Ursula scowled at the girl, one brow arching with annoyance, but thankfully, she skipped the scolding. "Do you recall the family history lesson I *tried* to enlighten you with last year?" she asked, staking me with a wide, patronizing glare.

"Uh…parts of it." My cheeks burned as I looked down at my lap and picked at an invisible thread on my sweater.

"How about the parts regarding Lilith's arrival in the New World?" Ursula tried again. The low drone in her voice told me she knew she was wasting her breath.

"She came over with the pilgrims, right?" I stammered. "Lili was some distant cousin of Pocahontas or—"

"She was *Powhatan*," Ursula corrected. "Lilith promised Lili—who went by Matoaka, at the time—immortality in exchange for being her guide in the New World. They traveled from Jamestown all the way to the southern tip of Illinois."

"It wasn't known as Illinois in 1611," Dante interjected. Ursula smacked his arm.

"I'm telling the story," she snapped. "You had your chance all those nights you were bedding her rather than taking over those history lessons you promised you would."

Dante's expression remained stoic, completely unphased by her teasing. "Apologies, Your Majesty."

"So," Ursula continued, "Lili led Lilith and company— her scions, Adam and Gabriella, and the dozen or so humans and wolves in their service—along the Ohio River. They ventured much deeper into the New World than the mortal pilgrims dared, several hundred miles west of the budding colonies. Which, as you can imagine, took considerably longer than the average road trip does today.

"One fateful summer night, a violent storm upturned the wagons, and they were forced to take shelter in a cave near the river. Their supplies greatly diminished or damaged, Lilith made the decision to turn back. That same night, Lili requested her reward. And one hundred and seventy-four years later, they returned to this cave, the place where their blood bond was consummated, to lay Lilith to her forever rest."

I blinked at Ursula, trying my best not to appear too surprised by the story. It was highly likely that she'd told it to me before, during one of our mind-numbing sessions in the library last fall. Probably somewhere in between tales of her adventures at blood charm school and gossip she'd overheard about House Novak's sordid mortal affairs.

"And we're going to Lilith's tomb *why?*" Mandy piped in. She propped an untied boot against the back of Ursula's seat, removing it just as suddenly when the queen's eyes narrowed on her.

"You'll be staying behind, little pup." While I was relieved that Ursula had stopped using the term *mutt*, Mandy seemed to bristle at anything my sire called her. "Only vampires are allowed in the tomb."

"You didn't answer my question." Mandy folded her arms, then flinched and unfolded them. I imagined it would take another shift or two before her broken ribs were fully mended.

"I'm the queen." Ursula snorted. "I answer to no one, certainly not a—"

"Lilith's blood will reveal Audrey's location," Dante interrupted, earning a huff from my sire. "At least, in theory."

"In theory?" I frowned at Ursula. "Please tell me this plan of yours is not based on a crusty old legend." If we were screwing off on a childish quest while Audrey was being tortured in some shithole of a werewolf den, I would never forgive myself. Or my sire.

Ursula returned my sour expression, but it couldn't disguise the sliver of uncertainty that had emerged after Dante called her out. "It's a legend because there's only enough blood for one use. It's for dire circumstances. Like now."

"How is Lilith's blood supposed to tell us where to find Audrey?" I was still unconvinced.

"It's the last of her lifeblood," Ursula said as if that should explain it all. She swallowed and absently stroked her throat. Her gaze slid away from mine and wandered into the darkness beyond her window. We were well outside of St. Louis now, the city lights nothing more than a faint glow above the horizon behind us. A beacon to lead us home, whether Lilith's parting gift could save us or not.

A lot of mystery surrounded lifeblood among undead society. Lifeblood bonds, like the one I'd unknowingly forged with Roman, were rare. More novel yet were the medicinal uses of vampiric lifeblood—or rather the enzyme it created that could purge silver from the blood.

I guessed not enough vamps died with their lifeblood intact to warrant further research into the matter. And until now, I wasn't aware that lifeblood could be preserved for future use. Certainly not two hundred-*plus* years later.

I had a bad feeling I knew who would get to be the lab bat for that experiment.

Just the thought of Lilith's coagulated blood gumming up my throat had me swallowing to fend off a gag. If Mandy wasn't allowed inside Lilith's tomb, maybe I could bribe her into picking up some mouthwash at the nearest dollar store.

Legends, theories, and heebie-jeebies notwithstanding, I would try anything if there was even the slightest chance it could help bring Audrey home.

Chapter Fourteen

I didn't know what I'd expected Lilith's cave to look like. An Indiana Jones-ish tomb seemed too cliché. But something as unrefined as a Neanderthal hangout with fingerpaint wall art was equally unlikely. What we found was less assuming than either.

"That's it?" Mandy whispered as we neared an unremarkable cliff, no different than the dozen or so we'd passed along the way. The beam of Murphy's flashlight flickered over the jagged rockface, directing our canoes across the river and toward the small opening between the base of the bluff and the water's surface. It was maybe a foot tall and three feet wide and recessed so deeply that I suspected it was hidden in shadows, even during the day.

Ursula snorted. "What'd you expect? A flashing neon sign?" Her usual irritation was muted with uncertainty, and it echoed in a hushed whisper over the river, bouncing off the rocky cliffs before returning to us like a phantom warning.

Stars freckled the moonless sky above, their reflections dancing in the ripples we created. Their pale light painted dusty outlines over the treetops and vacant camp cabins in the distance and illuminated my frozen breath and the fog grazing the river's surface.

As we neared the cave entrance, Dante pulled his paddle

out of the water and laid it on the floor of our canoe. I did the same. Ursula sat on the bench between us, hands folded in her lap. Holland had led the way in a second canoe, while Murphy grudgingly manned the flashlight, and Mandy wrestled the second paddle to little effect.

After Ursula's refresher on the history of House Lilith, she'd explained why Lili's former wolf donor had been invited along, despite our reservations about his trustworthiness: No one else knew the precise location of the tomb.

Neither Ursula nor Dante had been here before. Their late sires—Morgan and Alexander—had shared the story of the cave off the Ohio River, but the clues they'd given were so vague that we could have easily spent weeks if not months searching for the *hidden opening beneath the bluffs*.

Lili had forbidden her scions from visiting after river pirates turned a neighboring cave into a hideout—some two hundred and twenty-plus years ago. Well before Ursula or Dante had joined the family. The pirate cave was a popular tourist attraction to this day, but Lili occasionally sent a trusted donor or guard to check on the tomb during the off-season. Just to make sure the entrance hadn't been disturbed or vandalized.

Beyond that, Holland couldn't help us navigate our way to Lilith's final resting place. But at least he knew how to get us inside.

The beam of Murphy's flashlight searched the narrow, dark tunnel under the cliff. "We're going in *there*?"

"Yes," Holland confirmed. "It takes a bit of finesse, but I believe we can manage it—even in your frail condition." Murphy growled a low warning, but Holland continued obliviously. "We will have to lie on the floors of the canoes to fit. Even then, the water could be too high, requiring us to push up on the rock to sink the boats deep enough to pass— though we mustn't push too hard, lest we take on water or become unstable and roll over."

"And the icy currents carry us off to a watery grave," Mandy grumbled. "Super."

"The trick is to spread your hands wide and stagger your movements with your partner's."

Murphy huffed. "I thought you came out here alone."

"Yes," Holland said, unruffled by the accusation. "I use my feet when necessary."

I was beginning to feel sorry for him. Maybe it was the good-natured way he took everyone's criticism. Or the fact that his partner had ditched him—quite possibly for the dark side.

To be fair, I'd been suspicious when the late queen had *gifted* Holland and Clyde to us at Midwinter. The general consensus was that they were transplants sent to spy and report back. Technically, we were on the same team. But

Dante and Ursula had opted not to share certain things with Lili. I was sure they had their reasons—though I wasn't curious enough to pry. One less person knowing my deepest and darkest was not something I could bring myself to complain about.

"The royal family should go first," Murphy said, almost as if Holland had suggested the opposite.

"Of course," the werewolf agreed. "It would be impossible to assist them from inside, should they have any difficulties."

"Yeah, but who's gonna help us?" Mandy asked, wincing as she pulled her paddle out of the water.

Holland hummed thoughtfully. "You're tiny. Even if the boat drags across the rock ceiling, you should emerge unscathed. Though I imagine, despite Mr. Murphy's incapacitation, he will adequately weigh down your end."

"Incapacitation?" Murphy barked and twisted in his seat, causing their boat to bump against ours. "Keep it up, pal, and I'll show you just how incapacitated I ain't."

"Please, Mr. Murphy," Dante groaned through clenched teeth.

"Forgive me, Your Highness," Holland said before Murphy could reply. "I was unaware it was a sensitive subject."

Murphy mumbled an apology under his breath, and I

became keenly aware of how different Lili's expectations of her guards must have been. That much decorum seemed suffocating to me. To Dante too, I guessed, considering the more casual way his guards behaved around him. I wondered if Holland's manners would grow lax under Ursula's rule—or in close proximity to Mandy, who had plenty of bad habits to share. I was just glad our swanky neighborhood didn't have a stray cat problem.

"Well," Ursula said, sliding off her bench to sit on the floor of our canoe, "we're wasting darkness."

Holland riffled through the duffle bag he'd brought and produced a second flashlight and several elastic head lanterns that he passed out. We worked quickly and quietly. The river was less busy in winter and at night, but any chance of exposing the tomb to humans was a risk that couldn't be taken lightly.

I adjusted my head lantern and nestled down into my small corner of the canoe. It was a tight fit, and despite the teeth-chattering temperature, I gagged at the rotten, fishy stench coming off the river.

Mandy tilted her head back and inhaled a lungful. "That's some toxic funk, now. Like, super-villain-grade shit."

"The human authorities do not advise swimming in it." Holland cleared his throat. "I do not recommend it either. Mercifully, I've only tipped a boat once."

Mandy reached over the side of their canoe and rapped her knuckles on the aluminum hull. Then, as if only just realizing it was not made of wood, swore under her breath. She lifted the blade of her paddle and knocked on it instead.

The glare of Dante's head lantern drew my attention, and we simultaneously blinded each other. I clicked my light off. I wouldn't need it until we made it inside anyway. Dante curled one hand over his lantern to dim it, bracing his other hand on the lip of the cave entrance.

"Ready?" he whispered, eagerness and dread tightening his voice.

Ursula had already curled herself into a tight ball in the space between us, clutching the braid draped over her shoulder. She hadn't turned her head lantern on yet, and her eyes were pinched closed, like a child waiting for the scary part of a movie to be over. I was tempted to do the same.

A stiff breeze dragged my hair across my throat, and I shuddered. I took one last look at the river behind us, then turned back to Dante.

"Ready." I lowered my head to the floor of the canoe and twisted onto my back to gaze up at the stars, waiting for the shadow of the bluff to swallow us whole.

The rock curve of the cave entrance was surprisingly smooth. It was wet and cold against my hands, but the water level wasn't so high that we needed to apply more pressure than was required to tug the canoe along until we were inside.

Dante's head lantern had lit the tunnel, but the abyss of the cave devoured light. Even after Ursula and I clicked on our lanterns, the damp walls were only revealed in slices.

"There," Dante said, bobbing his head toward a flat rock ledge angled into the water. As soon as the canoe scraped against it, he grasped a rock jutting from the wall and heaved us farther up the slope. And just in time.

Lights flickered at the end of the tunnel, signaling the arrival of the second canoe. Holland and Murphy appeared first, then Mandy's hands slapped the inside wall. She used the leverage to torpedo the boat out of the hole.

"Whoa there," Holland hissed as his end nearly collided with mine. I held out my forearm, leveling it with his so we could push away from one another. The motion rocked both canoes.

"Get me out of this thing," Ursula snapped, crawling toward Dante. He'd already stepped onto the rock ledge and was doing his best to hold the canoe in place.

The extra lanterns and flashlights painted a larger picture of the cave. It was a tight space, consisting mostly of the pool and a narrow walkway that began at the water's edge and coiled upward around the grotto's perimeter. Murphy angled his flashlight at the ceiling, but Mandy caught his arm and shushed his gruff protest.

"Don't wake the sky puppies," she whispered, pointing at the cluster of dangling shadows above us. "They're not supposed to come out of hibernation for another few months."

Bats. A real live bat cave. Of course it was. This little nook was a perfect roost.

Holland offered his hand to Murphy. The senior guard gritted his teeth, but he opted to keep his mouth shut this time. Instead, he smacked his flashlight in the werewolf's open palm before wrangling himself out of the boat one-armed. Mandy gripped the gunwales and did her best to stabilize the back end of the canoe. She and I were the last to come ashore, slipping on the wet rock as we dragged the boats farther up the ledge behind us. Being stranded in a dank, bat-filled cave was the last thing we needed tonight.

"Here we go." Holland pulled an electric lantern from his bag. The gadget was small—not much larger than a can of hairspray—but it was bright. The lumpy formations dripping from the cave walls glistened in its glow.

"I have one bar." Mandy gasped and waved her phone in the air. "Yeah, baby!"

Holland gave her an apologetic smile. "It only lasts

halfway to the top tier."

"Then she shall remain with the boats," Dante said. "We need someone ready to call home the second we return from the tomb with Audrey's location."

I supposed it was a better use of Mandy's time than sending her on a mouthwash run, regardless of my doubts about the usefulness of Lilith's blood—and its shelf life. Dante's hope was so fragile, I just couldn't bear to wound it. He'd regressed back to his distracted brooding ever since Audrey had been taken, and I hated seeing him this way.

Holland handed me the electric lantern and then hung the strap of his duffle bag over my shoulder. "There's a first-aid kit in there, as well as a thermal lunch pouch with a few bags of blood and some other miscellaneous camping gear like flint and rope."

"Is all of that really necessary?" Ursula tugged at the end of her braid and chewed her bottom lip. "Just how far is the tomb from here?"

"I don't know." Holland removed his head lantern and raked a hand through his mussed hair. "I've never gone beyond this cavern. Those were Lili's orders. I was to stick to the walkway around the pool and report any discrepancies."

"Well, that's helpful." Murphy rolled his bound shoulder and groaned under his breath. "I should come with you."

"It's super slick, and you're still recovering," I pointed

out, earning a scowl.

Ursula sighed. "As much as I'd love the extra security, the princess is right. You'll only slow us down, and time is of the essence."

Murphy grunted in offense, but Holland cut in before the guard could launch an argument.

"I'll take you to the tunnel passage that leads to the tomb," he said, flicking the beam of his flashlight up the slope. He stepped carefully over the slimy rock path, searching out the most even footholds. Dante and Ursula followed closely. I gave Mandy's arm a squeeze and tossed Murphy a two-fingered salute before tailing after my sire.

Rust-colored stalagmites bordered the walkway on either side, their spindly columns casting sharp shadows. I didn't see any stalactites, but I knew they were there—every few seconds, a cold drip of cave dew peppered my face or soaked through my hair to my scalp. More drops echoed all around, the depth of their notes ringing as they struck rock or water or the assortment of manmade things we'd brought to their stage.

As we neared the end of the walkway, I adjusted the panels of the electric lantern to keep the light from rousing the snoozing bats above.

"The tunnel is hidden behind these formations," Holland said, turning to paint the beam of his flashlight across a section of thick stalagmites I'd just walked past. They were situated right before the grade of our path leveled into a narrow, empty precipice.

I could see how someone might overlook the secret tunnel. The top tier demanded one's full attention. There were no formations to give the illusion of safety here. Just a slippery, sharp drop into the dark waters below—or the jagged edges of the walkway if one were even less fortunate.

"There's a steep slab," Holland continued, still waving his flashlight at the formations behind me, "but the rocks create a natural stairway farther down. The tunnel entrance opens beneath the slab, so you won't see it until you reach the bottom. I've never gone that far, but that's the direction Lili went the last time I brought her here."

"When was that?" Dante asked, stealing a cautious glance over the end of the walkway.

"Late nineties. Right after Princess Morgan—" Holland paused to wet his lips, and his gaze settled on the queen. "Lili wanted to personally deliver her ashes to the tomb."

I had been on the verge of suggesting that Ursula wait with the guards. She'd managed the canoe ride and the squeeze through the narrow cave mouth—which, honestly, was more than I'd expected of her. She wasn't cut out for daring adventures in the wilderness. Her blood school training had prepared her for hosting fancy parties and charming—or intimidating—diplomats into submission. She was a fully bloomed version of Audrey. But there was no stopping her now.

"Morgan's here?" Ursula curled a fist to her chest and sucked in a ragged breath. Then she was gone, vanishing around the stalagmites Holland had pointed out.

"Wait!" I called after her. "I should go first. I have the lantern."

"And I have the Eye of Blood," her voice echoed back, sounding much too far away.

Dante grasped Holland's shoulder. "How long did it take Lili to return from the tomb?" he asked, genuine fear hitching the inner corners of his eyebrows. Beyond this point, everything was an unknown.

"Almost two hours, but who's to say she didn't spend most of that time ruminating in her sire's company?" he added hopefully.

"Two hours." Dante swore. "If we're not back in three, you have my permission to enter the tomb to retrieve us. If we take any longer than that, we'll be spending the night in this cave."

I knew staying at a hotel, even one that catered to vampires—hell, probably *especially* one that catered to the undead—was out of the question. The Free Blooders had eyes and ears everywhere, and our few guards were not exactly in top shape.

Holland nodded. "Yes, Your Highness."

"Good man." Dante released his shoulder and motioned for me to go ahead of him around the wall of stalagmites.

I held the lantern high as we emerged, shining light down the long slab until I spotted Ursula. Her dilated gaze remained fixed on whatever lay beneath the slab, but she pointed a finger at the broken layers of rock on the far side of the cavern. Dante and I navigated the steps as quickly and carefully as we could manage.

"I think we have a problem," Ursula finally said as we joined her.

In the stark, artificial light, I couldn't disagree.

Chapter Fifteen

A hollowed entryway, the most obvious route to the tomb, stood before us. Filled to the brim with crushed rock. Dante ran a hand down the barricade as if he needed to feel it to believe it.

"I don't understand," he said. "Lili was just here…"

"Twenty years ago," I reminded him, which I realized in hindsight probably didn't seem like an eternity to him the way it did to me. "Wasn't there an earthquake in '08? Maybe that's when this happened."

"It doesn't matter now, does it?" Ursula hugged herself. I wanted to be angry with her for this needless waste of time, but she was plenty disappointed for both of us. Her chin quivered as she stepped away from the dead end and wandered past the slab, deeper into the room. The lantern light followed her to a lumpy half-wall of rock, and when she spoke again, her voice echoed in some distant chamber I hadn't realized was there. "That must be where the tunnel ends."

She pointed past the uneven rocks, and I tilted the lantern over her shoulder, spilling light into a grotto below. A matching hollowed entryway waited at the bottom, near another dark pool that consumed most of the space, save for a narrow lip that lined the cavern. There was no spiraling footpath this time, but the walls weren't as smooth either. Large, shadowy holes pocked the inside of the grotto. I noticed a few cracks and small ledges, too.

"Maybe we can still reach it." I hitched an eyebrow at the duffle bag nestled against my hip. "Holland said he packed some rope."

I handed the lantern off to Dante and moved aside so he could inspect my intended descent while I rummaged through our supplies.

"This drop is even more perilous than the one over the first pool," he said, a deep line cutting across his forehead. "I don't like it."

"Do you have a better idea? Look, I'm not leaping for joy here either, but we don't have a lot of options. Audrey is counting on us, and"—I waved the lunch sack of blood bags and the small medical box at him—"we've got a first-aid kit."

Ursula nudged Dante out of the way and stuck her head over the half-wall of rock to get a better look. "If you fall from this height, I think it will take a great deal more blood than that to patch you up."

"Let's hope we don't have to find out." I set the lunch sack and medical box on the ground and finally unearthed the coiled bundle of nylon rope at the bottom of the duffle bag. I was sure it was too short to reach the bottom of the grotto, but if I could make it to one of the larger hollows in the rock wall, maybe I could loop the rope over a lower ledge and finish the journey down that way.

Of course, if I couldn't clear the tunnel, there was a good chance I'd be stuck with no way of climbing back out. I supposed I'd cross that bridge—or not—when I came to it.

I went back to the window overlooking the cavern and took the lantern from Dante. The rockface wasn't as consistent or predictable as the climbing wall in the gym at home, but it wasn't impossible. At least, not for me. Ursula and Dante, on the other hand…

"Maybe I can travel back up the tunnel and try to dig it out," I offered.

"It's worth a look," Dante agreed. "But do not waste time if the task demands too much attention. Retrieving Lilith's blood should be our main priority."

"Yes," Ursula agreed, though she didn't look happy about it. "However, if I leave here tonight without seeing Morgan's final resting place, I'll be returning with an excavation team to have the path cleared."

Dante scoffed. "You would reveal the location of our bloodline's tomb to strangers?"

"Are you volunteering for pickaxe duty, cousin?"

I waved a hand between them. "Can we save the arguing for *after* I inspect the tunnel?"

Dante had the decency to look ashamed, though Ursula

bristled at the chiding. They remained silent while I counted the number of times the rope hooked around my forearm. Two loops from my thumb to elbow equaled roughly five feet. The drop was at least forty. I had seventy-five feet of rope to work with. Without any harness equipment, I'd need to double it over to rappel down the cave wall safely. Add in the distance to a nearby rock pillar that looked strong enough to support my weight…and I was looking at a ten to fifteen-foot freefall at the end of the line. Finding a secondary anchor was a must.

"Do you know what you're doing?" Ursula asked, watching as I wrapped the middle of the rope around the rock pillar and then tossed the ends into the grotto below.

"Sure," I said, trying to sound more optimistic than I felt. "My mom taught me how to do this when she took Laura and me camping as kids." It had only been down a ten-foot slope to reach a secret fishing spot, but they didn't need to know that part.

I stood between the two lengths of rope and turned my back to the cavern opening, trying to remember the steps the way Mom had explained them to my ten-year-old self. *Criss-cross, hopscotch, butt floss, wristwatch.* I mouthed the words to myself as I coiled the two stretches of rope around my waist and through my legs.

Dante made a face at my final setup. "That looks… uncomfortable."

"Bet it feels better than splattering my brains on the cave floor."

He blanched at the comparison. "Do be careful, my dear."

I nodded solemnly and then lifted my arms. "Mind giving me a lift?"

Dante grasped my waist and hefted me up onto the edge of the rock wall. He pressed a quick kiss to my forehead before backing away to stand beside Ursula. I couldn't help but smile at their agitated expressions. For all their knowledge of vampire politics and supernatural war strategy, this was unfamiliar territory. It felt good having something useful to bring to the table—or at least, I hoped it would be useful. We'd see.

I wrapped one hand around the paired rope coming from the pillar. My other hand pulled it taut where it wrapped behind my right thigh. I'd coiled that end around my forearm once too, just in case it slipped out of my grip—the *wristwatch* step of the process. Inch by inch, I let the rope slide through my clenched fists until my back was parallel with the grotto pool. I braced both feet on the edge of the opening and pushed myself out into a standing position.

"Jenna?" Dante's worried face appeared over the edge, and he loosed a sigh.

"See?" I said. "Easy-peasy." My voice trembled, but I managed not to squeak.

I angled my head lantern down between my legs to gauge my next step and slowly released another few inches of rope. Everything glistened with the light, making it hard to determine which footholds were slick and which were safe. It was a dangerous guessing game, but I avoided the worst of it by choosing the most textured and angled ledges I could find, testing them one foot at a time.

The deeper I descended into the cavern, the louder the dripping music of the rock formations rang in my ears, clicking and crackling off the cave pool and the bumpy walls. I passed a few smooth hollows, but nothing deep enough for me to fit inside while I re-anchored the rope. Not that I'd found anything worth anchoring to.

I was running out of options when I noticed a wider hole in the rock a few feet below. If I could squeeze inside, then I could at least give my aching wrists a break while I searched for a way to finish the climb down.

Canon-balling into the dark pool at this distance was too risky. In the low light, I couldn't tell how deep it was or if there were any spear-shaped formations lurking beneath the surface, ready to impale me. I wasn't dismissing the idea of creepy cave monsters either.

Hey, if vampires were real, why not?

I was so caught up in my phobic water search, I completely missed the garden-variety creepy crawlies waiting for me in the pit-stop hole—until I was right on top of them.

A dozen copperhead snakes lay piled on top of one another in the back of the small hollow. At my surprised yelp, a few lifted their spade-shaped heads and hissed. One snapped at my boot, extracting another shrill of protest from me. Then everything turned red as my blood vision flared to life.

"Jenna?" Ursula called from above. "What's happening? Should we pull you up?"

"Nooo—" My voice cut off as I was wrenched upright, and my forehead connected with the rock wall. The rope slipped from my hands, but I caught my balance on the lip of the copperhead den.

The rudely awoken snakes were not thrilled by this. Neither was I. One snapped near my fingers. I let go of the ledge and plummeted a few feet before my hands clenched around the rope again. I quickly descended several more steps as one of the copperheads poked its head out to hiss at me.

"Jenna?" Dante's voice echoed through the cave. "Are you all right?"

"Do. Not. Touch. The. Rope," I shouted through clenched teeth. I could already feel the goose egg sprouting on my forehead. The friction burns against my waist and palms didn't feel too hot either.

"Sorry," Ursula huffed.

My muscles were shaking. It was half from the effort of scaling the wall and half from nerves. Anger and fear swirled in my gut, tightening my breath and quickening my pulse. Not a great combination. Certainly not when I was at the end of my rope. *Literally.*

I took another backward step, and my right hand came up empty. The rope uncoiled from around my thighs, and I clutched the dangling ends with both hands, holding them together to keep from slipping.

The grotto pool was still a good fifteen feet below. I twisted my neck and shined my head lantern down into the murky water. I'd already gone for one freezing, unintended swim tonight. I hadn't planned on a second, but the uneven ledge surrounding the pool looked even less inviting.

"Jenna?" Ursula called, disrupting my train of thought and sending a jolt of panic through me as I anticipated her yanking on the rope again.

"I'm okay! Just…thinking." I sighed and blinked as something dripped off the ceiling and onto my cheek. "I changed my mind," I shouted, caving now that my fingers were screaming for mercy.

"You're *not* okay?" Ursula's voice hitched anxiously.

"No—I mean about you touching the rope."

"We should pull you up, then?" Dante asked.

"Not what I had in mind," I clarified before they jumped the gun. "I'm going to let go of the left side of the rope. I want you to slowly lower the right side until I reach the bottom. Okay?"

"This one?" I heard Ursula ask.

"No, no—*her* right," Dante said.

"Fine. Ready when you are, princess."

I felt a slight tug on the rope and loosened my grip on the left side. The right end slipped an inch and then stopped.

"We have you," Dante's voice echoed through the grotto.

"Slowly, okay?"

"Slowly," he repeated.

I took a deep breath and let go of the left side of the rope.

Three backward steps, and it was out of my reach. I dangled by one end, completely at Dante's and Ursula's mercy. My actions were less stable than before, having no way to pause or recalculate if a ledge was too slippery to gain purchase. I lost my footing and cracked first my hip and then my shoulder against unforgiving swells in the wall. But then my feet touched flat ground.

"I made it!"

The rope stopped moving, and Dante and Ursula peered over the edge.

"Thank heavens." Dante sighed and pressed a hand over his heart.

"Well," Ursula said, blinking stiffly at me. "Go check the tunnel already."

Dante glared at her. "Give her a moment, you tyrant."

A moment wasn't going to cut it. I opened and closed my hands a few times, wincing at the blisters and bruises spread across my palms. Digging through a rockslide right now sounded like pure hell. But it was nothing compared to the hell I envisioned Audrey enduring, held hostage by the Free Blooders. At the hands of *Marcel*, no less.

I followed the narrow ledge around the pool to the tunnel exit. It was clear as far as the light from my head lantern carried, though there were plenty of twists and bends along the ascending path. The walls were crumbling and partially collapsed in a few places, littered with broken rock formations. Water trickled down from the ceiling, creating puddles and slimy, slick spots that caught me by surprise and sent me to my knees more than once.

When I finally reached a section of the tunnel that was completely impassable, I used the toe of one boot to dig out the larger stones for fear of discovering another danger noodle sleepover. Then I set to work clearing the mound of smaller rocks, using the crook of my arm for scooping where I could to spare my damaged hands.

Soon, muffled voices seeped through the barricade.

"Dante! Ursula! Can you hear me?" I worked faster as bits of light slipped through gaps in the rock. A hand pushed through the rubble, and then the top portion of the tunnel crumbled open, revealing the queen and prince.

"Well done." Ursula beamed. She held the lantern as Dante and I finished clearing the entrance. When there was enough room for them to pass through, Dante's hands found mine and squeezed. I sucked in a sharp breath and pulled out of his grasp, turning my palms up for him to see.

"You poor dear," he cooed. "A little blood should remedy this on the ride home, yes?"

I pressed my lips together and nodded.

"Come along, children," Ursula ordered, slipping past us and heading down the tunnel the way I'd come. "Who knows what other horrors await us."

"Us?" I sniffed.

Dante gave me a weak smile. I imagined it was the best he'd be able to summon until we had Audrey back. He laid a soft kiss on each of my palms before opening an arm to one side, directing me to follow my sire.

There was only one other hollowed archway in the second grotto, tucked in a shadowy corner behind the tunnel exit. And, fortunately, it was passable and led to our final destination. Lilith's tomb.

Unfortunately, our Mother of Eternal Blood hadn't known how to leave well enough alone.

Dante squinted at three box-shaped indentations in the top of Lilith's sarcophagus. The white stone monstrosity sat in the middle of the small room, leaving less than six feet of space between any given side and the chiseled-smooth walls. The floor was flat and even, too. Someone—or several someones—had spent a good deal of time in here. Any pretense that this was just an average, random cave was gone.

The lid of the sarcophagus featured a sculpted effigy of the first undead queen of the New World, floating in a bed of skulls and apples. She was remarkably realistic. Her face constantly drew my gaze, as though I expected her to sit up at any moment, wipe the milky dust from her eyes, and demand why we were disturbing her.

One of her delicate hands rested above her heart, her index finger angled up the column of her throat, pointing at two tiny bite marks that oozed blood drops made of tiny rubies. Her other hand curled around the underside of her belly, flat except for the strange, boxy indents Dante was fixated on. His brow furrowed as he read the riddle engraved in the stretch of stone between the depressions and Lilith's décolletage, muttering the words under his breath for the hundredth time.

"Three scions mine, gifts earned in time, point them home, and my blood is thine."

He'd been at it for at least half an hour, though we were no closer to understanding what needed to be done to open the stone sarcophagus—where we assumed we'd find Lilith's blood.

Ursula stood before an alcove carved in the wall opposite the entrance, near the stone effigy's head. There were three niches in the rock, one stacked on top of the other two, each holding an ornate urn. Ursula traced a finger over the glossy surface of one painted with tiny pink blooms.

"This has to be Morgan's," she said, a hazy note in her voice. "Cherry blossoms were her favorite thing to paint. Besides me."

I glanced up at the urn tucked in the highest nook. It was decorated with feathers and leather strings dotted with turquoise beads. "I suppose that one is waiting for Lili's ashes." My gaze slid to the remaining urn in the nook beside Morgan's, painted with Greek tragedy and comedy masks. "And that one for Alexander."

"Point them home…point them home," Dante muttered in the background.

I sighed and left Ursula to her melancholic pondering to circle the room. Alcoves had been carved into all four walls, though only two held additional urns, and only one each.

I didn't know much about Adam or Gabriella. Just that neither had created a scion before their interment in the cave. It didn't take a detective to discern that the vessel covered in roses and swords belonged to Gabriella, the warrior scion Lilith had found on the battlefield. Leaving the one painted with apples and a crown around the lid as Adam's.

The elaborate stonework on all sides of Lilith's sarcophagus told a more detailed story that matched up with the scions showcased on each wall. And the panel at the foot of the casket, the only one without a coinciding urn, depicted a well-known scene from the Garden of Eden—Lilith with the serpent. Ivy vines trimmed every edge of the sarcophagus, the corners embellished with fanged skulls wearing crowns. It reminded me of the history tome I'd discovered in the BATC library.

"Damn it!" Dante pounded a fist on the stone lid. "There has to be something we are missing in this room. Something that fits in these openings."

"We've got urns." I shrugged. "Want me to open one up and take a look inside?"

"Jenna!" Ursula snatched Morgan's container off the shelf, clutching it to her chest protectively.

"Kidding." I lifted my hands in surrender. "Mostly," I added under my breath.

When Ursula turned around to replace the urn inside its nook, she froze. Then I saw it, too. There was a square-shaped hole in the rock shelf, right below where the vessel had been sitting. And in it rested a small stone cube, not much larger than a wooden toy block.

I stepped around Ursula and extracted the piece from the hole before retreating so she could put her late sire's ashes back where they belonged. Five of the block's six sides were smooth, but a line of textured stone—a relief carving, I realized—created a tiny ridge down the center of the remaining side. I held it under the lantern light as Ursula turned to get a better look.

"It's a paintbrush," she said, pointing out the extra detail marking the bristled end.

"Would something this size work?" I asked Dante, holding up the block for him to see.

"Bring it here," he demanded, waving his hand to hurry me along. He plugged the piece into one of the stone depressions. It was an awkward fit, but it was a step in the right direction. "Check under the other urns," Dante instructed.

"There's nothing under Alexander's," Ursula announced, one step ahead of us. She reached up to search under Lili's urn next while I checked Gabriella's.

"Found another one!" I winced as my bruised fingers scraped the inside of the hole under Gabriella's urn, too eager in my retrieval of the next block. Like the first, only one side was carved. This time it was a sword.

"Lili's had one, too." Ursula handed a third block off to Dante as I pulled a fourth from under the last urn—Adam's.

"This one has a crown," I said, turning the piece over in my hand. I added it to the others on top of the sarcophagus, but Dante's frown only deepened.

"There are three openings. *Three scions mine…* I believe we can count Morgan's block out of this equation." He handed it to Ursula to replace beneath her sire's urn.

"*Gifts earned in time,*" I read the next bit of the riddle inscribed on the tomb.

Dante nodded and held up each remaining piece. "We have Gabriella's sword, Adam's crown, and Lili's… fish?" He blinked at the carving on her block. "That can't be right."

"It could be a hairbrush," Ursula suggested.

"It's a mirror," I said, remembering the first anointment vision the Eye of Blood had shown me. "Lilith gave it to Lili the night she turned her." Dante and Ursula's curious stares sent heat into my neck and cheeks. I ignored them and continued reading the riddle. *"Point them home…"*

"Right." Dante rotated the blocks inside the carved openings. "Home being…their ashes on the walls, perhaps?" He stepped away from the sarcophagus and gave the lid a push, but it wouldn't budge. "No, we're still missing something."

"Gifts earned in time," I repeated, retracing our steps. "Did Adam's crown or Gabriella's sword come first?"

"Adam was her first scion," Dante pointed out.

Ursula scratched her head. "True, but Adam didn't become Lilith's *royal* consort until they were established in the New World. Gabriella had her sword long before then."

Dante rearranged the blocks again. This time, before he had a chance to try the lid, it popped open like a sprung lock. A gap spread behind one side of Lilith's effigy, weaving between the skulls and apples carved into the stone around her.

Ursula fetched the lantern we'd hung from a dusty torch sconce in the corner. It was brighter than my and Dante's head lanterns, fully illuminating every corner of the silk-lined sarcophagus. It was surprisingly shallow—less than a foot deep—and pristine. A stone-sealed time capsule.

I'd half-expected to find Lilith's skeletal remains, or a mummified version of the effigy above. She was the only one without an urn, after all. Instead, lovingly laid among the glossy red folds, we found a sword with a golden hilt, a crown set with emeralds, and the oval hand mirror, its brass now covered with a dull green patina.

Nestled in the center, framed between the three heirlooms, sat a spherical vial of dark blood.

Chapter Sixteen

"I can't do it." Dante ran both hands through his hair and backed away from the sarcophagus. A feral darkness swirled in his eyes. "What if it doesn't work? Or what if it does, but I can't tell where she is? What if she's…what if she's dead?" he whispered.

He'd been given a key to a cage he wasn't sure he wanted to see inside. After the horrors my blood had revealed, I couldn't blame him. If Audrey's location could be found in Lilith's blood, the details would be in real-time, not through a glimpse of some distant past she'd already survived.

"Jenna?" Ursula asked, holding the vial out to me. Her bottom lip trembled. "I'd do it myself, but you know the city best. If there's some clue as to where Audrey is being held, you'll notice it before either of us. You also have more experience with the Eye of Blood, oddly enough."

At least it wasn't another cave wall to scale. I'd expected this, and I supposed some part of me was curious, but Dante's reaction had alarmed me—still alarmed me. He paced the cramped tomb, eyes wide and hands fisting his hair. When I finally accepted the vial from Ursula, he stopped and blew out a shuddering breath. His hands slipped away from his head, and he laced his fingers together, wringing them over his chest.

"I should do it," he whispered. "I know I should. It is my duty to protect my scion. No one else's—"

"Dante." I wrapped my free hand over his. "She belongs to us all."

I didn't wait for a reply. Every minute Audrey remained with the Free Blooders was a moment too long. It was time to bring our duchess home. I broke the black wax seal of the vial and threw my head back, pouring the syrupy contents down my throat.

Lilith's blood was tart with an herbal aftertaste as if maybe sage or frankincense had been burning in the room when it had been extracted from her. I rolled my tongue against my cheeks and the roof of my mouth, trying not to gag on the strange flavor.

"That wasn't so bad, I guess," I said, glancing up at Dante—or to where I'd last seen him. But he was gone. So was Ursula.

I spun in a complete circle, trying to understand why the room felt different. Who had lit the sconces in the corners? And where the hell were my shoes? The stone floor was cold on my bare feet, and the hair lying over my shoulders was stained red by the torchlight. My gaze shifted from my hair to the white silk gown, and then I understood.

I'm in Lilith's head.

It shouldn't have been so surprising. My taste of Lili had

taken me back farther in time than this. Except…except Lilith seemed to *know* I was there. Or at least that *someone* was there. Watching through her eyes, through the lens of time and circumstance. And why not? She'd left the vial of blood behind for this very reason.

"This part will not be pleasant," she whispered, gentle humor coloring her words. "The last of my blood will give you the last of my life. It is this final gift the Eye of Blood bestows. Then it will trickle away from me, into the veins of tomorrow and beyond. It will reveal the living pulse of my line—of *our* line, dear child of the night." Her voice dropped lower as I heard footsteps approaching from outside the tomb entrance. "Do not look away. You have come seeking truths, and truths you shall have. Use them well."

Lilith turned and faced the door, taking my gaze with her. Others soon entered the tomb. Lili, Alexander, and Morgan. The two women were in elaborate, ruffle-sleeved gowns and dark cloaks, while Alexander wore a navy riding coat with gold embroidery, and a frilly ascot.

A man I didn't recognize soon joined them. He was handsome despite the sorrow dragging down the corners of his full mouth. Like Lilith, he wore white, though his robe looked more ceremonial than the queen's delicate negligee. Unlike Alexander's powdered George Washington coif, his dark hair was thick and unbound, and paired with the white robe, it made him look more like a graveyard angel than a vampire.

"Adam," Lilith said, holding her hand out to him. He took it without hesitation and drew her into his arms. His warmth engulfed me. As Lilith lay her head against his chest and combed her fingers through the curls lying over his shoulder, I inhaled his smoky, herbal scent.

"She looks just like you," Lili said, peering down at the effigy on the open sarcophagus. She cupped the statue's pale cheek and sniffled.

"Sweet child." Lilith opened an arm, inviting her youngest scion into her and Adam's entwined embrace. And then Lili was pressed in amongst them…*us*, her salty, floral notes cutting through Adam's musk. Her sobs made me uncomfortable, but I couldn't decide if that was because I was used to her having a more intimidating presence, or if I experienced Lilith's remorse for her scion's pain.

"Be strong," Lilith whispered against Lili's cheek.

"Yes, my queen."

"*You* are queen now," Lilith reminded her.

Lili sniffled again and nodded as she pulled away. She disentangled herself from the group hug and slipped a hand between the folds of her gown, producing the mirror from a hidden pocket. The dark brass I recalled from the vision of her final anointment had already taken on a good deal of green patina.

Lili kissed the rim of the mirror's decorative, oval frame before placing it in the sarcophagus beside Gabriella's sword and Adam's crown. She took a deep, shuddering breath and turned back to Lilith and Adam. "I'm ready."

Something pinched in Lilith's chest, and therefore pinched in mine. The tender throb doubled between one heartbeat and the next. I could sense Lilith's weariness, and the haunting, aching sorrow that lingered in the shadows of her mind. Her eyes snagged on the hilt of Gabriella's sword, and the shadows thinned, letting her heartache bleed into me.

How did one recover from losing a scion they'd loved for nearly three centuries?

She hated to leave Lili behind, but this was what she'd been preparing the girl for. This was the legacy she'd promised her youngest scion, once she tired of this world's pleasure and suffering. Gabriella's departure had cleaved the former and made the latter intolerable.

The rough pad of Adam's thumb pressed against Lilith's cheek, wiping away a tear. When she looked up into his face, I saw her grief mirrored in his eyes.

"If she awaits us in the realm beyond, we shall find her," he promised. "And if there is no realm beyond, then at least we are now together in this one."

Lilith nodded, and I felt her swallow the lump that had

formed in the back of her throat.

Adam released her and turned toward the sarcophagus. He pressed his fingertips into several notches and nooks hidden among the engraved scene that faced the wall displaying his urn. A mechanism inside the stone clicked, and then he grasped the upper ledge that bordered the panel and pulled. A table wrapped in black leather rolled out before us.

Above the scene at the head of the sarcophagus, Adam revealed a hidden drawer. This one contained a divided wooden box filled with glass orbs and sticks of black wax. From another compartment, Adam pulled a wide hand brush. He ran his fingers over the soft bristles, loosening a bit of dust that shimmered in the torchlight. Then he handed it to Morgan before retrieving his crown-and-apple-painted urn.

This was it. The answers to any question I'd ever had about a forever rest were about to be answered. The anticipation filled my stomach with acid, and my breath was suddenly too tight in my lungs. I couldn't tell if the reaction was more mine or Lilith's.

Adam set the urn on the leather table and stripped out of his robe. Alexander took the garment and draped it over his arm, bowing his head with reverence. His eyes glistened, but he hadn't said a word since entering the tomb. Morgan, too, remained somber and silent, clutching the brush to her chest.

Something low in Lilith's stomach fluttered at the sight of

Adam's naked body, and a bittersweet giggle purred in my chest before it bubbled from her lips. "All these years, and you still stir my blood."

"And you mine," he said, eyes tracing her figure as her gown slipped free and puddled on the tomb's floor.

Adam sat on the table and pulled his legs up, stretching them over the leather before opening his arms for Lilith, inviting her to come to him. She did, slowly. And with each careful step, I felt her fangs extend just a little more until they dug into the flesh behind the corners of her mouth.

As Adam's hands curled around Lilith's waist, her lips parted with a blissful sigh. She draped her arms over his shoulders, and I shuddered as I felt her breasts graze the soft patch of hair that covered his chest. Then Adam's mouth found her collarbone, his searing tongue slipped out to taste her as he kissed his way up to the column of her neck. When he reached her ear, he nipped at her lobe and whispered, "It is time."

"Yes," Lilith agreed, struggling to rein in her thirst for more than his blood. A tender ache between her thighs told me it was a craving they'd attempted to sate before the ceremony. "It is time," she echoed, a warning I felt was intended for me.

Adam's fingers brushed through Lilith's hair, and then his palm cupped the back of her neck. He tilted his head to one side and pulled her in—pulled *me* in. "With this blood, I anoint thee mine forevermore."

Lilith struck with precision. There was no awkward navigation around muscles or veins. It was the sort of expertise I imagined came with centuries of practice. Adam didn't even flinch.

His blood was hot and bitter, reminding me of Dante's. Only I'd stopped after a small sip of my lover's. Lilith was determined to drown in hers. She gnashed her fangs in deeper, tearing at the holes in Adam's flesh until his blood nearly choked us. It burned in my sinuses and made my eyes water. Lilith's fingernails dug into his back as the vision of his final anointment took hold of us both.

Wherever we were, it was dark and rainy. Lilith didn't seem to care, sprawled beneath Adam on a damp blanket in a clearing surrounded by woods. Just as entwined in one another as they'd been in the tomb. My head swam from the spell they were under, and from the jarring transition of experiencing a vision within a vision, trapped in two memories at the same time.

Lightning streaked through a lush canopy of trees above, but it was clear that Lilith's labored breath had more to do with the way Adam's hands moved beneath her gown. His deft fingers created an electricity of their own as they worshiped her skin, the delicate veil between so much hot blood and the crisp night air.

"Thou art certain?" Lilith whispered against his mouth as he leaned in for another kiss. "Will thou not yearn for the fellowship of dear Michelangelo?"

Adam scoffed. "Divine as my friendly foe may be, I've outgrown him. He prefers the male form, and I'm afraid thine hath ruined me for all others. Thou art my muse. Forevermore, my hands will seek thee in the stone, as they seek thee in the flesh now."

Lilith's laughter rippled up through her core, but then she threw her head back with a groan as Adam's hands picked up where they'd left off. Her fangs extended without warning, razoring over her bottom lip. Adam surprised her again when he swept his tongue over the twin lacerations and suckled at her mouth. Pressure built low in her stomach and then blossomed as the next crack of lighting broke the sky.

Then we were wrenched back to the cave tomb, the wave of pleasure interrupted with all the grace of a sucker punch. Adam was cold. He trembled in Lilith's arms. Her mouth hurt from the effort it took to pull from his veins now. There was so little left, but his blood felt like a lake of fire in her stomach. Still, she drank, ignoring the thrum of power resonating beneath her skin, rattling her ancient bones.

A moment later, Adam ran dry. Lilith extracted her fangs as his flesh grew brittle and gray. His dark eyes blinked up at her in peaceful wonder. Then those, too, turned to ash. His body folded in on itself, crumbling to dust over the leather slab.

Horror and relief rose like bile in Lilith's throat, but she swallowed it down. This would all be over soon. She stepped back and shot a sideways glance at Lili's scions. It was all the cue they needed to set to work. Alexander opened the urn and tilted it under the lip of the table, while Morgan used the brush to painstakingly gather Adam's ashes into the mouth of the vessel. When they were done, they dutifully replaced the urn in its nook on the wall.

Then Lilith took Adam's place, stretching out on her back over the dark leather. Lili approached timidly, her gaze fixed on the urn that now held her sibling scion's remains. And now she was expected to repeat the process, to turn her sire to ash before emerging from the cave as the new queen of the American undead.

"Fetch a vial," Lilith ordered. *So maybe not the* exact *same process?*

"Aye," Morgan answered first, replacing the brush in its hidden slot and taking up one of the glass orbs. She reached out her free hand to squeeze Lili's, offering moral support.

"Sire to scion, and scion to sire," Lilith murmured. "The eye is well-fed, and now the blood will reveal all."

"Yes, my queen," Lili replied. Confusion puckered the

skin between her brows as if she couldn't understand why her sire was explaining something she'd already learned. She didn't understand the lesson was meant for me.

"*You* are queen now," Lilith reminded her again. She reached up to touch Lili's cheek, the only comfort she had left to spare. "And you will be magnificent." She turned her wrist up, bringing it to Lili's trembling mouth until I could feel her breath against Lilith's skin.

My desire not to die struggled against her resolve that this was the bittersweet end of everything, my urge to see the world fighting her conclusion that she'd seen all there was to see. Or maybe the conflict resided in her, and I was simply holding tight to the end of her survival instincts. Either way, the vision trapped me in her eldritch calm, and together we waited for true death.

Lili's fangs pressed tenderly at first, entering Lilith's flesh almost painlessly, relieving the pressure of Adam's heady blood coursing through her veins. Then Lili deepened her bite. The brook became a river, rushing past a broken dam of flesh.

A scorching line trailed from Lilith's wrist and pooled in the bend in her elbow. Her pulse slowed, and her eyelids drooped, obstructing my view of the tomb.

"The vial," she instructed, her voice barely a whisper. "I'm near the end. Take what you must."

I felt the glass press against her arm, and heard the blood as it trickled inside the container. Then Lili's fangs returned, tugging gently at Lilith's vein until a strange sensation spread over her skin. It felt like…a sunburn. It had been so long since I'd had one. It wasn't entirely unpleasant. Just a tingling tightness that promised to peel—or in this case, ash.

"Be strong," Lilith whispered as Lili's fangs slipped free of her brittle flesh. I couldn't decide if she was talking to Lili, me, or herself. But it was her scion who answered, one last time.

"Yes, my queen."

The tomb went black, and my stomach did a little summersault as if I were on a rollercoaster going through a tunnel. When the lights came back on, I was in a dark bedroom, standing near a window that overlooked a patio.

Scraggly shrubs bookended the concrete slab, and cheap solar lights dotted the yard. Beyond the dead grass, empty fields stretched as far as I could see. Something about the scene felt familiar, though the mangled hand pressed against the window drove me to distraction.

The cold surface of the glass was soothing even with the suffocating gloom that hung like smoke in the air. I'd expected panic and terror from Audrey. A guard or some restraints maybe. This window was something she could easily break through. Why wasn't she trying to escape?

All these thoughts flitted through my mind before I considered the molten flesh and thick scabs between my host's knuckles and across her fingers. Even if the Free Blooders had tortured Audrey, without proper care, she wouldn't have had time to heal even this much.

Who the hell is this then? Had Scarlett or Raphael left behind another secret scion? My brain scrambled to connect the dots, but a deep voice broke my focus.

"You need more blood." My gaze drew away from the window, and I found Clyde leaning against the open doorway. The rogue wolf didn't look so good. Even in the dim hall light that spilled over his shoulders, I could see the sickly hue of his skin. One sleeve was rolled up above his elbow, and several fang impressions lined the inside of his wrist.

Before my host could reply, Lilith's blood ripped me away.

I blinked and was suddenly back in the tomb. My throat and eyes burned as if I'd been crying, and panic stabbed at my chest. Dante squatted on the floor, hunched over a body. *My* body.

"Maybe we should give her the first-aid blood," Ursula said, my mouth moving with her words.

"It won't do her any good if she can't swallow it," Dante said. He pried open one of my eyelids and shined his head lantern into my dilated pupil to no effect.

"We have to do something!" Ursula screamed. Her mind felt unhinged, as if the world around her could explode at any second—as if she might be the one to blow it up. My scalp throbbed as she reached up to yank at her hair. The abuse continued as she dragged her hands down her face and began pacing the tomb.

Lilith's blood spell gripped my insides once again, and my consciousness leapt once more, this time to Dante. I peered down at my expressionless face as he fingered open my other eyelid to inspect the pupil beneath.

My poor prince was no better off than my sire. Tension squared his shoulders, and I felt his teeth creak in protest at how tightly he clenched them. A dull ache swelled behind his breastbone. The twinge of misery felt more desperate than the grief I'd tasted in the vision of his final anointment. But then again, I wasn't *dead*-dead. Not yet, at least. He swept my ponytail over my shoulder and pressed two fingers to the side of my neck.

"She has a pulse," he announced, breath rushing out in relief. He leaned over me as if preparing to kiss my forehead. As his eyes closed, I felt Lilith's blood take flight.

An icy blast whipped my hair back. Someone's hand squeezed my thigh, and when my new host opened her eyes, I was staring into the face of a man I'd only ever seen in grainy security camera stills.

Marcel.

He grinned back at me, white teeth and liquid eyes gleaming under the strobe of streetlights. Without looking at the road, he jerked the wheel of the convertible, navigating around the thin traffic of the witching hour. The night air tousled his almost-mullet, giving him a John Stamos from the eighties vibe that was ruined by the perma-sneer he shared with his brother.

I waited to hear Audrey's scream of displeasure, her demands to be released…but then a hand with long, black nails reached across the divide to grope Marcel's thigh in return. I cringed as the hand migrated toward his crotch, taking me along for the ride. Marcel's growl-laced groan sent a thrill through my host. The laughter that howled up from her throat as she threw her head back was *not* Audrey's. But it wasn't entirely unfamiliar.

Before I had a chance to place it, the rollercoaster of blood visions dropped me down another steep hill, and I found myself back in the tomb, one eye staring up at Dante's headlamp as he examined me.

I tried to move but couldn't, paralyzed by the Eye of Blood. My dread swelled as Ursula joined Dante, looming over me. She grabbed my shoulders and shook me like a rag doll, rattling my skull against the stone floor.

"Jenna! Wake up!"

Dante swatted her hands away. "She might yet be in the throes of a vision."

"What do you know of visions?" Ursula spat.

Dante's face flushed. His mouth opened and closed, but I didn't linger long enough to hear his explanation. The slingshot of Lilith's blood hurled me into another mind, one I could finally identify.

Audrey's helpless moans ripped at my heart. She sat in the corner of a small bedroom. The carpet was filthy, and there were bars over the window. And her *pants* were missing. I was going to murder someone.

My vision blurred with Audrey's tears, but I could make out the blood dried to her fingers and caked under her nails. She'd put up a good fight, but apparently, it was only with her dinner. She stroked the dead cat in her lap and whispered apologies in between sniffles and scrubbing her lips with the sleeve of her stained sweater.

Look out the window. Look out the window. Look out the window. I silently pleaded.

By some stroke of luck, sirens wailed in the distance. Audrey cradled the cat in the crook of one arm and crawled toward the window. A tiny flicker of hope sparked in her. I prayed she'd hold on to it a little longer. A little longer was all she would need, because when her gaze dropped to the liquor store on the corner, I knew exactly where she was.

Lilith's blood finished its journey by dumping me back into my body in the tomb. I sat up so fast that I nearly headbutted Dante.

"Pawnshop near Fountain Park," I blurted. "The address is in the Scarlett Inn case file. We need to get back to the boats so we can call it in. *Now.*"

Chapter Seventeen

Being almost two hundred miles out meant we were forced to take a back seat during Audrey's rescue mission, both figuratively and literally. Though Dante remained on the phone with Radu the entire time, shouting over the roar of the SUV's engine as Holland pushed it to go even faster than he had on the way to the cave.

At a hundred-plus miles per hour, it really didn't matter how great a ride's suspension was. Especially not from the very back seat. I felt like I might upchuck the two bags of O-negative Ursula had insisted I drink. Of course, there was also the possibility that Lilith's ancient blood cocktail wasn't agreeing with me. Either that, or I'd been concussed by Ursula's maraca treatment.

My temples throbbed. The idea that a vampire could have a headache annoyed me, but more than that, I was irritated by the visions I couldn't explain—two female vampires of House Lilith's bloodline, unaccounted for.

I tried to convince myself that I hadn't mentioned them yet because Audrey took priority, and because Ursula and Dante were distressed enough. But as much as I hated to admit it, a part of me just wasn't ready to out them.

I knew what it was to be an unsanctioned royal scion. My situation was unique, and I'd gotten lucky. They wouldn't have the same opportunity to prove themselves worthy of our name—not that I believed the tart feeling up Marcel had any interest in joining the royal fam. She was far too cozy with the king of creeps. But that first vampire…

I felt sorry for her. It was more than the mangled flesh that drew my sympathy. I could feel the heaviness in her heart, and knew it was something she carried with her all the time. I wanted to know who she was and what had happened to her—and why Clyde had bailed on us to go to her aid.

If I outed Marcel's girlfriend, I'd feel obligated to share both visions. So, I kept my mouth shut. For now.

Mandy nudged her shoulder into mine. "They picked the lock on the back door, and they're in the building," she whispered, relaying what her wolfy ears overheard of Dante's call. Radu's men were reporting to him. Radu then reported to Dante, and Mandy reported to me. It was a tense game of telephone. "Three guys in the back room—*and* now there's one. They're keeping him for questioning."

"They have her!" Dante cried, pausing to press the phone to his chest. Then it was right back to his ear. "Is she well? Does she require medical attention? Do you have plenty of fresh blood on hand?"

Mandy squirmed beside me, unwilling to repeat whatever Radu's reply had been. I thought of Audrey's missing pants and the dead cat. That wasn't exactly something a little blood would fix.

"I see," Dante answered. A shadow passed over his face, spoiling his relief. "Take her to the manor. We'll be there shortly. And, Vlad—thank you. I owe you a debt I can never repay."

Less than an hour later, we made it home. Audrey met us in the foyer. Or rather, she hadn't made it past the foyer since Radu's men delivered her. She was still without pants, but an oversized suit jacket swallowed her arms and hung down her thighs, several inches past the hem of her sweater.

Two harem donors trailed after her, sloshing oversized mugs of blood anytime Audrey shrieked at them to leave her alone. She paced the foyer, eyeing the guards on duty as if they'd all betrayed her. When Dante approached, she turned her wrath on him.

"I want Levi. Where is my wolf?" she shouted in his face. Her bloodshot eyes locked on Ambrose, standing near the doorway that led down to the basement. "They told me he's alive. I have to see him!"

"And you may," Ambrose answered. "Just as soon as you have some blood, Your Grace."

"It was a cat!" Audrey sucked in a ragged breath and

clawed her hands through her curls. "It was a cat," she repeated more evenly. "I would never do that to someone I cared for."

"Hey, you won't get any judgment from me," Mandy said, momentarily drawing the duchess's attention. "I snacked on a stray or three back in the day."

"Where. Is. Levi?" Audrey demanded through clenched teeth. Her eyes welled, but when Dante opened his arms to comfort her, she slammed her fists into his chest. "Why are you keeping him from me?"

Dante hugged her anyway, ignoring her protests as he stroked her back. "Have some blood, my scion, and then we'll go see him together."

A banshee wail swelled up from Audrey's throat, growing louder the longer Dante held onto her. I knew he was only trying to soothe her anxiety—and his own—but after being manhandled by a bunch of Marcel's thugs, a bear hug probably wouldn't do her much good.

"Hell have mercy." Dante gave Ursula a pleading grimace, but she held her hands up.

"Don't look at me," she said. "You labeled my brand of scion control heartless and barbaric."

"Just bring the goddamn blood downstairs with her," I finally snapped.

Audrey's wailing cut off with a gasp. "Downstairs?"

Ambrose gave me a wide-eyed glare. He braced himself in the doorway, preparing to guard it with his life as Audrey wrenched free of Dante's embrace. But it was Levi who saved us from whatever violence she had in mind to get to him.

"Let me through, doc."

Ambrose waited for Dante to nod his approval before stepping aside and letting Levi hobble up the stairs on crutches. His hair was a disaster, and dark circles ringed his eyes. But that wasn't what captured everyone's attention. His right thigh was wrapped in gauze. All the way down to where it ended just above where his knee had once begun.

Even in his exhausted, mutilated condition, Audrey's fangs snapped out at the sight of him. She covered her mouth with both hands.

"I'm sorry." Her muffled voice seeped through her fingers. "I'm *so* sorry, Levi."

"Don't be." He shook his head and limped a few steps closer, not at all concerned by her inability to control her new teeth. "This is what I signed up for. I'd do it all over again to keep you from harm." Then he took in her bloody hands and bare legs. "Didn't I…keep you from harm?"

Audrey burst into tears. Her knees buckled, and she sank to the foyer floor. Levi hopped closer before handing Ambrose his crutches.

"You really do need more rest," Ambrose scolded him.

"And absolutely no giving blood until we confirm the silver is out of your system."

"I heard you the first ten times, doc." Levi took the arm Murphy offered and let the guard help him onto the floor beside Audrey. She couldn't even bring herself to look at him.

Dante's hands opened and closed helplessly. He wanted to comfort her—we all did. We just didn't know how. It was Mandy who finally yanked the throw blanket off the piano bench and draped it over Audrey's shivering legs. Then she took both cups of blood from the harem donors and plopped onto the floor beside the duchess. She tilted the first cup up to Audrey's mouth.

"Drink," Mandy ordered, her voice calm but demanding. Audrey obeyed, swallowing loudly until she'd drained the entire mug. She drank the second cup without help. "Need more?" Mandy asked.

Audrey shook her head and wiped her nose on the sleeve of the borrowed suit jacket. She was still a wreck, but at least she wasn't battling her thirst on top of trauma now. Baby steps.

"Where's Sweet Pea?" Dante asked, searching the room for the little ball of fluff that always seemed to cheer the duchess.

"She's terrified of me." Audrey sniffled and turned her swollen eyes up at us. "Ran and hid the second I got here. It's like she knows what I did. Like she thinks she might be next. Oh, God. I'm a horrible vampire!" She pressed her hands over her face again, her sobs beginning anew.

"You're not a horrible vampire," Levi said, rubbing circles over her back. "You're new at this. It takes practice, just like being a werewolf. Hell, the first time I shifted, I marked my sergeant's bunk and got latrine duty for a month."

How he could be recovering from losing a leg and still have empathy for a vampling crying over a mishap with a cat was beyond me. Levi was one of a kind. Not a pessimistic bone in his body.

"I drank cow blood from a butcher shop," I admitted, squatting on the floor beside Mandy who snorted at me.

"Which is way worse than fresh cat, let me tell you," she said, turning back to Audrey. "But that's what happens when you look a gift wolf in the mouth."

Dante cleared his throat and awkwardly sandwiched himself between Levi and me, sitting cross-legged on the hardwood floor. "I once tried chicken blood—"

"Dante!" Ursula gasped.

"What?" He stared up at her, cheeks flushing. "I was quite young and longing for mortal pleasures. I thought it might taste akin to the roast chicken my mother used to prepare for holidays. Sadly, it did not."

Audrey sniffled and pulled her hands away from her face.

Her fangs had budded again, but I'd expected that with all the talk of food. "Can't a donor alter the taste of their blood through diet?"

"It's hardly the same thing," Ursula answered. A small frown hooked the corners of her mouth. "But don't fret, dear. Your human cravings will dispel before you know it."

We'd all experienced our fair share of violence and abuse, but somehow, it was easier to talk about our supernatural growing pains instead—*those* we'd outgrown. The trauma of abuse was trickier. Just when you thought you'd overcome it, some cold premonition would slither its way into your gut and remind you that it wasn't that simple.

Audrey hiccupped and looked down at her hands as if noticing them for the first time. "I think… I think I'd like to take a shower."

"Better make it a quick one, Your Grace," Murphy said, glancing down at his watch. "Sunrise is in thirty minutes."

Panic widened Audrey's eyes again. Her mouth opened but no sound came out as she stared at the empty south-wing hallway.

"I'll go with you," Mandy said, looping her arm under Audrey's to help her stand. Dante stood too. He didn't try to reach for Audrey again, but I could tell that he wanted to.

"Would you like me to stay with you tonight, my scion?" he asked, lacing his fingers together over his chest. Audrey stiffened at the offer.

"No. No, thank you." She pressed her lips together. "But…could Jenna?"

Dante's smile was too slow to hide his disappointment. "Of course—I mean, as long as that is all right with the princess?" he added, looking to me.

I nodded. "Sure. I'll go change and be right there."

Mandy took the cue and led Audrey off to get showered while Ambrose and Murphy helped Levi up and onto his crutches again.

"Is someone gonna tell me what happened?" the werewolf grumbled under his breath. "How'd she end up suckin' on a cat? And is that really all that's the matter with her?"

"The Free Blooders took her," Ursula answered bluntly.

I gave her a withering look before heading off Levi's outrage. "We got her back a few hours later, and now you know as much as any of us. Whatever else Audrey feels like sharing is her business."

"And it will have to wait," Ursula added. "Dawn approaches." She turned for the south wing but then paused to touch my shoulder. A tender expression softened her face. "You made me proud tonight, princess. House Lilith is lucky to have you. *I* am lucky to have you. Rest in peace."

"Rest in peace," I echoed as she walked away. Praise from

Ursula was rare, and I treasured it despite how frequently she infuriated me.

Dante waited for Levi and the others to disappear down the basement stairs before folding his arms around my back and squeezing me with all the anxious intensity he'd refrained from smothering Audrey with.

"Thank you," he whispered against my neck. "Thank you for finding her, for staying with her tonight, for…for everything."

We kissed good morning and headed our separate ways, no time to spare with the sunrise just around the bend. Another day, another death slumber spent apart. But if it would help Audrey battle the demons that had invaded her mind, it was worth it.

Chapter Eighteen

When the sun set Saturday night, I woke atop Audrey's floral comforter. Mandy was curled up on the opposite side of the bed with the duchess snuggled in between us. Neither of them had said much that morning, though sunrise had taken care of the awkward silence.

"Someone from the harem delivered a blood pot," Mandy mumbled around a yawn before nodding off again. Audrey stirred beside me and sucked in a soft gasp, her first breath of the night.

I sat up and reached for the blood pot on the bedside table, filling one of the full-sized teacups and handing it to Audrey. Breakfast was more often served with espresso cups, but I supposed Dante had instructed the harem to take extra special care of his scion. Vampling bloodlust was worse than puberty. I was green enough to recall my own cringe-worthy growing pains—my recent cow blood confession, case in point.

Audrey gulped down her breakfast and then licked her lips. A thoughtful pinch formed between her brows. "When do you suppose Levi will be able to give blood again?" she asked, her face immediately flushing with shame. "Oh, God. He nearly died, and all I can think about is how good he tastes. What the hell is wrong with me?" Her eyes watered, and her bottom lip began to quiver as I refilled her cup.

"You're a new vampire," I answered with a shrug. "There's a period of adjustment. As to your first question, we'll be more subtle when we ask Dr. Starling how severe Levi's silver poisoning is. You'll want to wait for his injuries to fully heal, too."

"Right. Of course." Audrey nodded and tilted her cup to her lips again.

We sipped quietly, listening to Mandy's snores and wolfish whimpering in her sleep. It was a comfortable, nostalgic sound that reminded me of when we'd first moved to the manor in Ladue. It seemed like a million years ago. Now, I spent most days in Dante's bed, though I still had the room between Ursula's and Mandy's for my personal effects and my drawing desk.

"I'd like to see Levi now," Audrey said, handing me her empty teacup.

"Sure." I slipped off the bed before she attempted to crawl over me and stacked our bloody dishes on the service tray as she made for the door. "Don't you wanna change first?"

Audrey paused and glanced down at her pink flannel pajamas. "Oh…I guess I should, huh?" It wasn't like her to disregard her appearance. She'd arrived from Darkly Hall in a frilly gown, and it had taken some time to convince her that formalwear was not required day-to-day around the house.

"I'm going to throw on some jeans and a sweater," I said. There were too many new people under our roof for me to feel comfortable prancing around in my silky bat-print PJs. "I'll meet you back here in ten, okay?"

Audrey nodded and stepped into her closet while I dashed across the hall to my room. The purple heather and white roses from my sister's wedding sat in a vase on the corner of my desk. Ursula had caught the toss-away bouquet, but she'd instructed someone from the harem to deliver it to my room. The petals had begun to wilt around the edges, but the flowers were still lovely. It was hard to believe how happy and carefree we'd all been just the week before.

I dressed quickly, knowing Audrey wouldn't wait for long. But also, I was eager to know how Levi was doing, too. Someone would have to fill in for him as Audrey's primary bodyguard—maybe permanently—and I doubted Levi or Audrey would handle that well.

When I stepped back into the hallway, I found the duchess pacing outside my door in a peach-colored jumpsuit. Her hands were red from wringing them over her stomach. "Ready?" she asked, a pained smile tugging at her lips.

"Are you sure you've had enough blood? It's normal to need more when you're—"

"I'm fine," she snapped, then quickly covered her mouth.

When her hands fell away, she folded them under her chin as if in prayer. "I'm fine, really. I just want to see Levi."

"All right." I nodded and headed toward the foyer, staving off an encore performance of her pre-sunrise meltdown.

Audrey fell in step beside me. Her fingers moved again, this time to the sash at her waist to fiddle with the bow knotted there. I didn't like how uptight she was, but I had a feeling vampling bloodlust wasn't fully to blame for that. The jumpsuit alone told me she was still reeling from her time with the Free Blooders. I'd only seen her wear the garment once before—after which she'd dubbed it a fashion casualty of her first post-Darkly shopping trip. But it would be harder for someone to take her pants away if they were attached to her top and belted tightly enough to cut off circulation.

I wasn't one to point fingers at irrational behavior brought on by trauma. I hadn't fully unpacked my own emotional baggage, so Audrey would have to get her head shrunk elsewhere. Unfortunately, the most qualified person for the job, at least under our roof, didn't fall on Dante's most-trusted list.

We crossed paths with Ambrose at the base of the basement stairs, already dressed in his white doctor's coat. Audrey bristled as if she expected he would try to stop her from seeing Levi again.

"I've already had breakfast," she blurted before he even had a chance to greet us.

"That's very good to hear, Your Grace," Ambrose said. "I was just on my way to check on Mr. Bishop. Would you care to join me?"

Audrey gave him a brittle smile. "Lead the way."

"Please and thank you." I dipped my head, trying to make up for her rudeness. She was too fragile for lectures on manners.

"How long will he take to heal up?" Audrey asked as Ambrose directed us down the hallway that led to the guards' living quarters.

"I'd say at least another week. Maybe longer, depending on his lab results."

"But...but he's a werewolf." Audrey pressed her lips together, steadying the tremble in her chin. "Don't they heal faster?"

"Usually." Ambrose paused and gave us an apologetic frown. "But silver inhibits that ability, and Mr. Bishop had quite a lot in him. We're doing all we can to purge it from his blood. Amputating his leg helped a great deal—and, in fact, it saved his life."

"Oh, God." Audrey closed her eyes. "I...I don't know if I can hear this right now."

"He's going to be just fine," Ambrose assured. "In fact,

his silver levels are low enough now that we've ceased blood transfusions. However, he'll continue with an herbal detox regimen—mostly milk thistle and burdock tinctures—until his test results come back clean. Then his body should begin healing at a normal rate for a werewolf."

Audrey nodded. "Can I see him now?"

"Yeah," Levi's muffled voice called through the door we'd stopped in front of. "Can she see me now?"

"Certainly, Mr. Bishop." Ambrose rolled his eyes, but he opened the door and allowed Audrey to enter first. The show of trust softened the square that hadn't left her shoulders since we'd bumped into him.

I'd expected a sterile hospital setting, but the Tennessee Titans poster and bookshelf loaded with comics told me this was Levi's regular room. Other than the stark white sheets and a cart of medical supplies, everything appeared perfectly normal.

"Levi." Audrey sighed the werewolf's name and sank onto the edge of the bed as he sat upright. His right thigh was freshly wrapped, and there was a little more color in his cheeks. The dark circles under his eyes were gone too, but the five-o'clock shadow had evolved into the beginnings of a scruffy beard.

I was a little surprised that Audrey didn't shy away from his touch like she had with Dante. But then again, Levi had saved her life. Whereas Dante had watched as she'd been dragged away. Sure, he had pleaded with the Free Blooders to take him in her place. And he was far from the only one who'd been unable to stop her captors. But Dante was her sire, and as such, he had sworn to keep her safe. He was the reason she was a royal vamp and on the Free Blooders' radar in the first place.

No one had twisted Audrey's arm, but years of training had groomed her for this. Rejecting a royal house, even during a war—maybe *especially* during a war—would have disgraced her family and her school. It didn't matter that she hadn't picked this life for herself. I supposed that was another reason she felt more at ease with Levi. And with Mandy and me. We'd all been denied a say in our fates.

After my taste of Dante's blood, I knew he hadn't exactly been the master of his destiny either. But Audrey didn't know that. Not yet. She'd understand in time. Human, vampire, or werewolf, none of us got what we wanted all the time. Doors closed. New ones opened. People we loved hurt us, and sometimes we hurt them. Whether we meant to or not. That was just life.

I lingered in the corner of the room, watching Ambrose go about his doctorly business while Audrey and Levi snuggled and cooed at one another as if they were in a bad soap opera. Their Southern drawls were always thicker in each other's company.

"Don't you worry, Miss Audrey." Levi pressed another kiss to her knuckles and patted the top of her hand. "They make some mighty fine prosthetics these days. I knew a feller at Renfield who ran marathons—and he was missin' both legs."

"Well, I'll be. Ain't that somethin'." Audrey beamed, flashing her budded fangs. When Levi's gaze dropped to her mouth, she pinched her lips closed. "I…I'm so sorry. This is embarrassin'. I had two full cups before we came downstairs. I don't know what's wrong with me."

"I do." Ambrose sighed. "He was your first donor, was he not?" Audrey nodded sheepishly. "It's natural to crave your first. There's a pheromone pairing similar to the bond between a nursing mother and child. I'm sure Mr. Bishop is feeling the pull, as well."

Audrey and Levi cringed at the comparison and reclined away from one another.

"Maybe you should have a third cup?" I suggested. "Just to be safe."

Ambrose seemed to agree. "I'll be visiting the harem to check on patients there next. I'll request a blood pot delivery so you can extend your visit," he said, softening Audrey's scowl. But when her gaze slid back to Levi, he frowned. "I must warn you, Your Grace. If you should happen to cave to your thirst, Mr. Bishop's blood will make you quite ill. The residual silver may not be potent enough to kill you, but it will be most unpleasant. And the blood loss will prolong his recovery."

"I understand." Audrey tugged her hands away from Levi's and folded them in her lap. The scowl was back, but her voice remained even. "Now you understand this. We're not children. I think we can handle a few minutes alone." She gave me a pointed look this time, letting me know that it wasn't just the good doctor they were trying to get rid of.

I tried and failed not to think of the limp cat from my vision as I followed Ambrose out of the room. Would I come back later to discover Audrey whispering apologies and petting Levi's corpse? Surely, her self-control was better than mine had been as a vampling. She'd studied the undead condition since grade school.

"Don't worry," Ambrose said as we reached the main hallway that led back to the stairs. "If she does take a sip, it'll only be a small one. The taste of silver-tainted blood is enough to turn any vampire's stomach."

"Good to know." I gave him a weak, fleeting smile. It was the best I could manage after the chaos of the night before. And I knew it was far from over.

"Mr. Bishop is going to require physical therapy," Ambrose went on. "And I believe they could both benefit from trauma counseling. The duchess especially. Crawling inside her head and helping her find the peace she's lost will be a long and tedious process. Even if our dear prince were to trust me with such a precious obligation, my hands are quite full with the harem survivors from Evergreen. Perhaps you could refer them to your therapist?"

"Yeah. I'll do that," I said, intentionally not dropping Delph's name. I had the feeling that's what Ambrose was after. When he paused at the end of the hallway and shot me a sly grin, I was sure of it. But before he could pry further, Radu and his scion appeared at the base of the stairs leading down from the foyer.

"Good evening, Your Highness," Radu greeted me with a bow. Zane stuffed a thick folder under his arm and mimicked his sire's gesture, but his jaw flexed as if he resented me for it. "Doctor Starling," Radu added, shaking Ambrose's hand. "Always a pleasure."

"Likewise, Mr. Vlad." Ambrose hiked his chin at the stairs. "Forgive my swift departure, but duty calls." As he made for the harem, I detoured to trail after Radu and Zane on their way to Murphy's office.

"What brings you back to House Lilith?" I asked, trying to keep my tone friendly. Radu's men had rescued Audrey. I didn't want to seem ungrateful, even if the old vamp did make every hair on the back of my neck stand at attention. That

Radu seemed aware and amused by it didn't help matters.

"The queen made me an offer I couldn't refuse—in exchange for our continued alliance against the Free Blooders." Radu placed a hand to the side of his mouth, and his voice dropped to a whisper. "Though I must admit, I am looking forward to paying Marcel back for what he did to my opera house."

"Is that all you got?" I nodded at the folder under Zane's arm.

The vampling scoffed. "It's more than *your* people have."

"Come now," Radu scolded. "We are all the same people here, are we not? We want the same thing. Perhaps you would like a progress report, Your Highness?"

I couldn't quite decide if his royal address was mocking or sincere. He'd used the same calm, cheery voice when he threatened to *dirty his hands* with me last year—before I'd been dubbed Ursula's adoptive scion. Such a casual, nothing-personal tone that brought back the image of him in his silk Hefner jacket, holding a rocks glass of blood as he sized me up. Somehow, it made the sleek black suit he wore tonight more unassuming.

"Of course," I said, realizing he was waiting for an answer. Clearly, it was not the answer Zane had been hoping for. He ground his teeth as he held open the door to Murphy's office for us.

Radu flipped on the light, revealing a pair of long tables that the guards congregated at during the weekly briefings. I'd only sat in on a few, but Mandy updated me if there was anything of interest.

"Here, here," Radu said, holding his hand out to Zane for the folder. "Let us not keep the princess waiting." The vampling obeyed with another grudging glare in my direction.

"Congratulations on finally tying the knot," I said, my gaze darting to his mouth. The fake perma-fangs were gone. I'd let him believe that had been my clue. "Suppose I can't call you Count Denturla anymore."

"Yeah, thanks. And I suppose your fancy new title means I can't call you—"

"Zane," Radu warned. "We are guests in the queen's house."

"Apologies, sire." Zane gave me a crooked grin. We were both more comfortable with the gritty club banter than the niceties of undead high society.

"Did you find anything useful in the Blood Vice databases last night?" I asked Radu, focusing my attention on the photographs and documents as he arranged them across the table.

"I believe so." He pointed to a phone call transcript. "One of your agents managed to piggyback a hidden recording app on an *erotic* advertisement that ensnared one of

Marcel's underlings. They speak in code, but Marcel's lot…
How should I say?"

"Can barely manage pig Latin?" I suggested, scanning the
highlighted portion of the transcript.

Heisters: They blew the coop before the hen came home to roost.
Fanning: The fox won't be happy about this.
Heisters: Managed to save the freshest egg though.
Fanning: And the others?
Heisters: Too slippery. They rolled under a bush.
Fanning: Take the one you've got to the north-central market.
Might earn you enough for a trip to the moon.

So, we were only alive because the Free Blooders assigned
to take us out were incompetent. They'd mistimed the airport
explosion. Then, when it became clear they couldn't salvage
the job, they'd taken Audrey as collateral in hopes of
appeasing their boss—or cashing in on whatever a *trip to the
moon* meant.

I tossed the page back to the table and huffed. "I don't
know if I should feel lucky that we're up against idiots or
insulted that we haven't taken them down yet—who's that?"
I asked, my attention snagging on a photograph of a man
standing in front of a rusty trailer. A chain-link tattoo covered
his upper arm.

"Eddie Yates, from the Raymore Pack out of Kansas City," Zane answered. "That's their mark," he added as I traced a finger over the capital RM inside a paw-print outline on the man's shoulder.

"One of the men who attacked us at the crash site had matching ink."

Radu nodded as if he weren't surprised. "Marcel likes to move his people around. It's a control tactic, keeping them divided and far from home. They're less likely to default that way."

"It also makes it more difficult for local law enforcement to ID and track them," Zane added. "Eddie here was spotted outside a moonsmack lab near Dallas."

"Moonsmack?" I frowned, unfamiliar with the slang. Though from Mandy's previous involvement with the Moreau Pack during her time at the Scarlett Inn, I knew they enjoyed their hell dust. "Do you mean heroin?"

"If only." Zane snorted and dug another photograph from the pile, tossing it in front of me. This one featured a plastic-sheeted grow house packed with tall stalks of pale blue flowers.

"Is that...wolfsbane?"

"Wolfs*boon*." Radu clicked his tongue. "A rare, night-blooming hybrid of lupine, to be precise."

"Ain't nothin' *boon* about it." Zane shook his head. "The

Free Blooders cook the seeds down and mix them into a cocktail of heroin and steroids. When one of Marcel's wolves *pays the man in the moon a visit*, it forces a partial shift."

"Why would anyone want that?" I imagined Mandy at the halfway mark of her transition and made a face.

"Think about it," Zane said. "All the bite of a wolf, but with opposable thumbs."

"Yeah, if you don't mind looking like you just stumbled off a B-horror movie set."

"True." Zane snorted. "But they can open doors, climb trees, drive cars, dial the boss."

"Yes," Radu agreed grimly. "And the drug is quite addictive, giving them another reason to remain loyal to Marcel."

I shuffled through a few more pictures of Eddie and the drug lab. "Is this site still active?"

"Nope." Zane heaved an annoyed sigh. "One of your *brilliant* Dallas agents discovered it three days ago and torched the place. Luckily, we were able to locate a second lab near Austin by tailing an associate of Marcel's with that new Hanson facial recognition software y'all got. The place is under drone surveillance now. We're just waiting to see where the next delivery leads—as long as your people don't fuck it up first."

Radu clicked his tongue again. "These vampling agents,

they dig the grave before building the coffin."

"Everyone's eager for a pat on the head right now." I shrugged. "Can't hardly blame them after everything that's happened."

Zane fiddled with one of his gold cufflinks before turning back to the paper trail spread across the table. His brow furrowed as he resumed arranging the photographs and transcripts into whatever timeline or map they were constructing. I wondered if he was looking for a pat on the head, too. Or maybe some sort of validation that Radu still appreciated him even if he couldn't take a bite out of him anymore.

"We also have men on the ground at several Free Blooder hotspots." Zane unfolded a city map and then pointed to a stack of printed emails. "Without the leash y'all work against, we're able to deep-dive into more personal networks."

"You mean *hack* into them?" I hitched an eyebrow but refrained from balking about privacy rights.

Discretion was a human privilege, which Blood Vice pretended to respect as a division of the FBI. Our databases sometimes overlapped, so we had to be cautious. Radu's men, on the other hand, belonged to his private organization. They had free rein to dig wherever needed to get the goods their boss wanted. And they had the skills to get the job done, too.

"The pieces are coming together." Radu picked up a fat

stack of photographs and began sorting them on top of the various piles of transcripts and emails. There were pictures of burning buildings and smoking fields—all the damage undead society had suffered in the past twenty-four hours. I recognized the flaming airport I'd only seen briefly through an oval window before falling out of the sky. Radu handed me the last photograph of our half-submerged plane and waved a hand at the spread, now covering every inch of the table.

"The twelve attacks from last night have been matched to communications between Marcel and his generals. We have but one remaining mystery."

"Where the hell the big bad wolf is hiding?" I ventured.

Radu pressed his lips together. "Not quite."

"Where the hell he's planning the grand finale," Zane answered, smacking the back of his hand against a stapled bundle of pages. The printed text messages were full of random numbers. The more sophisticated code made me long for the farm lingo of the twats who had botched our landing in Columbia.

"Event number thirteen." Zane scratched the back of his head. "All we know is that it will be happening in St. Louis and *soon*."

"But maybe not soon enough to save you from the council's wrath." Radu gripped my shoulder. I was sure the gesture was meant to comfort, but it just made my skin crawl.

"These attacks were all aimed at the assets of members who openly support the hemoarchy," he said, a warning note in his tone. "They will demand blood for this injustice. If House Lilith does not deliver…"

I laid the plane photo on top of the others and swallowed. "Then they'll come for ours."

Part of me wanted to play the princess card, retreat to Audrey's bedroom and curl up under the covers with Mandy until this whole nightmare was over. But when I made it upstairs, the familiar sound of Dante's and Ursula's bickering seeped through the closed office doors.

They were up and at it early tonight. Of course they were. We were in the middle of a war, as everyone kept reminding me. Not that I could do anything constructive about it. Looking at Radu's and Zane's case file was one thing, but going into the field to search for Marcel with Blood Vice? There wasn't a chance in hell Ursula would get behind that plan. She still regretted taking the council's bait during our one-year evaluation and allowing me to investigate the Nightfall Opera House bombing.

Ursula's muffled voice grew louder and sharper behind the closed doors, until Dante finally snapped, "They are but babes! Blood Vice does not abduct children."

Our new queen was bending to the council's will much sooner than I'd expected. Dante and I had our disagreements, but this was certainly not one of them. The guards on duty in the foyer struggled not to make eye contact with me. I could tell none of them had listed kidnapping as a job skill on their resume either.

I didn't bother knocking before barging into the office and was awarded a glare from both the queen and the prince. Dante clenched a small manual in one fist. I assumed it went to the shiny new phone that had replaced the one he'd smashed last night. Ursula paced behind the pair of guest chairs in front of his desk, arms folded over her gray cashmere sweater dress. Her braid was unkempt, and she was sans makeup, but I was relieved to see her looking more alive and playing an active role in House Lilith's operations—even if we were about to butt heads in a big way.

"How is Audrey?" Dante asked, his expression softening. "Did she have enough breakfast?"

I nodded. "Yes, though Ambrose is having the harem deliver more blood to Levi's room where she's camped out for now."

"Good. Good." Dante rubbed a hand over the stubble along his jaw and sighed. "We were just discussing the messages we missed last night."

"Messages?" Ursula scoffed. "They were *threats*, cousin. The council expects action. *Immediately*. At this point, they're less concerned with the moral high ground than they are with results—"

Dante groaned and ground his teeth. "Bartering with the lives of children is not the answer."

"Agreed," I said, drawing Ursula's lethal stare. "Spero Heights is not a can of worms we should be opening right now—or ever. Besides, Selena Chase will devour anyone who comes after those kids. Seriously. She'll eat their faces clean off."

"Well, we have to do something!" Ursula threw her hands into the air. "The most prestigious vampire houses have been attacked. Lord Sorano is furious about his factory. We *must* call him back tonight—the sooner, the better. He intends to bring the council together for a veto vote regarding the retrieval of the Raymore pups. If we don't make that decision first, we'll be overruled. It's a slippery slope from there, children."

Dante dropped the phone manual onto his desk and folded his arms over the back of his chair. "We have Marcel's brother, but that has proven useless."

"Has it?" I asked, recalling Ambrose's comment about how someone needed to crawl inside Audrey's head. "Maybe we're just looking at Arnie from the wrong angle."

"What do you mean?" Ursula's gaze narrowed, but I refrained from reminding her of the long shot she'd based our last adventure on.

"Maybe it's time we play our wild card," I said, looking to Dante. He was already shaking his head.

"The council will not allow Dr. Delph on base—there are too many military secrets at risk. I doubt he would agree to such a meeting regardless, and he most certainly would not allow us to bring such a high-profile Free Blooder into his sacred community."

Dante's unraveling of my suggestion cued a melancholic sigh from Ursula. She closed her eyes and hugged herself, and a lightbulb flickered in the back of my mind.

"Leave the venue to me," I said, remembering the vamp's-eye-view of the sad, mutilated woman from my vision. I *had* seen that backyard before. "I'll even return Sorano's call. We're going to need his help."

"He will take offense." Dante grimaced. I knew he hated to remind me of how the council viewed vamplings. But in this case, only a vampling would do.

"Trust me." I picked up the handset of the new phone and nodded down at the keypad. Dante reluctantly punched in the number from memory. Lord Sorano answered on the first ring.

"I must say, I am surprised you had the valor to return

my call so swiftly."

"Valor?" I said. "Oh, I like the sound of that."

Lord Sorano scoffed. "Am I not worth the prince's time now?"

"The prince? Does the time of a princess mean so little to you?"

"I am not in the mood for games, Your Highness." His voice rasped, dangerously close to a growl. "I have important matters to attend to this night."

"Well, then. I won't take up any more of your time. I thought you wanted vampling impulsiveness. My mistake—"

"Wait!"

I grinned at Dante and Ursula, taking my time replying. "Yes?"

Lord Sorano cleared his throat. "What did you have in mind?"

Chapter Nineteen

"Clear," Murphy called from the back bedroom of the farmhouse. Mandy echoed him in the kitchen before returning to the living room where Dante and I waited. She tilted her head back and sniffed the air.

"Someone was here," she said. "They bleached the place to cover their scent."

"That's something Clyde would do," Holland admitted from the open doorway as he holstered his firearm. "The backyard and fields are clear, so it's doubtful they left on foot."

"Or recently. Bleaching would take time." I crossed the living room to check the thermostat. Fifty-five degrees. A werewolf—especially one recovering from excessive blood loss—would have cranked that sucker up to eighty. "There's no way they knew we were coming. They must have only stayed here for a short while."

"They could not have gotten far." Dante scowled. "Your visions are not yet forty-eight hours old."

I shot a wary glance in Holland's direction. My reaction to Lilith's blood had made it damn-near impossible to lie about who had drunk it and gone on the vision quest. I was sure that the fact I wasn't a true heir of House Lilith would eventually spawn questions from Holland and Murphy about how all of that worked.

Maybe we could convince them that the ancient queen's blood was capable of working its mojo on any ol' vamp. It wasn't like there was any left over to test that theory. Though I really hated the idea of lying to our own—especially to Murphy. He deserved the truth after everything we'd been through together. I'd been trying to work up the courage to tell him for weeks now. Of course, I hadn't mentioned this to Dante yet. Maybe I'd wait until he was less irritated with me.

The prince shook his head and gave me another withering look. "If you had mentioned this vision sooner—"

"What?" I snapped. "You would have pulled agents off the Free Blooder mission to hunt down this mystery heir of House Lilith?"

"Perhaps not, but…but the vision of Marcel would have been useful."

"How? Because of the convertible?" I pressed my lips together and breathed through my nose, trying to keep my composure. "In a car like that, you know he couldn't have been anywhere near a major city. Not with Blood Vice out in full force looking for him."

"That is not the point." Dante's jaw flexed. "You should have told us straight away, regardless."

"Leave her be." Ursula slipped past Holland and glanced around the living room, taking in the floral curtains and mustard-colored carpet. It was hard to imagine her living here, hiding from her family and the council. Mourning Morgan and relying on Annie to survive. She clicked on a floor lamp in the corner, and yellow light spilled across the room.

"Who owns this place?" Dante asked, curiosity granting me a small break from his displeasure.

"A friend of a friend in Spero Heights." Ursula ran a finger over the dusty lampshade, tracing the lace pattern. "They rent out the surrounding fields to a local farmer and earn enough to maintain the taxes and utilities on the house."

"Why bother?" Mandy's nose crinkled as her gaze migrated from the peeling wallpaper to the sunken sofa. The décor lingered somewhere between late seventies and early eighties. Which was probably the last time the place had had a legitimate resident.

"It's nothing special," Ursula said, pausing to straighten a framed painting of a little girl playing with kittens. "But they sometimes use it as a processing depot for newcomers hoping to gain residency in Spero Heights. Annie found out about it while doing odd jobs for some gardener up there. We were only here a month before…" Her voice trailed off, but I knew how the story ended.

Before Mandy and I showed up and dragged her back into the fold.

Ursula's brow pinched, and she turned away from us before wandering off toward the kitchen.

The last thing I wanted to do was dig up the past, but it was a risk worth taking. The farmhouse was the perfect meeting spot. Secluded, a stone's throw from Spero Heights, and abandoned—except for the most recent guests we'd just missed. The venue choice had also meant revealing the vision of Clyde and the wounded woman. And taking my lumps for keeping it to myself. I'd decided to clear my conscience all at once and shared the vision of Marcel and his girlfriend, too.

"I'm fine," Levi grumbled from the front porch steps. "No need to baby me, doc."

"Very well." Ambrose heaved a sigh that I was sure he intended for me, considering how vehemently he'd argued against Levi coming along when he should have been on bedrest. But, with the duchess in tow, there was no leaving her wolf behind.

My suggestion to get Audrey some *real* help while we had Delph at our disposal was probably the only thing keeping Dante from coming completely unglued for me keeping secrets. *Again.*

One step forward, two steps back. Story of my life.

"Look at these cute rockin' chairs, sugar. Let's give 'em a whirl." Audrey's *oohs* and *ahhs* were a little over-the-top, but she got brownie points for helping Levi without patronizing him. I imagined the task kept her mind out of that locked room above the pawnshop, too.

"Car's coming up the drive," Mandy said, her eyes glowing yellow as she listened closely to something I couldn't hear. Holland had gone still, as well.

"It's misfiring in a cylinder," he said.

"And burnin' oil," Levi added from the porch.

Mandy shook her head. "He really needs to put that thing out of its misery."

A moment later, the headlights of a 1970s yellow Datsun flashed across the living room window. The car knocked and rattled over the gravel driveway as if some part or another were loose and clinging on by its last bolt, before it finally sputtered to a stop behind the SUV and the sedan we'd arrived in.

The driver's side door creaked open, and Dr. Delph emerged. His gray hair was pulled back in a low ponytail that disappeared beneath the collar of his tweed jacket. He removed his glasses and tucked them into his breast pocket before rubbing his hands together beneath the frozen fog of his breath.

"Good evening," Ambrose called out first. Levi and Audrey parroted the greeting, adding their Southern inflection that somehow made it sound more friendly. Though Delph's guarded smile made me question their sincerity. Or maybe it was their confusion that he was picking up on.

Dante and Mandy knew what the doctor was capable of.

I'd tried to explain it to Ursula, but she was still unconvinced. As for the others, I'd let them believe that he was some retired, elite interrogator. It was the only way Delph would get a clear look at Audrey's state of mind.

"Good evening," he replied slowly, then dipped his chin as I stepped out of the shadow of the threshold. "Jenna—Your Highness."

"Dr. Delph." My voice trembled, but I quickly stuffed my hands inside my coat pockets, letting the cold take the blame. I'd spent most of the ride to the farmhouse brainstorming all the things I should absolutely *not* think about in the presence of someone who could read minds. What had started out as a cautionary exercise now felt like a spring-loaded Pandora's box.

I tried to clear my head and focus on something insignificant. The knit scarf hugging my neck. The chilled night air. The buttons on Dr. Delph's jacket. The amused line of his mouth suggested that I wasn't the only one who had tried this method with him.

"Selena has requested that I express her immense gratitude," he said. "The twins will not leave her sight until this business with the Free Blooders is resolved. To that end, I hope I can be of assistance."

I nodded. "Thank you for coming."

As he made his way up the porch steps, I introduced the

others. It was an unnecessary formality, seeing as how Dr. Delph had probably already helped himself to their thoughts and whatever their first impressions were.

"A pleasure to make your acquaintances." He made eye contact with each of them, lingering a bit longer on Ambrose's curious gaze. "Might I request a private word, Your Highness?" he asked, turning back to me. "Before your other guests arrive?"

"Of course." I waved an arm toward the open doorway, directing him inside.

"What's up, doc?" Mandy grinned and welcomed Delph with a warm embrace. Shameless affection was a rarity for her, but I supposed he'd earned the privilege by helping her overcome addiction and accept her wolfish nature.

I was a work-in-progress on the acceptance end, but I was grateful for his earlier advice about Roman. Even if I hadn't taken it right away.

"Thank you for agreeing to meet us here," Dante said, shaking Delph's hand as soon as Mandy released him. "Your service to House Lilith will not go unrewarded."

"Please, Your Highness." Delph waved him off with his free hand. "Anything for a friend of Graham's." He stole a quick glance around the room as if searching for someone. Ursula maybe, or the other guards.

Despite the queen's skepticism about the doctor's psychic

ability, we'd decided it was best that she not meet Delph. Especially since she'd been so ready to cave to the council's wishes regarding the Raymore twins. That and she could be quite abrasive when she felt cornered or compromised. She'd been banished to the back patio under Murphy's and Holland's supervision.

"Ah, I see," Delph said, replying to my unspoken thoughts—or possibly Dante's, I decided when the prince blanched and withdrew his hand suddenly.

"The bedroom," I said, pointing at the hall that branched off the living room. "Let's have that private word. The others will be here soon." My stomach knotted in anticipation and dread.

"I haven't been out here in years," Delph commented as he followed me through the house. "Of course, there are more comfortable accommodations for guests in town these days."

I thought of the Velvet Casket where Roman and I had stayed. The accompanying memories set my face ablaze with shame when I realized I'd just given Delph an involuntary peep show. I retreated to my mind-clearing exercises. *Funky carpet. Quilted bedspread. Night sky through the window.*

To Delph's credit, he didn't mention whatever naughty bits he'd witnessed. Instead, he closed the door and pointed me to the far corner of the bedroom, dropping his voice to a whisper, lest the wolves in the house overhear.

"There are enough issues here to start a second clinic. Where to even begin?" He sighed and pinched the bridge of his nose. "The vampling duchess and her wolf are clinging by a thread."

I chewed my bottom lip and nodded. "Yeah, they've been through a lot recently."

"They should come back to Spero Heights with me," Delph said matter-of-factly. "What the duchess has endured… It's not something the prince can fix with gifts and smothering—and I think you know as well as anyone that those are precisely his intentions.

"And the wolf is optimistic to a fault. He thinks a few more days and a prosthetic are all he needs for his life to return to normal. I commend him for his noble heart and devotion to the duchess's needs, but he must not forget his needs in the process. His efforts should be focused on physical therapy. In both his human and wolf forms. I don't believe he's yet considered how this will affect his hunting skills or rank among the new pack he's still assimilating into."

"But you can help them, right? Both of them?" I wrung my hands over my chest, wondering how much it would take to convince Dante—and how much convincing Audrey and Levi would require. And how long they would have to stay in Spero Heights.

"Yes, I can help them," Delph answered. "And I'd say at least six weeks. Dante wishes above all else to be a good sire, who does right by his scion. I do not believe he would have brought her here if he did not intend for me to offer my services. The duchess will agree to this for the sake of her wolf, and he for her sake."

"Fair points." I cleared my throat and tried to think of a tactful way to inquire about Ambrose, but that in itself was enough.

"Dr. Starling's only crime is curiosity," Delph said, a wry smile curling one corner of his mouth. "Though I believe the unraveling of a mystery is his favorite part. He would find a gift like mine tedious. For the record, he has no nefarious plans for you. He misses his niece, and you remind him of her. You loathe polite pretense and prefer courage over comfort. He suspects you will make life interesting—as Sonja once did. A rare treat for an old, jaded vampire who has seen it all. Still, it would be safest for you to keep your secrets close to the vest."

I snorted. "Won't get an argument there."

Maybe Ambrose wasn't the sneaky villain I'd suspected, but I didn't like the idea of anyone having life-or-death leverage over me. Not even friends—or old lovers.

Dr. Delph sighed and squeezed my arm. "I told you it would get worse before it got better."

"W-what?" I stammered. "No. I'm not…attached to him anymore. It *is* better. The lifeblood bond is broken."

"Broken?" His eyebrows hitched as I mentally replayed my last encounter with Roman for him. "His blood may be out of your system, but that does not change the fact that it once saved your immortal life. Nor that yours once saved his. A bond like that is never truly broken."

"I love Dante," I said, feeling foolish for how defensive I sounded.

"*Love* need not have anything to do with it." Delph cocked his head. "Though love—or lust—often initiates the forging of a bond. It's much like a child. Creating one does not guarantee the love or commitment of either parent. But the child exists, nonetheless. And as such, your bond exists. Regardless of love or nurturing."

"When I see Roman, I feel nothing," I insisted, my rasping whisper growing louder. I hugged myself and turned toward the window to avoid Delph's piercing stare.

Okay, maybe I *did* feel something. But it was definitely *not* love. More like the queasy regret after eating an entire pizza all by oneself. Not that I'd done that in quite some time, but I'd witnessed Mandy do it plenty.

"It is your choice not to nurture the bond," Delph said. "But it would be unwise to mistake your denial for closure. There will always be an invisible string that connects him to you, as long as you both shall live. Acknowledging it does not give it power over you—quite the opposite, really."

"Why are we discussing this?" I snapped.

"Because it's weighing on your mind." He gave me a dry smile and tapped the side of his head. "And for good reason."

Lights flickered across the upturned fields surrounding the backyard. My mouth went dry, and my pulse picked up the pace, beating out a warning rhythm behind my temples.

Arnie.

He was finally here. Though after Delph's little pep talk, I was second-guessing my reaction.

Lord Sorano had agreed to my plan. That didn't mean he liked me or gave a shit about my comfort. In fact, I was sure he'd taken sadistic pleasure in arranging Arnie's transport. The assignment had been given to Vanessa.

And Roman.

The ambulance was a smart choice. We had to be cautious of spies and drone surveillance, and what better way to disguise Arnie than to call him a corpse and cover him with a sheet? Just some poor sap who hadn't survived training, being returned to his sire for proper burial.

Vanessa and Roman wrestled the gurney through the

front door. They'd traded their fatigues for dress shirts adorned with paramedic patches before leaving Lord Sorano's private plane and loading into the ambulance we'd sent from Blood Vice, offering up the same unfortunate cadet story for anyone who asked. They'd also rearranged the base guard schedule, clearing out the senior werewolf barracks so that no one would notice that Arnie was missing. This was a strictly need-to-know operation.

Vanessa made a slow assessment of the room, dipping her head in a nod to Dante where he stood near the sofa with his hands clasped behind his back. Meanwhile, Roman kept his gaze locked on the lumpy form under the sheet. It rose and fell, detailing Arnie's peaceful, drug-induced slumber.

Mandy pinched her nose and backed into the mouth of the hallway where Dr. Delph and I waited. "Ugh," she groaned. "Couldn't you have at least hosed him off first? He's ripe enough to draw flies from three counties over."

"We had to work quickly to smuggle him off base," Roman confessed, his gaze still pinned to the dingy carpet.

Delph sucked in a sharp breath and gave my shoulder a squeeze. "It seems your invisible string has tangled itself into quite the web," he whispered. The skin between his brows creased as his attention wandered from Roman to Vanessa to Dante.

Like I wasn't struggling with enough guilt.

"Yeah? And what exactly am I supposed to do about it?" I hissed.

"There is nothing to be done. Except make your peace with it."

"Super helpful, doc." I sighed and pulled away from him to go close the front door.

Ambrose, Audrey, and Levi had been instructed to wait with Ursula and the guards on the patio. Holland was a seasoned wolf, so he would smell trouble coming from a mile away. Still, I peeked through the curtains over the front window, tapping into my blood vision to scan the shadows in the distance.

I turned around to find Roman folding back the sheet from Arnie's head. An elastic sleeping mask covered the werewolf's eyes. His chest was bare, save for a thick leather strap that held him flush against the gurney top.

"Does he need to be awake for this?" Vanessa asked, eyeing her watch. "Because if not, I'm supposed to inject him again in another twenty minutes."

Time was of the essence when transporting a high-profile creep associated with a supernatural terrorist outfit. I supposed that was another reason Lord Sorano had chosen his grandscion for the task. Vanessa had been the one to first tell me about Dr. Delph's psychic mojo, which meant we could skip the shock and awe and get right to the point of this gathering.

Dr. Delph cracked his knuckles. "Let's see what we can find in his subconscious first." He took a step toward Arnie but then froze. "Will you *all* be staying for the extraction?"

"Not gettin' stage fright, are you, doc?" Mandy teased. Dante gave her a pointed look that she took for the cue it was and stomped off into the kitchen. I heard the patio door open and close as she joined the others outside.

Dr. Delph took another look around the room as if he might request that we cull the audience further, but whatever he saw in our minds must have made him decide it wasn't worth the effort. "Okay, then," he said before crossing the room to stand near Arnie's head.

Roman stepped back from the gurney and went to stand behind Vanessa. Once out of her peripheral vision, his icy blue gaze darted up to meet mine. I looked away, suddenly realizing I'd been staring. My embarrassment doubled when my attention snagged on the line cutting across Dante's brow. He pressed a hand over his chest as if stanching a wound. Maybe looks couldn't kill, but they could injure.

Tangled web, indeed.

Dr. Delph cleared his throat. The sound had a reprimanding edge to it. "If I could have some quiet, please."

"No one said anything," Vanessa replied, her ears turning bright red as Dr. Delph shot her a dark look.

"If you were thinking any louder, I'd be deaf," he said. "If it will help ease your mind, you should know that the answer is without a doubt: *no.*"

"To which question?"

"All of them," Delph said. "Take comfort and meditate on whatever peace that brings—at least until I emerge from the abyss of this diseased creature's psyche."

"Yes, doctor." Vanessa bowed her head and turned her back to the lamp until her face was hidden in shadow.

Delph raised an eyebrow at me. "The rest of you are not making this easy either. Please, if you could quiet your minds for just a moment. Try thinking of the ocean tide or falling snow. Something simple and soothing."

I nodded and resumed my earlier mental exercises. Granted, it was harder in this room and with these people. *The black silk of Arnie's eye mask. Vanessa's shiny boots. The glint of Dante's wedding ring. The sparkle of the diamonds and sapphires in mine...*

"I suppose that will have to do." Delph huffed and peeled off his tweed jacket. He tossed it over the arm of the sofa and unbuttoned the sleeves of his shirt before rolling them up to his elbows.

The air in the room suddenly felt too dry. I licked my lips and clutched the ends of my scarf. This was it. Our entire plan hinged on this moment.

Dr. Delph's hands trembled as he lowered them over Arnie. He pressed his thumbs and middle fingers together, forming a circle that he planted on the werewolf's forehead, his palms resting against either temple. Then his eyes rolled back in his head until only the glowing whites remained.

I held my breath, begging the powers that be, whatever they were, to grant us this break we so desperately needed. If this didn't work, we were lost in the woods. Waiting for Marcel to make his final move. And when he did, House Lilith would fall like a king on a chessboard.

The room was deathly quiet—so silent that I could hear the soft *tick* and *tock* of a clock from some other room in the house. Maybe the kitchen.

Seconds stretched into minutes, but Delph's eerie, unblinking eyes remained white as his mind's eye traversed Arnie's gray matter, searching for breadcrumbs. If he were breathing, I couldn't tell. He stood mannequin-still, a soulless husk awaiting the return of its master.

When he finally emerged, he rasped in a harrowing breath, and his skin gleamed instantly with sweat. It coated his upper lip and forearms and curled the hairs at the base of his neck that had slipped free from his ponytail. His hands recoiled from Arnie and gripped the edges of the gurney.

"I…I found it," he said through panting gasps. "The alpha bond…I've seen one before…but I've never followed it back to its source.”

“And?” Dante pleaded. “Do you know where Marcel will strike next?”

Delph’s eyes glistened as he looked up at us. “He’s already there.”

Chapter Twenty

We were a good two hundred miles away from Bleeders—where Marcel and the Free Blooders were busy enacting their next phase of anarchy. Radu and Zane had said it would take place in St. Louis, and that it would be soon. I just hadn't realized it would be *this* soon. Or this depraved.

I should have known better. We were dealing with Marcel, after all. He'd turned Mandy and countless other girls against their will. Of course, that had been one at a time. Not an entire club in a single night. Ambitious bastard.

"Bleeder's average capacity is twelve hundred, and at least eighty percent of their patrons are human," Roman said under his breath, mindful of the call Dante was making from across the room. The prince had reached for his phone the second Delph dropped the news, though I wasn't sure how much damage control we were capable of on such short notice.

"But tonight is a new moon," Vanessa said, her sharp brows twisting with confusion. "It's not like they'll shift."

I pressed my fingers over my eyes and groaned as the pieces began to click into place. "They will if Marcel pumps them full of his designer drugs. Then he'll have a raging new insta-pack ready to do his bidding."

"That does seem to be the idea," Delph said, dabbing his face with a handkerchief he'd dug out of his jacket. He still seemed spooked from tapping into Arnie's alphic link to his brother. "However," he continued, "I am uncertain if a partial shift is enough to claim their wolves or pledge themselves to an alpha. There is a chance the condition could be reversed if they are treated in time."

Dante tucked his cell phone into the crook of his neck before adding his two cents. "That's if Marcel does not brainwash them into joining his cause first." He pulled the phone back to his mouth as someone answered his call. "Radu Vlad, is he at the house? When did he leave? Zane? The vampling scion? Put him on."

Dante stabbed a finger through the knot of his tie, prying it away from his neck as he turned to pace the room. The low, muffled hum of Zane's voice filtered through the speaker of the phone, but I couldn't register anything beyond his distress.

"Yes, we know—I will explain how later," Dante barked. "We will be there as soon as possible. Do *not* approach the building before we arrive. We need you to get us in through Vlad's private entrance… The micromoon? I see…"

"We could help them," Roman said, more to Vanessa than anyone else.

"We could," she agreed through clenched teeth. The tight line of her jaw told me that was a maybe at best. "But we have orders to return Arnie Moreau to base as soon as House Lilith is done with him."

"And we are not yet done with him, Agent Sorano," Dante said. He tucked his cell phone into his pocket and turned to face us. "It would appear that Marcel has reached the pinnacle of immoral chemistry with the latest version of his drug. It still triggers a deformed shift like before. But under a micromoon, it induces a *full* shift that will allow an alpha to mark and receive them. We have until the new moon rises— three minutes before sunrise—to stop this madness."

"He has explosives," Dr. Delph reminded us. "Marcel is zealot enough to blow the entire block if he feels his plan will fail—"

"Not before he attempts escape," I interjected. Marcel's dark, self-assured eyes and ravenous smirk replayed in my mind. "He thinks too highly of himself to give up that easily."

Vanessa's nose crinkled. "How would you know that?"

My heart skipped at the cautious glance Dante gave me. I had to think fast. "Why else would he have stayed hidden for so long?"

Dr. Delph nodded, but I had a feeling his agreement was based off a stolen peepshow of my remembered vision. "Marcel also has the help of a vampire. One you've *seen* recently," he added, confirming my suspicion.

"We can't just send in a Blood Vice raid team," I said, hoping to distract Delph from spelling out my illicit vision quest for Roman and Vanessa.

"No, we cannot." Dante's shoulders squared. "I am done hiding behind Blood Vice. My sire has been murdered, and my scion abducted. Now this atrocity against our blood faction…"

Vanessa blinked stiffly, shock seeping through the stoic mask she wore most of the time. "Your Highness, you can't mean to go in there yourself."

"But I do, Agent Sorano." Dante lifted his chin. "House Lilith's relationship with the public is fragile and on the cusp of ruin. If we have any hope of containing this disaster or preserving our regime over supernatural society in this country, it is vital that we make a strong showing tonight. I will face Marcel and handle the negotiation myself. I may not get my pound of flesh tonight, but I want him to know that I'm coming for it."

"I'm going with you," I said, reaching for his hand and lacing my fingers with his. "We're in this together. For better or for worse."

Dante swallowed and gave me a weak smile. His palm was moist, but I would have been more concerned if he weren't worried about confronting a psychotic tyrant werewolf.

"Thank you," he said, squeezing my hand until it ached. I wondered if he already regretted his newfound courage. We were rolling the dice with death—in a few short hours—and we didn't even have a game plan.

"So, Zane is sneaking us in through Vlad's private entrance?" I asked.

Dante nodded. "And we are using Arnie as a bargaining chip in hopes of freeing over a thousand hostages." The flat, faithless tone of his voice didn't instill much confidence.

"Marcel left him to rot in Denver," Vanessa pointed out. "Do you really think his life is worth anything to his brother?"

"Maybe. Maybe not." Dante rubbed a hand over the back of his neck. "But if we try—if we make an appearance and show our subjects the lengths we are willing to go for them—"

"There's a chance we might sway them from joining the Free Blooders," I finished. "Turning them is one thing, but they have to accept the alphic bond of their own free will. Of course, we might still go boom if Marcel gets away from us before we're able to evacuate the building."

"If we can distract him long enough to slip in a few agents from the bomb squad—" Vanessa bit her bottom lip, but not before a dry laugh slipped out. For all her aversion to helping us, she couldn't resist a covert operation when one was coming together. "Fred still running the St. Louis office?" she asked.

I snorted. "Straight into the ground, if you ask me."

"Is he as heavy-handed with the red tape as everyone says?"

"Let me deal with Captain Nicks," Dante said, reaching for his phone again. "You will ride with me so I can grant clearance as needed while you make arrangements with the necessary agents."

Vanessa winced. "Even with Arnie sedated, I wouldn't dare leave my scion to supervise him alone."

"I'll go with Roman," I offered without thinking, and earned uneasy stares all around. "Mandy can ride with us, too."

Dante's gaze fell away first. He pressed his lips together. "Very well. Let us gather the others and make arrangements for the queen's and duchess's return home."

"About that…" Dr. Delph cleared his throat and gave me a pinched smile, a silent request to spell out his earlier recommendation.

"Audrey and Levi need therapy," I said. There was no sense in beating around the coffin, not with so little time to spare. "They deserve the best, and they can have the best"—I blinked at Dr. Delph, making my point clear—"but you'll have to be willing to part with them for six weeks."

"What?" Dante blanched. "I…I don't know if…"

Arnie groaned, and we all jumped. His head twisted from side to side, and he made a wolfish, whimpering noise like Mandy often did in her sleep. Vanessa checked her watch again before yanking the sheet up to cover Arnie.

"Time for his next dose," she said, nodding to Roman. He grabbed the end of the gurney near Arnie's feet and tugged it toward the front door.

Dante waited for them to be out of earshot before turning back to Delph. "Six weeks? Is that really necessary?"

Delph shrugged. "I suppose that depends on how important your scion's mental health is to you."

I could tell the answer was too accusatory for the prince's liking, but it served its purpose. "They may return with you to Spero Heights tonight, but I will be calling tomorrow to confirm that Audrey is not distressed by this arrangement."

"Naturally." Dr. Delph motioned toward the kitchen. "Time is short, Your Highness. Would you like to say your goodbyes before we depart?"

"Yes, of course. Excuse me." Dante nodded to Delph and then to me, though he didn't make eye contact before heading out to let the others know the plan.

"He still grapples with your past," Delph said, fetching his jacket from the sofa. "It is getting easier, but Roman's presence is a painful reminder of the choice he denied you. It makes him reckless with the need to prove he is worthy of your love and respect."

I already knew all of that. Though I had no idea how to fix it. My breath rushed out in a sigh I felt as if I'd been holding in for ages.

"Roman will go back to Denver once this is over, and things will return to normal." It was an automatic response that I wanted to believe. That I *needed* to believe.

Delph cupped my chin, gently lifting until I looked him in the eye. "Please, heed my counsel this time. Make your peace with the bond before he leaves."

I swallowed and nodded as he released me. "I'll try."

"Your Highness?" Holland called from the entrance to the kitchen. His gaze flitted between Dr. Delph and me, and I wondered what he feared the doctor might see in his mind. "The queen would like a word before we leave."

"Of course." I smoothed my hands down my coat and tightened my scarf before saying goodbye to Delph and heading out to the back patio.

The solar lights created a halo of pale light around the modest garden spot set with lounge chairs and bookended by hedgerows. I had the strangest sense of déjà vu, especially with Ursula stuck somewhere between sulking and spitting mad.

"This is a terrible idea," she said, twisting her fingers in the elastic at the end of her braid. "I don't suppose there's anything I can say to talk you out of it?"

"I can't let Dante face Marcel alone. He needs me—and so do a thousand hostages."

"You don't have to do this," Ursula insisted. "We can

send in Blood Vice."

"I *am* Blood Vice." I shrugged at her scowl. "Agent Jenna Lilosa. Got the badge and a gold star sticker from the council to prove it, remember?"

"You're a princess, and Dante is a prince."

"Only because the Free Blooders murdered our predecessors."

"This is absurd!" Ursula threw her hands into the air and stalked away from me, pacing the edge of the concrete slab. "And I don't care for Dante throwing around his authority as commander of Blood Vice either."

"Guess you should have turned Blood Vice over to me while you had the chance."

Ursula hitched an eyebrow at me. "Are you saying that you would have handled this any differently?"

"I guess we'll never know." I gave her a teasing grin and shivered as a wintery breeze nipped at my nose and ears. I almost wished it would penetrate my wool coat and offer relief from the nervous sweat that had broken out as soon as I'd volunteered to ride with Roman.

Ursula shook her head and glanced out over the barren fields surrounding the backyard. Her pale skin glowed in the darkness, nearly as bright as the solar lights. Even without the crown, there was a regal air about her. There always had been.

"I sometimes wonder what would have happened if you

hadn't found me out here," she said, pulling her knit shawl tighter around her shoulders before folding her arms.

"Do you still regret that I did?" I asked.

"Do you?" she countered. Her gaze twisted back to me, and a sad smile pinched one corner of her mouth. "I regret my poor handling of Raphael and Scarlett. And I regret that Annie gave her life to prove me innocent of Morgan's murder. I don't want my incompetence as queen to cost you and Dante your lives, as well…" Her voice trailed off in a choked whisper.

That was a lot of guilt to carry around. And for the longest time, I'd held her responsible for the actions of her scions, too. But really, she was only responsible for them in the way that Hitler's mother was responsible for his crimes. All Ursula was guilty of was getting lost in the grief of Morgan's death and shutting out her family.

I knew a thing or two about grief and lack of communication. I knew how it could tear a family apart. I didn't need to learn that lesson the hard way a second time with my undead family. And while I couldn't absolve Ursula of all her guilt, I could at least put a dent in it.

"You're my sire and my queen," I said, stepping in front of her. "But you don't get to take credit for my every action. You didn't order Scarlett to open a brothel. You didn't order Annie to come to your trial. And you're not ordering me into battle with the Free Blooders. If I go down tonight, it will be because of my incompetence, not yours."

"Is that supposed to be comforting?"

"You know what I mean. But for the record, I fully intend to come home—"

Ursula threw her arms around me, dragging me in for a hug so tight it stole my breath. If her strength hadn't, the shock would have.

"You better," she whispered, pressing her cheek against my hair. "You better."

I hardly had a chance to say goodbye to Levi and Audrey before Delph stuffed them into his little yellow car and headed off to Spero Heights. Ursula, Ambrose, and Holland left next in the SUV, homeward bound. We passed them on the highway soon after, a la the emergency express route.

"Are you…warm enough?" Roman asked, fiddling with the thermostat dial on the ambulance dashboard.

"Yeah, I'm good." I pressed my lips together and resisted the urge to lecture him about keeping his eyes on the road. The speedometer read just shy of a hundred. Although, the flashing lights and wailing sirens meant less traffic to navigate.

Murphy, Dante, and Vanessa were close behind us. I

could see the tinted sedan windshield every time I glanced in my side-view mirror, but I didn't waste my blood vision searching for Dante. I wondered if he was debating doing the same, insecure as he'd been lately. Surely, he didn't think Roman and I were capable of anything inappropriate in a vehicle traveling this fast or with the fate of supernatural society as we knew it on the line.

Mandy had insisted on riding in the back of the ambulance with Arnie, even after Vanessa injected him with enough sedative to last until we reached St. Louis. We were hoping by then he'd be semi-conscious and able to stand on his own two feet. He was an awful lot of dead weight to be dragging around inside Bleeders. That and he couldn't telepathically contact his brother unless he was awake—which we needed him to do if we were going to use him as bait and trading fodder.

As much as I hated the idea of releasing Arnie to his brother, I knew it was the lesser evil tonight. Mandy had to know that, too. Still, I was sure the idea was eating her alive. I'd almost withdrawn the suggestion that she come with us for fear she'd take a bite out of our bargaining chip. But everyone seemed less threatened by the idea of Roman and me riding together with Mandy playing our almost-chaperone.

I tried and failed not to think about the last time we'd been together without an audience. The dark gallery at Lili's manor in Evergreen where his blood had gutted me. It was gone now, nothing but charred splinters and dust. Maybe something new would be built atop the ruins. Maybe that's what I was trying to do now.

I knew this would be my last chance to talk privately with Roman about the lifeblood bond before he returned to Denver. Not that I was making good use of it. Half an hour had already slipped by with only the muffled howl of sirens filling the silence.

My eyes roamed the cab of the ambulance, lingering on every little detail. As if once I memorized the layout of the controls, maybe I'd have enough nerve to say more than two words to Roman. Admittedly, a flying, flashing emergency vehicle wasn't the best environment for a heart-to-heart. But this was what I had to work with, and I'd told Delph I would make an effort.

"Look, Roman," I began.

"Where?" His head twisted from side to side as he scanned the shoulder and the ditch of tall grass that separated us from the oncoming lanes. "I don't see it."

Great. He thought I was pointing out a potential hood ornament.

"There's not— I wasn't—" I blew out an aggravated breath and tried again. "I was just going to say that I…forgive you."

"What?" He blinked at me.

"Eyes on the road!" I clutched my seatbelt and pressed my foot into an imaginary brake on the floorboard.

Roman's attention snapped back to the highway in time to navigate around a truck straddling the rumble strip. Once we were past it, he shot me a sideways glance. "Sorry… You caught me off guard."

"Well, try not to put us in the ditch, but I also wanted to say that I'm sorry, too."

"For what?" He snorted and squeezed the steering wheel. "You did nothing wrong."

"You and I both know that's bullshit." I wasn't up for the full laundry list, but I'd humor him with the highlights if he needed the reminder. "I jumped off a building and tried to ride a van as if it were a rodeo bull. If I hadn't, you wouldn't have felt the need to save my life with your blood. Then I went and saved your life instead of letting you die in the line of duty so you could rise with a forgiven Blood Vice contract."

I skipped over the blood exchange after I'd been stuck with a silver syringe at Annie's old apartment. And the one at the Velvet Coffin in Spero Heights that I couldn't think about without the blood in my veins turning to lava. I was content letting both of those incidents fall under symptom rather than catalyst.

Roman's throat bobbed as he swallowed, but he didn't try to look at me again. "If I hadn't been so damn resentful and stingy with the information you requested, you would have known better. You were a vampling, and I'd been half-sired since before you were born."

It was a fair point, but I'd clung to that grudge long enough. I took a deep breath and let it go. "Regardless, the lifeblood bond is just as much my fault. You were big enough to apologize for...*you know*... So, I can be big enough to apologize for the things I got wrong."

Roman cleared his throat and stole another glance at me. "In that case, I forgive you, too."

"Good... Good." I nodded, more to myself than to him. Apologies and forgiveness seemed like a decent start. But that's all it was. A start. Definitely not the peace I suspected Dr. Delph had meant.

Damn it.

I stared out the windshield and chewed my bottom lip, keenly aware that Roman's attention was divided between the highway and me. As if he didn't believe *that was that* any more than I did.

"Is it...do you still feel it?" I finally asked.

After a long pause, he confessed, "Not like I used to. It comes and goes. You?"

"No. Well... I do a pretty good job of pretending I don't,

anyway. Delph says the bond will last forever—at least to some degree."

"Think we can live with that?"

"I suppose we'll have to." I sighed and offered him a tight smile.

"It could be worse, you know," Roman said, one hand leaving the steering wheel to mess with the dials on the dashboard again.

"Yeah, I could be *dead*-dead. So, thanks for that. A little blood nostalgia seems a small price to pay."

"Blood nostalgia." He grinned. "That sounds about right."

I sucked in a deep breath and braced myself before dropping the next question. "Was it all the bond, or do you think there's a chance we were ever in love?"

"Does it matter?"

"I guess not…as long as you're happy with Vanessa."

"We were never—" Roman sighed. "It's complicated. She enjoys playing with her food. And I'm no longer on the menu."

"Oh." I looked down at my lap. "I suppose I should apologize for that, too."

"Why?" He barked out a dry laugh. "Because your new boyfriend's the one who *chopped* me?"

"Something like that." My face burned with the

accusation, however playful it had been. Then I backtracked to his previous comment. *She enjoys playing with her food.*

Is that what I'd been doing with him at the Velvet Coffin? I could certainly understand the appeal. And Dante had mentioned something about Lili and Alexander's romance ending after he'd been fully turned, too.

Roman shrugged. "What I had with Vanessa was never a relationship—not in the traditional sense. After the first decade or so, she grew bored with me. It wasn't until she noticed my interest in you that she became jealous and decided to test the waters again. My initial refusal did not go over well."

"I saw," I said tightly. The Eye of Blood had played out the scene for me in vivid detail.

"I was afraid to lose another potential sire," Roman said. "I'd already lost two. I shouldn't have, but I caved. That was the last time Vanessa anointed me. And the last time she invited me to her bed."

"I'm sorry."

Roman shrugged again. "It is what it is."

I didn't know what else to say. I'd been so angry with him for cheating, I hadn't bothered to let him explain. At the time, I doubted any excuse would have sufficed. But now, after some distance, and after having moved on with Dante…I could see through that faded heartache and try to understand.

It didn't mean we were getting back together. At least half of my forgiving nature relied on that fact. It was easier to forgive someone for breaking your heart when you had no intention of handing it back over to them with a big red bow tied around it.

Still, we could be civil with one another. We were professionals, after all. I was ready to let our past be blood under the bridge.

"What about you?" Roman asked. "Are you happy with the prince?"

"Very." The answer was reflexive, and I realized too late how callous it probably sounded. "I mean, I wasn't at first. Obviously. I hated his guts and felt like I was under house arrest."

Roman grinned. "I think that's called Stockholm Syndrome."

"Har, har." I rolled my eyes.

"Neck-snapping aside, he seems like good people," Roman said, his smirk going slack. "Does he know...about your real sire?"

Of course he would have to go and ask a question like that. As if our lifeblood bond weren't difficult enough, we shared something far worse. A secret that could end us both—and anyone else who knew about it.

Maybe I didn't trust Roman with my heart anymore, but

I *had* to trust him with my life. There was no way around it. Sharing that truth with Dante had felt just as necessary—not only to unravel Kassandra's betrayal but also to claim my rightful place within House Lilith.

To everyone else, I could be the redheaded step-vamp of the royal family, but I'd demanded a level playing field with Dante from the beginning. It was one of the things he loved about me. Well, most of the time.

"He knows," I finally answered, unable to hide my smile.

Roman's jaw flexed. "Then it must be true love." The snarky attitude was back, but with less cheer this time.

"I had to tell him—he found Zajalvo's actual scion," I admitted. That seemed to surprise Roman even more.

"And he didn't report that to the council, I take it?"

"No." I immediately regretted offering up the explanation. What was it about disappointing Roman that still bulldozed my better judgment? I was sweating under my coat again.

"Then the prince has as much to lose as I do." Roman's icy gaze slid toward me again. "Or as much as I did."

Chapter Twenty-one

Roman turned off the flashing lights and sirens before exiting the highway. We had a couple of miles to go, but we didn't want to alert Marcel until everyone was in place. As far as he knew, we were oblivious to his psychotic plan. And the longer we could play dumb, the better. No sense in putting a rush-order on the mayhem.

There was a streak of evil genius to Arnie's brother that made my blood run cold at the idea of finally facing him. Engineering a drug that could create an instant pack to do his bidding was concerning enough on its own—because whether they pledged themselves to him or not, they would be a massive pain in the ass to round up. But then scheduling the anarchy to ignite just shy of sunrise when seventy percent of Blood Vice would be dead to the world? And during a micro new moon when the wolves on the force would be at their weakest? That was Lex Luthor-level wicked.

Bleeders was clearly a calculated choice, too. The human patrons that frequented the place were well-acquainted with supernatural society, and the vampire pheromones they were hooked on made for the perfect gateway drug. Marcel's moonsmack would be like candy tossed into the masses at a parade.

Roman pulled into the parking lot of an insurance office

a couple of blocks away from the industrial district that surrounded the club. A black Rolls-Royce waited under the only security light. Exhaust from the tailpipe formed a hazy fog along the pavement, and the chrome wheels glistened with frost. As I exited the ambulance, the driver's side window of the car rolled down, revealing Radu's agitated scion.

"He's alive," Zane said, pausing to take a long pull from a flask likely filled with one of Radu's blood cocktails. "I'd know it if they…if they did somethin' to him." Zane shook his head as if to dislodge whatever awful image his mind had painted. "Plus, the building's on cellular lockdown."

"Must be why no one has called this into Blood Vice," Roman said, walking around the front of the ambulance to stand beside me.

Zane nodded. "Vlad and I are the only ones with clearance to shut down the system. They must've forced him to. At least he was able to get a message out first. Still don't know how y'all found out."

"Friends in psychic places," I said, earning a dirty, disbelieving scowl that told me Zane was in no mood for jokes. With his sire's life hanging in the balance, who could blame him?

I decided against trying to explain it was the truth. If not for having experienced Dr. Delph's *gift* firsthand, I wouldn't have believed it either.

Headlights sliced across the lot as Murphy pulled in and parked on the opposite side of the ambulance. An unmarked SUV followed closely behind and parked sideways in the row behind us, taking up four spaces. I recognized Nicks' plate number and swore under my breath.

With Dante ordering him to turn over the reins to Vanessa, I should have known Nicks would make an appearance. I'd tolerate him only so long as he didn't waste time beating his chest like a territorial gorilla.

"It wasn't just the message from the boss," Radu whispered, eyeing Nicks' ride. Vlad and his people cooperated with Blood Vice under the radar when necessary, but they'd made no secret of their distaste for the current captain. If memory served, they hadn't been overly fond of Vanessa either.

"One of our drones followed a delivery truck here from that lab in Austin," Zane went on. "Bastards pulled right up to our back door. Vlad was furious. He thought a bouncer or bartender was dealing in the club and went to put a stop to it. I would've gone with him, but he'd sent me to check out another lead across the river. By the time I made it back to Ladue, all I had to work with was his message and the drone feed."

"And?" I said, waving my hand to hurry him along. With his aversion to law enforcement, I knew these details would dry up the second Nicks and Vanessa joined us. Playing nice with me was hard enough for Zane.

"The delivery truck was still in the back alley, last I checked. 'Course I came here to wait as soon as the prince told me where to meet y'all. Guess Marcel and company slipped in before the drugs arrived." Zane's lips pressed together, and his gaze wandered past me. "Mornin', cap."

"Morning," Nicks grumbled. Then he did the unthinkable and dipped his head in my direction. "Your Highness." I was too stunned to reply.

"Captain Nicks, I presume?" Roman extended his hand. "Agent Roman Sorano of the Denver division."

"Sorano?" Nicks harrumphed, but he took Roman's hand and gave it the obligatory shake. "The former captain's scion, right? I've heard about you."

"I'm sure you have," Roman said without missing a beat. "I was assigned to two high-profile cases during my short time in St. Louis. The Scarlett Inn and the Green Fang Killer."

I still preferred *Buffy*, even though the killer turned out to be one of Scarlett's butt-hurt former minions. And though I hadn't cared so much at the time, I kind of hated that my contributions to both cases were so off-the-books. It would've been nice to have more official cred with Blood Vice when the council had conducted their one-year evaluation.

"Oh, I've read your files." Nicks smirked. With his

enormous forehead, it made him look like a giddy Herman Munster. "I'm referring to the blood cooler talk at the office."

"Huh." Roman rubbed his jaw. "Every agent in Denver is working overtime in the Free Blooder search, and you're telling me you all have time for gossip? Interesting."

"What's interesting?" Vanessa asked as she, Dante, and Murphy crowded in between the ambulance and Zane's car. She tossed a hooded sweatshirt to Roman.

"Captain Nicks' philosophy on professionalism," I answered before Roman could, enjoying the way Nicks' brow furrowed, and his mouth opened and closed like a fish out of water.

Vanessa gave him an indifferent look and then jumped straight to business, forgoing any introduction or handshaking. As the former captain of the St. Louis division, I was sure she'd had words with him a time or two before tonight. There clearly wasn't any love lost between them.

"What I'd find interesting is knowing where our bomb techs are," she said, blinking expectantly at Nicks. He waved a hand at his SUV, signaling whoever was inside to join us.

I pounded on the side of the ambulance to get Mandy's attention, too. One of the back doors creaked open and closed, and then she slipped in beside me, shivering in her cropped leather jacket.

"Every available agent is set up along a half-mile

perimeter around the club, Your Highness," Nicks said to Dante as if addressing the prince made this more palatable to his ego. "They're equipped with all the naloxone tranquilizers we have on hand. Medical units are standing by. I've called in backup agents and resources from Kansas City and Chicago. They should arrive anytime now."

Dante glanced down at his watch. "Sunrise is in less than three hours. Every undead agent in the field will need to seek shelter long before then. We can't afford to wait for backup."

The two men who had climbed out of Nicks' SUV stopped behind Zane's car. I only recognized one. He'd been at the Hearty Harem warehouse, sifting through the debris after the place had gone boom and collapsed on top of Mandy and me.

"Vlad's private entrance," Dante said, looking at Zane, who was still cozy in his car and nursing his flask. "Can it be accessed without detection from the security cameras?"

Zane nodded before shooting Nicks a sideways scowl. Sharing his boss's secrets with the fuzz wasn't ideal, but it was his only option tonight.

"Vlad owns all the buildings around the club and rents them out to various businesses for surplus storage," Zane said. "Including one with a basement parking garage where we keep his Wraith and the Phantom here parked. There's a tunnel that cuts under the two storehouses in between, leads to a stairwell that goes all the way up to our—Vlad's—loft apartment."

"Does it have an entry point on the main level?" I asked, recalling the hidden doors in the back hallway of the club.

"Sure does." Zane frowned and cradled the flask to his chest, clinking it against the gold chain necklace that peeked between his unbuttoned collar. "The door's hidden behind a bookshelf in the office across from the juice bar, near the elevator. The computers in there are tapped into the security room upstairs."

"So likely compromised?" Nicks guessed out loud.

"And full of explosives," Zane added, blinking up at the ceiling of the car. His brow creased. "That's what Vlad's message said. It's all part of Marcel's ultimatum. Either join the Free Blooders or blow sky-high."

"Damn." Murphy pinched the bridge of his nose. "This prick don't pull no punches. Suppose this means he's missing his brother and willin' to deal?"

Dante offered a weak smile. "Let us hope so, Mr. Murphy."

"At least until these fine stiffs disarm any explosives on the premises," Nicks added, cocking his head at the two bomb techs waiting for orders.

"Any other entry points?" Vanessa pressed.

"No," Zane answered, clearly a little too quickly for her

liking. Vanessa leaned over until she was eye level with Zane and let him squirm under her scrutiny for a moment.

"It's vital that we know all options. There are a lot of lives at stake."

"My sire is in there," Zane snapped. "Don't you think I'd tell you?"

"What about the furniture place next door?" I asked. "We could use the hidden entrance in the back hallway. Is there any way to access that building from one of the upstairs levels?"

Zane shook his head. "Sorry."

"Not even from the roof?" Roman tried next. "Are there cameras up there?"

"Yeah, but they're aimed down at the parking lots and the back alley." Zane scratched his head. "If you stay clear of the edge and don't let your shadows fall into frame, I suppose you *could* get into the furniture place unnoticed. If you had the key, which is in the loft—"

"Which might be compromised, as well," Dante finished.

"However…" Zane held up a finger. "With the building on cellular lockdown, it's not like anyone would be able to call downstairs to let 'em know we're in."

"Okay, okay." Vanessa stood up straight and raked a hand through her hair. "We get in through the garage tunnel and fetch the furniture warehouse keys from the loft. Then we'll split into two teams. Nicks, Roman, and Zane, you'll go with the bomb squad down to the office on the main level.

"The rest of us will wrangle Arnie across the roofs and down through the warehouse entrance. We'll get in, get Marcel's attention, and hopefully hold it long enough for you all to take care of the explosives," she said, motioning back at the bomb techs again. They were beginning to look a little green around the edges.

"Then Mr. Zane can activate the building's cellular signal," Dante said, picking up where Vanessa had left off. "We'll call in the agents standing by to assist, and hopefully apprehend Marcel and his ilk as they attempt their getaway— though our main priority is to contain the patrons who require treatment."

"Put the sweater on Arnie," Vanessa instructed Roman. "Pull the hood up. Then grab the pair of cuffs in my bag. We might need them when he comes to."

I rubbed both hands over my face. "This is…quite a plan."

"Lots of ways for it to go wrong," Mandy said, spelling out my sentiments more bluntly.

"The cellular lockdown means we won't have any radio communication to work with either," Vanessa continued, ignoring our nervous rambling. She nudged Roman with her elbow and wiggled her wrist, signaling for him to hold up his watch and compare it to hers. "We'll have to time this just right so that we make our entrance before the coup in the office."

"And we can't trust anyone while we're in there." My gaze locked on Dante's. There was no safe way to share our knowledge of Marcel's House Lilith mystery heir companion without creating a fresh new hell to deal with later, but we couldn't let them walk into this without some sort of warning.

"The Free Blooders have recruited vampires," Dante explained. "Even ones from noble households. Revealing our presence or intentions to anyone is a risk we cannot take."

"Duly noted." Nicks adjusted his shoulder holster and checked the magazines clipped to his belt. There was a larger plastic case fastened near his hip. When he caught me staring, he rapped his knuckles against it. "I have a dozen tranquilizer rounds. Couldn't justify leaving any of my agents with less than I'm packing."

"We might be looking at a thousand brand-new, doped-up wolves," Murphy said, grimacing as he checked over his own firearms. "This thing goes south, we're gonna need a helluva lot more sedatives than that."

"This thing goes south," Mandy said under her breath, "*we're* not gonna need shit."

She had a point. A very cold, sharp point that dug into my resolve with increasing ferocity.

This wasn't a plan. It was hardly a Hail Mary. We were halfway to martyrdom, throwing ourselves to the wolves. What a way to go out.

I supposed we'd had a good run.

Arnie was still unconscious. The sedatives were hanging on longer than expected, though he groaned in his sleep as Roman and Nicks hauled him down the sidewalk, his socked feet dragging behind him. To any passersby, it probably looked like two guys helping an inebriated friend home from the club. Only they were going *toward* the club instead of away from it. And Roman and Nicks looked entirely too sober, clean, and annoyed to be friends with some scruffy drunk in sweats.

Mandy and Zane tailed behind them, prepared to make a scene if anyone tried to help with Arnie. Vanessa and Heath, one of the bomb techs, were half a block ahead, checking for scouts. The rest of us—Dante, Murphy, bomb squad Ned, and I—lingered half a block behind, spacing out our party so we wouldn't draw too much attention.

We made it through the parking garage tunnel and up to Vlad's loft at Bleeders without any major hiccups, but once inside, the dread seeped into my bones.

Blood-spattered sheet music was strewn across the floor. The piano bench lay on its side, busted and splintered with two legs missing. I searched the room for them, and my stomach sank when I found one crammed through the chest of a man wearing a satiny bouncer suit. He lay slumped against the wall, his blood smeared down the plaster above him.

Zane swallowed hard and passed his hand over the man's face, closing his vacant eyes. "Ben was one of our best," he said. Then his gaze migrated to the iron maiden in the corner. It was closed. The other broken bench leg had been slipped through two metal handles, holding the doors together, and a dark puddle spread beneath the contraption.

"Male human," Mandy confirmed, nostrils flaring. "Dead for at least an hour, I'd say."

Zane crossed the room, nearly slipped in the blood, and ripped the bench leg free. The iron maiden's doors creaked as he pried them open, and a wetter sound echoed in the chamber behind them as metal spikes were extracted from flesh. A younger man, this one wearing a set of blood-soaked silk pajamas, remained upright inside, skewered in place from behind.

"Fucking hell." Zane looked away and covered his mouth as his fangs slid free. The wide-eyed horror and disgust in his expression was familiar and practically a rite of passage for vamplings. If they didn't stay well-fed, any blood—no matter how friendly—flamed their appetite.

"Need a hand?" Murphy asked, stepping over the broken piano bench.

"Don't touch him!" Zane snarled. He gasped in surprise at his own outburst before his eyes drooped and he held up a hand. "I'm sorry," he choked out. "Peter was mine, from the harem. I just…need a moment."

Nicks and Roman took that as their cue to prop Arnie in a corner and then began stretching their arms and backs. They were strong, but I was sure carrying a load that large and limp for several blocks and then up four flights of stairs was no picnic.

"I'm real sorry about your friend," Murphy said, squeezing Zane's shoulder. "Believe me, I've lost favorites, too. But the more time we waste up here, the more time Marcel's got with the rest of your people downstairs."

Zane nodded and ran the sleeve of his jacket under his nose. His fangs were still out, and the sight of them reminded me of my own hunger. As if on cue, he stalked across the room to a minibar and pulled several bottles of blood out of the refrigerator.

"We really need to keep our heads clear tonight," I warned as Murphy accepted one of the bottles. Zane handed the next one to me, and I automatically accepted it on behalf of my budding fangs.

"Don't worry. This ain't the top-shelf sauce," he said. "Just run-of-the-mill, club-donor blood we keep on hand for the staff. I have a feeling we're gonna need it."

He was probably right. I cracked the cap of my bottle as he finished passing out the others and took a long drink, almost wishing it were the distilled diabetic Radu preferred. My hands were shaking, and I was sure Dante had noticed by now.

Radu Vlad, cousin of Vlad the Impaler, who was so feared and respected by undead society that even Blood Vice steered clear of his territory—for the most part—had been taken captive by the Free Blooders.

What chance did the rest of us have?

Chapter Twenty-two

Bleeders was sweltering. As we snuck past the curtain that hid the door to the warehouse and into the back hallway, it felt as if we were stepping into a sauna. The air was humid and tinged with the salty tang of a thousand-plus bodies pressed up against one another. It wasn't an uncommon odor for the club, but it was normally paired with techno music and laughter, not the hiss of panicked whispers.

Murphy carried Arnie over one shoulder as if he weighed no more than a wet towel. The handoff had baffled Roman and Nicks, but Murph wasn't the captain of the royal guard for nothing. Vanessa seemed relieved, anyway. Mandy was too tiny for heavy lifting, and no one would dare ask the prince or princess to help carry the likes of Arnie Moreau.

Thanks to Murphy's strength and agility, we'd also arrived fifteen minutes ahead of schedule. We would have remained in the warehouse a while longer, but there was no telling what obstacles awaited us inside without having a look for ourselves. I just hoped we had better luck with curiosity than Alice or cats.

No strobe lights flashed through the curtained archways that led to the dance floor, and even the industrial sconces that framed the restrooms were out. I'd expected as much. Werewolves had far better night vision than humans—better than vampires, too. Except for those of us with the Eye of Blood. Mine activated the second Murphy stepped on my toe.

I bit back a yelp and gave him a dirty look that I was sure he couldn't see. Murphy mouthed *sorry* as I hopped a step away from him. Speaking was a no-go this close to so many enemy wolves. Mandy had reiterated that fact as we'd gone over the finer points of the plan on our way through the neighboring warehouse. Now that we were finally in, it was time for some reconnaissance.

With my blood vision in full effect, I peered through the wall that divided the back hallway from the rest of the club. The room was filled with red. One giant, huddled mass of human flesh with a thousand hearts that fluttered like a time-lapsed night sky of twinkling stars.

In the closest corner, just beyond the wall that hid us, a small cluster of vampires cowered. Their coloring was crystal-clear, outlining their horror in vivid detail. These weren't Blood Vice agents or experienced nobles. They were just average vamps out looking for a good time and a quick bite. Several large men—likely Marcel's wolves—stood guard around them, rifles at the ready.

More made the rounds through the crowd of humans. A few carried medical cases full of syringes that they unceremoniously jammed into arms or thighs, occasionally an ass cheek if someone resisted and had to be held down.

The Free Blooders were moving fast. Too fast. Everywhere I looked, a patron rubbed an injection site or wobbled unsteadily on their feet, eyes glassy, breath slow and heavy. Several sat on the floor, nodding in and out of consciousness. A few moaned and groaned as they touched themselves or their dates—pleasure-seekers hooked on vampire pheromones, discovering a new vice.

The booths were empty, the curtains pushed back and behind the leather benches so that no corner of the room granted shelter. I picked out more Free Blooders in front of the juice bar, guarding the entrances to the back hallway on either side.

Mandy moved toward the curtain to steal a peek at the scene. I grabbed her arm and held up four fingers before nodding in the direction of the bar, warning her of the danger. Then I made a V with the index and middle finger of one hand and touched my fingertips to my canines before pointing at the corner where the vamps were being held.

Mandy swallowed and nodded before taking a step back to relay the information to the others as if it were her own. That detail of the plan had remained unspoken between us. A benefit of working together for so long and knowing which secrets required guarding from whom.

Dante was new to the eye. We had agreed that he should save his energy, but I had to wonder if fear had activated it for him regardless. How long had it been since he'd rushed into battle? Willingly, anyway.

The gunfire we'd taken after our plane had gone down was still fresh in my mind. After Lane's death, I'd assumed Dante would proceed with more caution. With Roman in the mix again, I supposed the prince's pride was stronger than his survival instincts. But more than that, I feared he was right about our relationship with supernatural society.

House Lilith's reputation was drenched in scandal. Betrayal, exile, incarceration, assassination. Those of us who had survived the rise of the Free Blooders were too young or unreliable to deserve respect of the American undead.

Marcel's timing was no coincidence—especially considering he was responsible for a good chunk of that scandal. But there was a decisive opportunity hidden beneath the mayhem. If House Lilith defeated the Free Blooders, we would also prove ourselves worthy of the crown. It was a big *if*, but it was also the only way we would secure our future. I clung to that silver lining…and I planned to strangle Marcel with it the first chance I got.

Arnie groaned, and every hair on my body stood on end as one of the guards near the juice bar turned toward us. He cocked his head and took a slow step in our direction, but then his attention slipped away at some commotion near the front of the club.

Thank God.

We needed to do something about Arnie. He would only become more problematic as the sedatives wore off. Before I could figure out how to address this without speaking, Vanessa unknotted Murphy's tie and silently slipped it off his neck before cramming it into Arnie's gaping mouth.

Problem Solved. And just in time for the next one.

"Well, aren't you a fine bunch of blood bags?" A booming voice echoed through the club. I quickly pinned it to the DJ stage set against the front wall near the main entrance where a warm-blooded figure paced the platform, hands tucked casually into his pants' pockets. A trio of spotlights shined down on him from an overhead rig, prompting the humans in the room to turn toward him like moths to a flame.

Mandy's fingers latched on to my arm, and her eyes found mine in the dark. Despair and vengeance raged within her, confirming what I'd already guessed.

Marcel.

Another line of armed men stood between him and the crowd of humans. Not that they could cause much trouble in their drugged condition.

"I bet you're all feeling pretty good right about now," he said in a slow drawl. "You're welcome. And there's plenty more where that came from. Apologies for the rushed dosing, but we're on a tight schedule. You see, here in a couple of hours, the micromoon is going to shuck off that tedious humanity you've been cursed with."

The whispers in the crowd grew louder. Someone gasped excitedly. Someone else burst into tears.

"Now, now." Marcel pressed a finger to his bottom lip, hushing them as if they were children. "I know what you're thinking. You haven't been scratched or bitten. It's not even a full moon. But I assure you, my moon juice will take care of everything. Even the pain of shifting."

Moon juice? So, we already had a new name to go with this caustic crap. Super.

A door slammed, and I caught movement out of the corner of my eye near the elevator. A square of armed Free Blooders hid someone from me despite the Eye of Blood. I strained to get a better look, but my abuse of the gift was taking its toll. My mouth was already dry, desperate for a sip of fresh blood. Not that I had any interest in sampling the spiked variety the club was now full of.

Marcel made a sound low in his throat that reminded me of the illicit joyride I'd witnessed in my vision.

"And, for those of you who get your kicks opening a vein for the fanged," he continued, stretching out his hand to the newcomer as they neared the stage, "you're in luck. Werewolf blood is a delicacy. Of course, you'll only be offering it up to

Free Blooder vamps from now on. Like your new queen and my consort, Kassandra."

A delicate hand slipped into Marcel's, and then she was on the platform beside him, staring out at the audience with unhinged emerald eyes and lips stretched into an obscenely wide, bloodstained grin. Her unbound curls were beyond mussed as if she'd just rolled out of bed—or more likely, a locked coffin—after taking a three-month nap.

Marcel wrapped an arm around Kassandra's waist and gave her leather miniskirt and thigh-high boots a lewd once-over. If he hadn't called her by name, I wouldn't have believed it was her. I still wasn't sure I believed it, even if it did explain the vision. The Free Blooders must have snuck her coffin out of Lili's manor in Evergreen before the bomb went off.

"I believe a demonstration is in order." Marcel snapped his fingers, and two Free Blooders dragged a man wearing a denim vest and a spiked choker up onto the stage. He was young, maybe in his mid-twenties, and moving sluggishly enough that it was clear he'd been dosed.

I glanced around the room, searching for the men brandishing the syringes, but they were gone. The deed was done. Marcel had waited until they'd all been drugged before making an appearance and explaining his intentions. We were too late.

Marcel ripped the spiked choker from the man's throat.

Then he twisted him around to face Kassandra. One hand gripping the man's shoulder, and the other clenched in his hair, he wrenched his head to the side. A tendon bulged in the man's neck.

"I am alpha to your beta," Marcel hissed. "You will hear my call and heed." He struck like a viper, his unshifted canines sharp enough to break through flesh and draw blood.

The man's garbled scream echoed as Marcel shoved him to his knees on the stage floor. I thought maybe he'd fainted. But then his back bowed up in an oddly sharp curve, ripping the seams of his vest. His arms curled over his head as if he anticipated being kicked, and I watched with horror as dark fur sprouted from his shoulders. It spread like moss down his biceps and forearms, stopping once it reached his knuckles. When he finally looked up, I saw more fur along his temples, merging with his thick eyebrows.

Gasps echoed up from the crowd, thankfully concealing my own.

"You see?" Marcel waved an arm down at the quivering wolfman. "Already, my alpha blood courses through your veins. All it takes is a little kick of adrenaline to ignite it. Pledge yourself to me, offer your blood to my consort, and we will welcome you into the fold of the Free Blooders. This is the future of supernatural society. Soon, the world will bow before us."

Kassandra crouched on the stage, giving the room a glimpse of the lace panties under her skirt. She hooked a finger under the wolfman's chin, forcing him up onto his knees. "What do you say, precious? Will you be a good boy and give Mummy a little taste?"

His bottom lip trembled, and tears streaked his face. A wolfish whimper muffled his words, but they were clear enough to reach me in the back of the club.

"I just wanted to see a vampire. I…I wasn't going to give blood." He held up his wristband as proof. It was tinted pink from my blood vision, but his reaction told me it must be white. The color was intended for exclusive harem members, but it was mostly requested by voyeurs and newbies who didn't want to risk a vampire encounter just yet.

Kassandra's sickly-sweet smile curled into a sneer. "Are you refusing me, mortal?"

"I don't want to be a werewolf—or whatever this is." He looked down at his furry arms and choked out a sob.

"Then you won't be." Kassandra grabbed a fistful of hair from the top of his head and twisted his face down toward the stage floor. Her fangs slid free, and she sank them into the back of his neck like a mother cat snatching up a kitten.

The murmur of the crowd swelled once more, along with my heart rate.

"No, wait!" the man squealed. But the only thing that

would sate Kassandra now was his blood. All of it.

Her back and shoulders heaved as she sucked from his flesh, gulping noisily until he went limp and fell to the stage floor. Kassandra tilted her head back and sighed blissfully. Blood oozed from the corners of her mouth and dribbled down her chin and neck.

When she stood upright, Marcel pulled her to his side and traced his tongue across her jawline, lapping up the mess she'd made. She purred in response, head bobbing unsteadily.

I jumped as Dante's hand closed over my shoulder. Our eyes met in the dark, and I realized that his blood vision had finally activated. Terror seeped through his gaze. His mouth opened, but no sound came out. I didn't understand his panic until Kassandra outted us.

"Looks like the in-laws finally made it to our engagement party, darling," she cooed.

My attention snapped back to the stage. Kassandra's gaze locked with mine. *Shit.* Alexander had been her sire as well as Dante's. She had the Eye of Blood. When her mouth stretched wider, it was clear that she knew I had the gift now, too.

"Lovely." Marcel closed his eyes and drew in a deep breath through his nose. "And they brought Arnold with them." He sniffed again. "Ooh, and my little pet."

Mandy's fingernails bit through my coat sleeve as her lips

peeled back into a silent snarl. We remained silent for a moment, mostly out of shock. But then Marcel's men were on the move.

I instinctively drew both Reaper TDs from my shoulder holster. Mandy and Vanessa unpacked a pair of pistols each, and Murphy managed to draw one despite having Arnie slung over his shoulder.

"Hell have mercy," Dante grumbled under his breath. He stuffed a hand between the lapels of his coat and clumsily retrieved the pistol I'd seen him practicing with at the bat cave.

Firing into a crowded club was never a great idea, but it was definitely not advisable with his aim. When he pointed the barrel at Arnie's head and motioned Murphy toward the entrance to the dance floor, I sighed with relief.

We entered the room before anyone could force us to. Though it only felt like a victory for the split-second it took the Free Blooders to surround us. I'd tried to take a headcount earlier, but I'd lost track after thirty. Outnumbered was an understatement.

A spotlight from the stage rig rotated in our direction. My eyes watered, but I kept them open and my aim steady on the two closest wolves. Vanessa's wrist grazed mine, using it as a guidepost as we fell into formation around Dante. She brought up the rear of our group, Mandy taking the opposite side from me, while Murphy inched us forward using Arnie's ass for cover.

"Is that the prince?" someone whispered from the dark corner the vampire hostages had been pushed into.

"There's the new princess, too!"

"Are they here to help us?"

"Who's that with them?"

"Brother." Kassandra still grinned like a devil, though it no longer reached her glazed eyes. "I'm surprised to see you so far from your gilded cage, mingling with the commoners."

"Kassandra." Dante clicked his tongue at her. "How could you align yourself with him? He killed our sire."

She giggled, but the sound soon warped into a high-pitched scream as she clawed her hands through her hair. "Alexander watched as I was stuffed into a coffin!"

"You had my potential scions murdered," Dante shot back. "And you sent an assassin after the queen. A locked coffin was more mercy than you deserved."

"Don't forget about poor Morgan." Kassandra snorted at Dante's lack of surprise. "I see you haven't."

"Why?" he asked, as if it mattered now. As if this level of crazy could be rationalized.

"Power, brother." The humor drained from her face. "And love. I wanted to rule as Alexander's queen. That was only possible with Morgan out of the way. Then your little vampling tart had to go and drag Ursula back into the mix and further complicate matters," she added, her loathing glare shifting to me.

I refrained from smirking at her. One wrong move, and she'd abandon her monologue to sic the wolves on us. Or spill my tea. I couldn't decide which would be worse. We just needed to buy a few more minutes.

"I knew the sooner our family grew, the sooner the queen would take the prince to her grave," Kassandra continued. "The only reason I allowed the redhead to live was so I could slip a spy into your household. I never expected you'd *actually* turn her. She's so…weak. Soft. Perhaps you intend to take her to your forever rest. She's certainly not fit to rule."

"And you are?" Dante scoffed. "Well, at least this psychotic, terrorist drug lord is a more suitable match for you."

"Marcel sees me for the queen that I am," she snapped. "He worships me like a goddess, and he dreams of conquering worlds as only a god can dream. Alexander accepted his true death long before my wolf king delivered it." She snuggled in closer to Marcel and rested her head on his shoulder. Vile satisfaction stretched his grin into creepy territory, but my attention fixed on his hand as it slipped behind his back.

Dante glanced around the room at all the frightened faces staring at us. Waiting for some sign that everything was going to be okay. This was our make or break moment, and it felt as if the entire club were holding its breath.

Arnie mumbled around the tie stuffed into his mouth and began to squirm enough that Murphy had to roll him off his shoulder and to the floor. He slipped on his socked feet, but Murphy kept him upright, pinning the werewolf to his chest with one hand while wielding his pistol with the other.

Marcel snorted as Arnie blinked around the room, trying to make sense of where he was. "Welcome back to the land of the living, little brother."

Dante stepped in closer to Murphy and pressed the barrel of his pistol to the side of Arnie's neck.

"You can have him back in one piece if you release these hostages," he said.

"Hostages?" The corners of Marcel's eyes crinkled as he laughed. "They're not hostages. They're my guests. The new nobles of the underworld, who will soon rule over the human chattel and any vampires who try to banish them to the shadows."

"We'll set them free soon enough," Kassandra said. "Our children will greet the dawn as harbingers of a new world."

Dante ground his teeth. "They'll be hunted and slaughtered by humans—we all will—and you know it."

"At first, perhaps," Kassandra agreed. "But in due time, we will have turned enough of them to level the battlefield.

Humans will be less inclined to wage war against supernaturals once they *are* supernatural."

"Besides," Marcel added, his sinister smile growing sharper, "all wars have casualties. True rulers must be willing to make sacrifices, starting with the useless runts of the litter." The hand hidden behind his back reappeared, this time holding a pistol the size of a cannon. "Like my brother, for instance."

A deafening shot echoed through the club, and then Arnie's hot blood splattered across my neck and cheek.

The room exploded with screams. They were muffled beyond the ringing in my ears—but not so muted that I didn't notice when they began to dissolve into grunts and howls.

Chapter Twenty-three

"Murphy!" I aimed at one of Marcel's men as he neared Dante's bodyguard. When he kept coming, I fired two rounds into his chest. Another man took his place, and I fired again.

"Damn it, Murph. Get up!"

"Fuck you," he grumbled before squeezing off a round in my direction. A Free Blooder collapsed behind me, screaming as he clutched his ruined kneecap. I finished him off with a round between his eyes.

"Thanks," I rasped over my shoulder. "Can you move yet?"

"I can cover ya just fine from here." Murphy shoved Arnie's corpse off his legs with a groan. Then he propped himself up against the side of the juice bar. His ballistic vest had saved him from a similar fate, but the wind had been knocked out of his lungs.

Dante crouched behind the bar in a puddle of fruit chunks, pistol gripped in both hands. Vanessa had immediately cleared a path for him and had taken up a post on the opposite side from Murphy and me. Mandy ducked behind the counter, too, popping up like a gopher every few seconds to fire at the stage.

The alpha of the Free Blooders hid behind the DJ booth, taking potshots at the vampire patrons now running loose in the club. The younger ones couldn't resist the sight of so much blood. Some fed on the injured, even at the risk of being shot or torn to shreds by one of the many mutated half-wolves frantically searching for a way out.

Wood splintered the stretch of bar between Murphy and me as another Free Blooder fired in our direction. I took aim, but before I could squeeze off my next shot, a spear sliced through the air. It caught the man in the throat and pinned him to the mirrored wall. The glass shattered, crackling ominously as it spiderwebbed behind him.

I glanced across the room, in the direction where the spear had come from, and found Radu. As our eyes met, he dipped into a short bow. Zane stood behind him, mashing the elevator button between firing shots at the Free Blooders.

I wondered why they weren't using the secret stairwell before remembering Zane's reaction to the dead harem donor in the loft. Maybe he was trying to spare Radu until we made it through this nightmare. I hoped the two of them would be enough to take down whomever Marcel had watching the security room upstairs.

In my distraction, a mutated wolf rushed in and slammed my back against the bar. I aimed before realizing he was just disoriented and looking for a place to hide. My hand snagged on the flap of shirt fabric that had survived his partial shift. I pulled him off me and shoved him toward the nearest entrance to the back hallway.

"This spot's taken," I shouted. "Try the restrooms."

He scampered off, slipping and sliding in spilled juice and blood.

When I turned back toward the elevator, Radu and Zane were gone. A few yards away, a Free Blooder headed for the office. I took aim, but as he opened the door, Roman's booted foot kicked the man square in the chest, sending him sprawling back toward the dance floor.

Roman slipped in beside Vanessa and provided cover as she changed out magazines. "Heath and Ned are working as fast as they can," he yelled over the cacophony of screams, growls, and gunfire. "As soon as Vlad has the cellular system back online, Nicks will call in the perimeter."

"We need to take out Marcel," Vanessa said. "Now, before he orders his men to unleash this hell through the front entrance."

"Go ahead." Murphy grunted and used the bar to drag himself to his feet. "I've got the boss covered." He drew his second firearm and squeezed off a round with a wince. His mark dropped, which seemed to satisfy Vanessa well enough.

She nodded to Roman, and they advanced on the stage. I almost followed until I spotted Kassandra along the far side of the dance floor, standing in front of the row of empty booths.

The wannabe queen had her fangs stuck in another moon juice victim, groaning like a porn star as her cheeks hollowed from the force of her appetite. She was too close to the mutated wolf for me to risk a shot at this range, but then another patron rammed into her from the side, knocking her fangs loose.

Blood arced through the air. Kassandra turned to hiss at the clumsy emo kid who had interrupted her meal. She lunged at him, but I knew a window when I saw one. I stepped out onto the dance floor, squeezing the triggers of both pistols as I moved in closer. One round caught her in the shoulder. The other went clean through her neck.

Any other vampire, on any other night, even one of those shots would have been enough to put them down—or out of commission, at the very least. But as Kassandra's narrowed-eye glare turned in my direction, her weeping flesh curled in, knitting itself back together at a rate I'd never witnessed before.

"W-w-what the—?" I blinked, and she was suddenly in front of me. Her hands clamped over my wrists as tightly as steel cuffs and squeezed until I couldn't feel my fingertips. My pistols clattered to the floor.

"Silly little princess," Kassandra hissed against my cheek. "I've drunk enough blood tonight to raise the dead. This is what *true* immortality looks like. Now, let me show you true death."

My shoulders screamed as she yanked me off my feet, and I was suddenly airborne. But only for a moment. My hip hit the mirrored wall first, followed closely by my elbow and then the back of my skull. Shattered glass peppered my hair and face as I bounced off a leather bench and landed on the floor.

There were too many bones in my body, I decided. And I was sure they were all broken.

I hooked an arm over the small table in the booth and tried to stand, but before I'd even made it off my knees, Kassandra was on me again. She ripped off my knit scarf, giving her fingers room to curl around my neck, then proceeded to crush my windpipe as she lifted me to standing and beyond. I grabbed her arm with both hands and kicked my feet, searching for the floor.

Kassandra cackled up at me. With her lips smeared in blood and her frizzy hair, she looked like a clown from a demonic circus. I could feel the heat of her metallic breath. There was a floral undertone to it as if she'd drunk enough tainted blood that the wolfsboon from Marcel's moon juice was detectable. The drug was certainly taking its toll. Her pupils were almost nonexistent, lost in the unnatural green of her irises.

"What's so special about you, hmm?" she asked. It was a rhetorical question, as my vocal cords were crushed in her grasp. "Was Zajalvo more powerful than he let on, or are you just a gifted liar? Maybe I should take a bite and find out."

My pulse spasmed in my neck at the thought. It was all the encouragement Kassandra needed. As she leaned in to make good on her threat, a pineapple cracked her in the side of the head.

Kassandra's outraged snarl rang in my ears. She jerked around to see where the produce missile had come from, only to take an apple to the eye. Dante popped up from behind the bar and lobbed a cantaloupe at her next. Maybe his firearm aim was lacking, but his throwing arm was Major League-worthy.

I made good use of the diversion and kicked my feet up onto the bench behind me, dragging Kassandra along for the ride. Her grip tightened around my neck, but now I had the high ground. And I was within reach of the curtain hanging in the corner of the booth.

I grabbed a handful of the material and looped it twice around Kassandra's head, pulling it taut as she tried to shake loose. With her face buried in velvet, her screeching was more bearable. Her hold on my throat slackened, but it wasn't until

I yanked up on the end of the curtain and dragged her over the top of the booth table that she finally released me.

I sucked in a ragged breath and screamed as her fingernails ripped through my pants. She set to work on the curtain next, clawing the soft fabric to shreds. I sidestepped into the opposite corner of the booth, holding tight and searching for something to fend her off with before she got free.

Radu's spear was stuck in the wall a few yards away. I leaned over the edge of the bench and reached for it, yanking my hand away as a rogue bullet ricocheted off the glass wall beside me.

Kassandra's muffled screams tore through the club, growing louder as she liberated herself from the velvet noose. The racket drew the attention of a nearby vampire huddled in a corner with a group of half-wolves. They all wore white wristbands. Paired with the trust of a vampire spelled them out as harem mates. And considering the relative calm of their master, I was willing to peg her as one of the elite regulars Vlad entertained.

I glanced around the room and picked out two others, both surrounded by white-banded wolves. Their attention had migrated toward me, too. Or rather, to Kassandra, I realized as they crept closer.

The harem donors followed. Some dragged their hands along the floor like chimpanzees. A few sniffed the air, testing out their heightened sense of smell. One unfortunate guy had lost his ears in the transition and now sported an oversized, furry set. They twitched with offense at Kassandra's shrieking. She finally destroyed enough of the curtain that her face could be seen again, and she took the opportunity to hiss at me, fangs extended.

"Release me, you filthy vampling!" she barked. Then she noticed the small crowd that had gathered around our booth. Wrath burned like coal in their eyes.

I held on to what was left of the curtain as Kassandra struggled to get loose. One of the half-wolves sniffed her leg that lay across the table. She kicked him in the face with her heeled boot, earning a chorus of snarls from the others.

"Looks like your new subjects have come to pay homage," I said, deciding I wouldn't need the spear, after all. I shoved her off the table. The patrons descended on her like locusts, and her screams were muffled once again.

"Jenna! Get down!" Mandy shouted from the juice bar. I followed the line her pistols drew across the room to the stage, in time to watch Marcel pop up from the DJ booth and launch a black orb into the middle of the dance floor—right between Roman and Vanessa.

Three. The countdown began automatically in the back of my mind.

Roman dropped his gun and grabbed the back of Vanessa's belt with one hand and her arm with his other.

"No!" she screamed, reaching for him as he hurled her up onto the stage.

Two.

Roman turned and glanced around the room, his eyes swelling at the hundreds of frightened patrons cowering in booths or clawing their way toward an exit. Then his gaze locked on mine. But only for a split-second before he threw himself over the grenade.

One.

The room shook, and chaos erupted anew. Everyone scattered. I scrambled out of the booth and pushed through the crowd, trying to reach Roman. It was no use. There were too many people going in too many directions.

A fur-swathed arm shoulder-checked me. Another elbowed me in the nose. I was lost in a sea of rabid half-wolves, suffocating in their collective body heat. More shots sounded, and my hands itched for my lost pistols.

Vanessa stood at the edge of the stage, her panicked gaze scouring the dance floor. Then Marcel appeared again behind her. The barrel of his pistol leveled with her head. I cried out a warning, but everything was too loud—the deafening gunfire, the screaming.

Marcel squeezed the trigger. The gun clicked, though the slide didn't open—likely a jam. He gave the pistol a disgusted look before using it to crack Vanessa across the back of the head. She dropped to her knees as Marcel leapt off the stage and disappeared into the horde.

I tried to activate my blood vision to track him, but I was too spent. Without my firearms, I was useless against an alpha werewolf anyway. The thought sent a stab of terror through my gut, and I began making my way back toward the bar.

Nicks grunted from the open doorway to the office, fending off a Free Blooder bare-knuckled before relaying an update. "Bomb squad is done, and Vlad has the system online. Help is on the way!"

I was too shocked to be relieved just yet. There was too much to process, and still so much to do. Would there be time to treat all the moon juice victims before the micromoon rose? Had Roman survived that blast? And where the hell was Marcel?

"Get back here!" Murphy yelled. I thought he was talking to me until I saw Mandy inching out from behind the juice bar. She held both pistols at the ready, hands bobbing as she followed a moving target through the crowd.

"Not a chance in hell he's getting away this time," she shouted, lips curling until her clenched teeth shone bright under the black lights over the bar.

A horn blared from the front of the building, which could only mean one thing—the entrance had been unbarricaded. Whether by the Free Blooders or Blood Vice was yet to be seen. The crowd was still too thick, but it was thinning near the back.

Marcel emerged and noticed the lack of cover right away. He snatched one of the injured half-wolves and used them as a shield as he headed for the curtained exit nearest Mandy.

"You coward!" she spat. When she made to follow him, he shoved the mutated wolf into her, knocking them both into the bar with enough force to crack the oak paneling.

Mandy paused to prop the kid up against one of the splintered barstools, blubbering a hasty apology. Then she was off.

Another spike of panic clawed at my heart, but this one came with a second wind.

"Mandy!" I tore after her. Dante snagged my arm as I passed the bar. He shoved his pistol into my empty hand.

"If you're going to run headlong into danger, at least arm yourself," he scolded me.

"Thanks," I rasped, then rushed through the back hallway and into the alley.

The cold air slapped me in the face, turning the blood splattered across my neck and the sweat in my hair to ice. I shuddered against it and blinked to clear the tears stinging the corners of my eyes.

Security lights painted the stretch of buildings in shades of gray. The space was generous for an alley, wide enough for two large vehicles to fit side by side. I searched the pools of shadows between loading docks, but I didn't see Mandy or Marcel. However, I did spot a delivery truck parked several yards down past a dumpster. I gripped Dante's pistol with both hands and headed that way.

An icy drizzle had begun in the time we'd been inside. It dotted the pavement, making it slick under my boots. I lost my footing and stumbled into the side of the dumpster, nearly tripping over Mandy in the process. She knelt, head bowed, arms curled in against her chest.

"Don't look," she hissed, turning her face away when she realized I was standing behind her. "He got me."

My heart lurched into my throat. I knelt beside Mandy and cupped her shoulder, but I was too afraid to wrest her around enough to see the damage.

"Where at?" I demanded, unable to hide the helpless quiver in my voice. "Where are you shot?"

"With the drugs," she clarified. A mournful cry spilled from her lips, bordering on a howl. "I was sober for two years, and now this." She finally held her hands out for me to see.

The moon juice didn't work exactly the same for everyone. Like the patron with the wolf ears, Mandy had gotten a little something extra. Her face was ringed in fur like the others, but the hair spreading from beneath her jacket sleeves hadn't stopped at her knuckles. Hooked claws extended from where her fingernails should have been. Her pistols lay useless at her sides.

I scanned the alley, ears pricked for any sound of movement. "Where is he?"

The delivery truck's headlights flashed on, blinding us as the engine turned over in answer to my question.

Mandy gritted her teeth and pushed off the ground on all fours, her deformed fingers scraping furiously against the pavement. She charged the truck, reaching it before Marcel could decide whether to put it in drive or reverse. And before I had a chance to aim at the bastard through the windshield.

"What are you doing?" I shouted as she climbed up the grill and onto the hood. Her clawed hands dragged down the windshield, screeching painfully as they left deep scratches.

"You piece of shit! Come out here and face me!" Mandy screamed. When she balled her fists and slammed them into the glass, Marcel hit the accelerator.

I fumbled to the opposite side of the alley, having nowhere else to go, and focused on the truck's tires. I only got off two shots before Marcel yanked hard to the right and stomped on the brake.

Mandy rolled off the hood and directly into me. My feet lifted off the ground for a second, and my back slammed against a brick warehouse wall. Dante's gun flew out of my hand, skittering across the alley and under the dumpster as we collapsed on the pavement.

"Sorry," Mandy groaned. I assumed the apology was less for involuntarily using me to break her fall and more for the fact that she was ready to do it all over again. She scrambled to her feet and took off toward the truck while I remembered how to breathe.

Marcel was trying to back out of the alley. But the truck was crooked, and he was going too fast. His side-view mirror scraped a warehouse wall and shattered as the frame broke loose. Then Mandy was on him again, her clawed fists smashing up the windshield.

The air brakes hissed, and Marcel threw the truck into drive. Mandy gripped the inside edge of the hood, anticipating an encore dismount, and continued beating the glass with her free paw—hand—extremity.

I pulled myself to my feet and sucked in a ragged breath as my spine tried to separate from my ribs. I wasn't the one trying to ride a vehicle like a rodeo bull this time, but somehow, I still felt like I'd been trampled half to death.

I staggered across the alley, toward the dumpster where I'd last seen Dante's pistol.

That's when the truck windshield finally decided to give.

Marcel was ready for it. He leapt through the gaping hole, dodging the lethal swipe of Mandy's claws, and landed in a crouched position. It was a wolf-like gracefulness that I didn't expect him to have in his human form. Mandy followed, landing on her feet this time, at least.

I realized too late that the truck was still moving.

Toward me.

Chapter Twenty-four

I grabbed the lip of the dumpster, squeezed my eyes shut, and braced for impact.

Metal scraped against metal. It screeched and squealed in my ears as I flipped ass over elbows, no longer able to tell up from down. My stomach catapulted into my throat, stifling a scream on the tip of my fangs. I had a vague memory of a carnival ride that had given me a similar jostling. Then my shoulder crunched and popped as it collided with a brick wall.

I found myself face-down on the pavement, right next to the upended dumpster now wedged between the truck and a set of stairs leading up to a loading dock. The smell of rotten produce stung my nostrils, and my ears rang. Chunks of pulpy oranges and strawberries squished beneath my sore fingers. Mixed in among the fruit scraps were hundreds of spent syringes, evidence of Marcel's crimes against science and humanity.

"Have you missed me, pet?" he crooned, sounding far too suave for a dead man.

I craned my head up and squinted through the beam of the truck headlights, straining to hear past the gravel hum of the engine. Nausea roiled through me, something that had nothing to do with the contents of the dumpster.

Mandy lay flat on her back with Marcel straddling her. He

pinned her clawed hands over her head, but when he leaned in closer, she snapped her teeth in his face. Her eyes glowed yellow. Despite the coming micromoon, it looked as if she might go full wolf at any second. She growled and thrust her hips, trying to throw him off.

"Mmmm," he purred. "You always were a feisty mutt. That's why you were my favorite. I bet if I gave you another hit or two, we could have ourselves a real nice reunion. What do you say?"

Tears streamed down Mandy's cheeks, and her screams turned into mewling sobs. The sound broke something in me—and planted something new. Something dark and vengeful.

I dragged myself up onto my hands and knees, swallowing every ache and pain that cried for mercy. My vision blurred as I patted the ground, searching for a weapon.

Mandy screamed again. My head jerked up in time to watch Marcel flip her onto her face and stomach. He pinned her hands to her lower back with one knee and fisted her ponytail, yanking it to the side.

"You're mine," he hissed in her ear. "Have you forgotten who made you? Maybe you need a reminder." He jerked her hair again, exposing more of her neck.

Mandy whimpered, which only seemed to encourage Marcel. He nuzzled her shoulder and dragged his tongue up the side of her throat before leaning back to get a firmer grasp on her. I found what I was looking for and inched closer. Every step ached. I clenched my teeth to keep from crying out.

Marcel's mouth opened wide, but before he could strike, I did.

I jammed a syringe into each of his eyes, shoving them down until my fists grazed sockets and moist flesh. A sick feeling curled through my guts again.

Marcel's gasp of surprise sounded like a death rattle as it echoed through the alley. His hands reached up slowly as if he might extract the needles. I wanted to turn away but couldn't. Mandy was still trapped beneath him, and he was still breathing. I wasn't thrilled about either.

With her arms suddenly free, Mandy rolled onto her back. I reached to help her up, but instead of accepting my hand, she slashed her claws across Marcel's exposed throat, carving trenches into his soft flesh. Blood gushed from beneath his Adam's apple, then bubbled from his lips. It splattered Mandy as she scrabbled away from him. She finally accepted my help, letting me pull her up by the wrists.

Mandy wrapped her arms around me in a crushing hug. I did my best to ignore the many bruises and possible broken ribs fighting for my attention as she trembled in my arms, her claws tucked awkwardly against my back.

Sirens wailed in the distance, growing closer as the drizzle turned into snow.

A door creaked open behind us, and then a dozen Blood Vice agents swarmed the alley.

"Skye!" Murphy shouted, pushing through the crowd. Dante and Nicks followed close behind.

"Oh, God." Mandy hid her face against my coat.

"You okay, Starsgard?" Nicks asked, taking in her blood-soaked jacket and Marcel's mutilated face and neck. "Need a medic?"

"No, just give me one of those tranquilizer darts," she said, holding out a clawed hand.

"But you're already a wolf," Nicks argued. "This ain't gonna fix that."

"Does this look like a goddamned wolf to you?" she growled and pulled away from me to show him her extra-furry face. "Put me out of my fucking misery before I die of embarrassment."

"Suit yourself." Nicks tossed her the last dart on his belt. She immediately turned the needle end down and jammed it into her thigh.

"Whoa, kid!" Murphy caught Mandy before she lost her balance, scooping her up into his arms. "You don't wanna take a nap right here, do ya?"

"Just find a nice rock to hide me under," she mumbled,

eyes drooping as the fur began to recede from her arms and face, and her claws retracted back into her standard-issue human fingertips.

Dante's hands slid up my arms, and he loosed a quivering sigh. "Paramedics are inside administering naloxone to the others. We are working against the clock, but I believe they will have adequate time to treat most if not all. Are you all right? Is that blood?" His fingertips brushed my cheek, then my hand as I reached up to tuck my hair behind my ear.

"It's not mine," I said. Dante's nose crinkled as he picked a chunk of strawberry off my chin. "That's definitely not mine."

"No injuries at all?"

"Just a little bruised," I answered, trying not to wince too hard as he embraced me. "Maybe some internal bleeding." I was sure he'd try to pull a medic off antidote duty if I confessed to anything more.

Nicks helped Murphy load Mandy into the back of an SUV. I frowned, wondering how long the tranquilizer would take to wear off. I wanted to be there when she woke up, though I had a feeling I'd still be in a sunshine coma.

"She'll be okay," Dante said, his hands moving timidly over my shoulders and back as if he were still unconvinced that *I* was okay. When he grew still, I looked up at him.

"What is it?"

The skin between his brows pinched, and he pressed his lips together. "The House Sorano vampling… *Roman*… is not well."

Someone had turned on the last-call lights in Bleeders. I squinted through the searing agony in my retinas and made my way out onto the dance floor, weaving around dazed patrons looking for their dates or a medic until I found him.

Roman lay on his back, his shoulders propped in Vanessa's lap. Bits of silver shrapnel had torn through his clothes and embedded in his pale flesh. Grayish veins spiderwebbed out from the wounds, pulsing darker with every clipped breath he took. Blood leaked from the corners of his mouth and his ears, telling me the damage was far beyond repair.

"Why did you do that?" Vanessa sobbed. "You idiot."

"I have a lot to be sorry for," Roman said, offering her a trembling grin. "But not this. Never this."

Vanessa gritted her teeth, smothering a miserable groan as Roman's breath stilled, and he relaxed in her arms. His gaze lost focus, but a soft smile curled the corners of his mouth. I turned away, suppressing a cry of my own as a strange sensation tugged at my veins and burned in my lungs.

When Raphael had killed me, and I'd been lost in that eldritch slice of no man's land between my mortal demise and rising as a vampire, I hadn't experienced my sire's death the way Dante had physically suffered Alexander's. But I imagined this is what it would have felt like if I had.

It wasn't entirely foreign—the hollow, throbbing ache in my chest. It was an echo of what I'd felt when my mother had died. The inequitable severing of a blood bond. A part of my heart and my past evaporating into the ether.

As much as I wanted to convince myself that I had no reason—no right—to feel this way about Roman, I couldn't deny it. It was biology. It was life. Some things even the undead couldn't escape.

Dante's arm slipped around my shoulders, and he pulled me against his chest.

"It was a noble death," he said gently, as much to Vanessa as to me.

"And he will be given a noble burial." Vanessa sucked back her tears as she stood and let a pair of agents pack Roman into a black body bag. Dawn was fast approaching. Grief would have to wait.

All around us, more medics and agents rounded up fallen Free Blooders and patrons alike. An injured vampire chugged from a bag of blood, and the more coherent half-wolves stood in line for a shot of naloxone.

The units Nicks had called in from Chicago and Kansas City had arrived with extra supplies. A local recruiter from Renfield found his way inside, too, and was now gathering up those who seemed less desperate to be cured before their condition became permanent.

I watched all of this from the shelter of Dante's embrace, tears clouding my eyes, and a chill settling in my bones.

"Where's Marcel?" Vanessa asked, forcing her gaze away from Roman as he was carried outside. "Please, tell me he's dead."

"Very." I shuddered at the fresh memory. It was nearly as horrific as it was satisfying. "The Free Blooders are finished."

Vanessa nodded and hugged herself.

"That *is* the new prince and princess," someone whispered behind us.

"And that one's from House Sorano."

"As in, Sorano Munitions? The vamps that make the silver bullets?"

Now that the chaos was winding down, and people weren't losing their minds over the idea of going perma-furry, the gawking and gossip had resumed.

"Your Highness." A young woman bowed as Dante glanced over his shoulder. "Thank you for coming for us," she said, revealing a stain of red across her teeth that gave her away as a vampire.

"You saved our lives," someone else called out.

"Long live House Lilith!"

More cries of gratitude bubbled up from the crowd, but they soon fused into a uniform chant.

"By the blood! By the blood! By the blood!"

The mantra sent a shiver through me when I realized how similar it sounded to Arnie's battle cry of *free the blood*. This night could have ended so differently. There was a lot to be grateful for, despite our losses.

The elevator pinged open, and several agents carried two more body bags out. Radu and Zane tailed behind them, their suits and faces spattered with blood. More stained their lips and teeth, and while an air of righteousness emanated from them, there was a distant, haunted darkness in Zane's eyes.

Radu, on the other hand, was perfectly at ease. Even more so than usual. He plucked a black handkerchief from his breast pocket and handed it to his scion, giving the vampling's mouth a pointed look. Zane scrubbed his lips and chin. He was no bloodier than his sire, but it gave him something to do besides sulk. House Vlad had an image to uphold.

"I've spoken with the queen," Radu announced as he joined us. "One of my half-sired guards will deliver a check to the furniture store that rents the neighboring warehouse. We're buying it out. All undead allies and guests are welcome to take refuge there for the day."

"You had to clear that with the queen?" Dante asked.

"Of course." Radu gave him an impish grin. "Who do you think will be reimbursing me?"

Chapter Twenty-five

The remaining moments before sunrise were a blur. We made it home, at least, where Dante and I managed to get a pot of blood and a shower in before the sun chased us under the covers. He refrained from lecturing, but I could tell from his heavy-browed appraisal of my injuries as he helped me bathe that I was in for an earful once the sun set.

After he returned a few dozen messages, anyway.

Within moments of rising Monday night, Dante's phone started ringing and wouldn't stop. Word spread fast, and every Blood Vice captain in the know wanted approval to end the Free Blooder search and put their agents back on a more manageable schedule. Then there was the council to deal with, lords and ladies seeking confirmation that Marcel Moreau and the Free Blooders had been eradicated—and validation that it was, indeed, House Lilith that had ended their reign of terror.

Not everyone was pleased by that last fact. If Ursula's lessons about modern undead politics were to be trusted, more than one fancy vamp was waiting in the wings, ready to swoop in and become the next sovereign of the American undead. Lady Beauclair—or Lady Butt Hair, as I preferred to call her—came to mind. For now, she and the other vultures were shit out of luck.

Audrey called, too, eager for an update. Dante put her on

speaker so I could listen in as she told him how well she and Levi were doing in Delph's care at Orpheus House. The prince fussed over her like a mother bat, inquiring if her accommodations were comfortable, and if she was drinking enough blood—and just whose blood was it? Was it organic? Should he send some harem donors to stay with her? Audrey seemed relieved when another call finally ended their conversation.

I left Dante to the rest of his messages and tracked down Mandy. I found her in her room, showered and changed into her angry unicorn pajamas. She lay on her stomach across her bed, watching reruns of *Henry's Courtroom*. A ball of white fluff—Sweet Pea—was nestled in the small of her back.

"They're running an all-night marathon," Mandy said by way of greeting. "Season two."

"That one's borderline pornography." I cringed as my sister appeared on screen in a bra and pencil skirt. This was the episode where she seduced a juror in order to sway the verdict in the embezzling defendant's favor—whom she was also sleeping with. Or whom her character, Anastasia van de Velde, was sleeping with, anyway.

Mandy buried her face in her pillow as things began to heat up on screen. "How can Hollywood stand to watch her suck face with these dudes all day?" she asked, her voice muffled.

I bit back the reflexive snark my new brother-in-law so often inspired and sighed. "I guess he doesn't have to anymore. What with the show being in its final season, and Laura having a bun in her oven. I imagine she'll want to be home with the baby for a while."

Sweet Pea's ears perked at the word *baby*. Audrey had called the dog all kinds of cutesy pet names. Not that the canine had answered to any of them since Audrey had risen as a vampire. Hopefully, the duchess's pooch would offer a warmer reception after her stint in Spero Heights.

"How are you feeling?" I finally asked, taking a seat on the edge of Mandy's bed. She shrugged, and then rolled onto her side, giving me her full attention.

"A little nauseous, but that's a typical withdrawal symptom. It was only one hit, so not anywhere as bad as I experienced before."

"Small mercy, huh?" I gave her a tender smile before adding, "And about Arnie?"

"What about him?" She snorted, and her gaze fell away, migrating back to the television. But not before I caught a glimpse of the yellow that flickered in her eyes. "He got better than he deserved, but I'm not sorry he's dead."

"Me either," I agreed. I dropped the subject and stretched out beside Mandy, watching the rest of the episode before heading off to meet Ursula and Dante for breakfast.

The back patio was freezing, but it stirred warm memories with the sparkling Midwinter lights that still hung from the roofline and trees. With Audrey off in Spero Heights, I had a feeling Dante would want to leave them up until she returned. Maybe we'd just go full-on eccentric and keep them brightly burning all year. It wouldn't hurt my feelings.

Ursula filled my mug to the brim with steaming blood as she scowled at me. "You were supposed to be careful," she said, eyes darting to the faint purple bruises along my wrists where Kassandra had practiced her death grip on me.

"I was," I insisted, earning a look from Dante.

"You nearly faced Marcel unarmed," he tattled. I resisted the urge to stick out my tongue at him.

"He's dead now, so what's it matter? And for the record, I didn't *need* a firearm to get the job done." My stomach still knotted when I recalled the slimy feel of his eyeballs under my fists.

"I recall." Dante cleared his throat and set his cup down on the patio table as if the memory had spoiled his appetite. "Regardless, I am relieved that this Free Blooder business is behind us."

"I, as well." Ursula sighed and pressed a delicate hand to her chest. "Though the rekindled prestige is quite welcome. House Lilith will thrive for years to come. Our improved reputation has already yielded some exciting new resources."

"Like a warehouse full of furniture, perhaps?" Dante hitched an eyebrow, but Ursula met his stare unphased.

"Among others."

"Do tell, Your Majesty. What plans do you have for this impromptu investment? Mr. Vlad will surely expect us to address the matter swiftly. Did you give it any thought at all before accepting such an absurd agreement?"

"As a matter of fact, I did." Ursula cupped her hands around the blood pot, warming them, and tapped her fingernails on the pale ceramic as her grin spread wider. "A proper queen needs a proper palace, and I intend to host the Midsummer ball here. Which will require a rather large addition, possibly two new wings—"

"I certainly doubt that will necessitate an *entire* warehouse of amenities," Dante said.

"The rest will be donated to Renfield Academy. After last night, they've had a sudden surge in wolf recruits. They'll be adding a new dormitory that will need to be furnished."

"Oh?" Dante sat forward, his eyes lighting thoughtfully. "Oh, I like that. We shall be needing more guards soon. Perhaps we could relieve them of a few senior cadets to help make room, as well."

"I'll also be adding a second harem—a private one near my new bedroom suite." Ursula didn't look away, but a pink flush filled her cheeks.

"I see." Dante tried to keep a straight face, but by now, I'd learned to read the lines at the corners of his eyes, the way they deepened ever so slightly when he was troubled. "I think a private harem is a wonderful idea, though I do have budget concerns about the size of this expansion. The estate in Evergreen will need handling, and while Mr. Vlad has agreed to take care of the staff in Texas, the property and its contents will need to be liquidated before those funds are available—"

"Never mind the budget." Ursula waved her hand dismissively. "As head of Blood Vice, you had the authority to oversee the Free Blooder assignment. But as queen, I have the authority to manage House Lilith's business dealings and finances. I've secured enough funds to cover the expansion."

"How so?" Dante asked, his voice pitching higher as if he might come unglued at any second. He'd been holding everything together since the Evergreen incident, and that control had kept him focused. Grounded. Now, Ursula was finding her footing as queen and complicating matters.

"Well…" She licked her lips and blinked a few times as her eyes watered. "I sold the West Coast estate."

Dante sucked in a sharp breath. "The home you shared with Morgan? To whom?"

"Vlad. He's going to open a second location for Bleeders," Ursula explained, her voice rigid. "And he paid a very handsome price. To be fair, I had just agreed to comp him for the vampire sleepover. The new club will also employ some of those displaced from Texas."

"A bold and admirable move, cousin."

"Don't look so surprised." She sniffed and gave him a dry grin. Dante chuckled and picked up his cup, silently toasting her before taking a sip.

"We still have many matters to attend to," he said. His gaze shifted to me, and those lines near his eyes deepened again. "Least of which is locating the remaining House Lilith heir and determining whether she poses any threat."

I made a noncommittal sound in the back of my throat and swallowed the last of my blood. I hadn't forgotten about the mystery woman from my vision. After Kassandra's reveal, I had to reevaluate the possibilities, and now I was certain I knew who it was. I just didn't know how to tell Dante and Ursula. It didn't feel like my truth to share.

The wind howled and tugged at my hair. I turned my face into it and breathed in the pine-scented night. Along the line of evergreens that bordered the property, lit gently by the Midwinter light display, a trio of silhouettes appeared.

"Call me crazy," I said, "but I don't think we have anything to worry about."

Dante stood, knocking over his chair. "That's—is that?"

"It is," Ursula answered, rising slowly. I stood and moved

instinctively to my sire's side, following as she stepped off the patio.

The figure in the center held up a gloved hand, directing us to stay put as Clyde and Holland escorted her across the lawn. Another guard called to Dante from the poolside entrance, but the prince waved him off, unable to peel his gaze away from our late-night visitors.

Her face was hidden behind a lace veil, and she wore a simple, wool trench coat. It was the ruby and onyx crown clenched between her hands that gave her away. After that, the proud tilt of her chin and the regal square of her shoulders became obvious. There was no doubt who she was.

"Your Majesty." Ursula choked out the greeting as she bowed. Dante and I stooped low behind her, rising only when she commanded us to.

"Enough of that. Get up," Lili hissed. Her gaze narrowed on Ursula. "A queen bows to no one," she added.

Ursula's breath quivered. "But you're—"

"Dead," Lili finished. "And I intend to stay that way."

"Why? How?"

"I share a lifeblood bond with Clyde," Lili confessed, her gaze flitting appreciatively to her werewolf companion. "I barely escaped the manor after it was bombed. I had to bury myself in the mud of a creek bed and wait for him to come to me." She peeled back her lace veil, and I bit my tongue to keep from gasping. Burn scars covered half her face, though she seemed much further along in her recovery than she had in my vision.

"Grandsire." Ursula clutched her hands over her stomach and swallowed. Tears lined her lashes and warbled her voice. "We have a healthy harem and the very best doctors. I'll oversee your recovery personally."

"Child." Lili sighed and cupped Ursula's cheek. "I have been planning my forever rest for some time. I had not intended for such a flashy exit, but it will offer certain advantages while I put my final affairs in order."

"Final affairs?" Ursula reached for Lili's hand as it slipped away from her face. "But you're our queen. We need you."

"Nonsense." Lili loosed a clipped laugh. "Holland has been my eyes and ears. You have everything you need in each other." Her piercing stare migrated to Dante and then to me. "You're not surprised to see me, vampling," she said, an amused note entering her voice.

"I…uh…" Didn't know what to say. Not without incriminating myself or the others. "I suspected you might still be alive—Your Majesty," I finally said, settling on a vague slice of truth.

"Did you come to this conclusion before or after drinking my sire's lifeblood?"

"After," I answered, abandoning the urge to lie through

my teeth. Lili's brows arched, but she seemed more surprised by my honesty than the confirmation that I possessed the Eye of Blood.

"I don't know how, and it doesn't matter," she said. "You have been blessed by Lilith's blood. Let that be all the explanation you ever need to offer those who question your gifts or your worth. You have earned your place in this family. All three of you have," she added, her gaze encompassing Ursula and Dante again. "My death rehearsal has gifted a level of peace and confidence not many sires can claim before leaving their children to take on the world without them."

Dante pressed a hand to his chest, gratitude and sorrow wetting his eyes. "How may we be of service in your last endeavors?"

Lili smiled at him, the gesture tugging stiffly at the scarred side of her face. "Grant my wolves extended leave and then meet me at Lilith's tomb in six weeks. Bring this with you," she said, handing the crown to Ursula, who accepted it and began to bow.

"Yes, my queen."

Lili's gloved fingers slipped under Ursula's chin, interrupting the genuflection.

"*You* are queen now. And you will be magnificent."

Chapter Twenty-six

Six weeks later.

"Special delivery." Belinda entered Dante's office with a stack of mail clutched in one hand. It was good to finally have her back from Texas. The house just didn't run as smoothly under anyone else's supervision, and she'd already memorized the names of the new donors we'd brought back from Denver.

Even Ursula was glad for Dante's assistant's return. Belinda was her right-hand gal when it came to fine-tuning the renovation plans. She knew which companies were vamp-friendly, and who all to call for recommendations for everything from landscapers to gallery brokers. And she'd convinced Ursula to add a new office for me in the north wing, across the hall from the gym.

I never dreamed I'd settle for being a pencil pusher. But even with every crucial Free Blooder having been rounded up by Blood Vice, Ursula was dead set on keeping me out of the field. Though she wasn't entirely incapable of compromise. I got to keep my badge on a special consultation basis, and I was given some clerical responsibilities, i.e. all the bullshit paperwork Dante didn't want.

Hence the new office.

In the meantime, the prince shared his workspace. It had seemed like a pretty sweet deal at first—especially the nights when the only thing that got done on his desk was me. But soon enough, the files and forms piled up, and we had to buckle down.

I'd had no idea just how many things in undead society required the review and approval of House Lilith. Whenever the BATC needed funding for new textbooks and equipment. Anytime a Blood Vice field office wanted to hire new agents or office staff. Sires nominating scions for the training program, and blood finishing schools looking to place graduates with noble households. Dozens of letters and requests flooded in nightly.

Belinda gave my bin of completed work an approving nod as she set the mail on the corner of Dante's desk. I snatched it up before he could, earning an annoyed glare.

"I do not believe I relinquished post duties to you, Mrs. Lilosa."

"I think relinquishing my panties to you before dawn this morning means I can take a peek at the mail if I want, *Mr. Lilosa.*" I blew a raspberry at him and stood to stretch my legs. "Besides, this one is addressed to me."

I held up a yellow envelope dotted with baby booties and cringed just a tiny bit at the return address label marked with a curly S for Steckleman. I used Dante's letter opener to slice through the pastel paper and dug out an embossed piece of cardstock. The cursive at the top read: *Debuting this August: Hazel Star Steckleman.*

A girl.

My sister was having a girl, and she was giving her my middle name and Mandy's nickname.

I swallowed the lump climbing up my throat and skimmed the rest of the page filled with details for a baby shower coming up in May, two months from now. I wouldn't be able to go, of course. Being dead and all. But Mandy would. And we could have a second party later that night, with just the three of us. Because I fully intended to fly out to California to rub my sister's swollen belly.

I set the invitation aside and flipped through the rest of the mail—though now it was more to torment Dante, who hadn't stopped frowning at me since Belinda had left the room.

"Junk, junk, junk," I muttered, tossing each piece in a haphazard pile on the desk. Dante propped his fist under his chin and huffed. His dark curls hung loosely around his temples, giving his brooding pout a swoon-worthy flavor that only encouraged me to vex him further. "*Ooooh*, furniture sale."

"Give me that," he grumbled, swiping the sale flyer out of my hand and feeding it directly to the paper shredder. The renovations wouldn't be complete for another month, so all of the furniture Ursula had purchased from Vlad's warehouse tenant was packed up in portable storage units that lined the driveway.

I snickered and then paused on a glossy postcard for the grand reopening of Nightfall Opera House. I read the main attraction three times before turning it toward Dante. "Did you know about this?"

He blinked at the bold announcement stating that the Queen of House Lilith would be singing *Coeurs Nocturnes* after a performance by the Le Mort Symphony Orchestra. "Huh." Dante scratched the stubble along his jaw. "Ursula did mention something about promising Vlad the impossible. And here I thought she was referring to intimate relations."

I made a face and glanced back down at the mail in my hands, trying to clear that picture from my mind. After my sip of Ursula's blood, I'd had all the visions of her getting her freak on that I could handle.

Speaking of visions, Audrey had talked me into agreeing to a more regular schedule with Dr. Delph. Over the phone, of course. The duchess waxed poetic about how much good he was doing her and Levi, and even Mandy had resumed sessions with him.

Our chats also yielded some useful information about the doctor who had stolen Vin's research. The man had abducted a vampling in hopes of creating a steady supply of his new experimental cancer drug. He'd only gotten the chance to treat a single patient in the trial, a teenage boy who had then busted the vampling out of lockup. Lifeblood bonds were tricky that way. The vamp turned the doctor into a chew toy before finding her way to Spero Heights.

So, no vampire secrets being published in human medical journals, and no council assassins after my neurotic ex. Crisis averted. Mandy relayed the information to Collins, and he passed it along once Vin regrew his backbone and checked in. I somehow doubted I had to worry about him attempting any more experiments with vampire blood.

I dropped the rest of the mail onto Dante's desk as the alarm on his watch beeped. He gave the clock on the wall an anxious glance and stood suddenly, no longer interested in the bills or our playful banter.

"It's nearly time. Perhaps I should change," he said, looking down at his long-sleeved Henley and jeans.

"Do you really want to go kayaking and cave trotting in a three-piece?" I hitched an eyebrow at him before turning to fetch Alexander's temporary urn off the bookshelf.

The late prince's ashes had finally been sorted out from the carnage in Evergreen. We would be laying him to rest with Lili tonight, alongside his queen as they had always intended. Dante took the urn from me and sighed, the inner corners of his brows pulling upward with his melancholy. He was still in mourning, and I imagined he would be for some time to come. But honoring this final wish of Alexander's was a step in the right direction.

"Good evening, Your Highnesses," Ambrose called as we exited the office. "Are you ready for the big night?"

Dante dipped his chin and held the urn tighter to his chest. "As ready as any scion can be to lay their sire to rest."

"And as ready as any sire can be to have their vampling scion home, safe and sound," I added, reminding him of the good we had to look forward to tonight, too.

Audrey and Levi were returning. Just in time for the field trip to Lilith's tomb.

Ursula appeared in the foyer, wearing a sweater dress and hiking boots. Her red hair was pinned up in a French twist, the ends sculpted to fit inside the band of her silver and sapphire crown. She carried a wooden box that I suspected held Lili's ruby and onyx headpiece. The ceremonial dagger was sheathed in the belt around her hips.

"Almost time," she said, her voice hardly more than a whisper.

Tonight, she would be made queen again. Officially. At least among our family. As far as everyone else knew, we were just interring the late prince's ashes in the family tomb.

Headlights flickered through the front windows of the

foyer. Dante's sagging shoulders squared. He set the urn on top of the piano, and two guards pulled open the front doors, revealing Audrey and Levi as they exited the back seat of a sedan.

The duchess's wolf sported a sleek steel prosthetic with a C-shaped foot, and he seemed to be well-adjusted to it. He climbed out first and offered Audrey a hand before running around to the back of the vehicle to help unload their luggage. The look Audrey gave him was filled with enough heat to melt the ice off an igloo. When she noticed us watching from the front porch, her mouth fell open in a startled *o*.

"Goodness," she giggled, tugging at the silk scarf around her neck. "I hope we didn't keep y'all waiting too long."

"Not at all." Dante rushed down the steps, then hesitated as if recalling how she'd reacted after Vlad's men had recovered her from the Free Blooder den. But Audrey didn't recoil from him this time. She threw her arms around his neck and squeezed until Dante grunted in surprise.

"Sorry!" she squeaked. "I'm just so happy to see you. All of you," she added, hugging me next, and then bowing to Ursula. The queen wasn't big on the touchy-feely to begin with, but the fancy crown added an extra layer of untouchability.

"Chop chop, children," Ursula said as Murphy's SUV pulled in behind Audrey's car. Mandy had already claimed the front seat. I could see her crumpled bottom lip through the windshield and guessed that her plan to convince Murph to let her drive had been foiled.

Dante slipped back inside the house to collect Alexander's ashes and his coat, while Levi and Audrey loaded into the very back seat of the SUV, snuggling in, all nice and cozy with one another. Ursula clicked her tongue at their blatant display of affection.

"She's going to spoil the brutal reputation you've earned House Lilith with all this cuddly bunny business," the queen complained. I turned to grin at my sire.

"I hope she does." My smile stretched wider at her exasperation. "We could stand to kill a few people with kindness. Don't you think?"

"I swear," Ursula balked, "you've learned nothing since your mortal death." She thrust the crown box at me and climbed inside the SUV, leaving me to wait alone for Dante.

My teeth chattered as a stiff breeze blew across the lawn, bringing with it the damp, grassy scent of spring on the horizon. The nights were getting shorter. I could feel the waning darkness like a counterweight to the life swelling in the earth. As a human, I hadn't paid much attention to the cycles of nature—at least, not beyond the weather segment of the morning news that told me whether I needed an umbrella or scarf.

Now the moon and sun were an integral part of my life—or unlife, rather. Every bit as relevant as the tides of joy and grief that had washed me up on this strange shore. And yet, I kept wandering back into the surf. I kept choosing to pick myself up and move forward. No matter how often I got knocked down or how much it hurt. That was the beauty of life. And sometimes even death.

Ursula was wrong. I'd learned plenty since becoming a vampire. That my mistakes could only define me if I let them. That immortal didn't mean infallible. And that the past was a miserable place to dwell for anyone, but especially for creatures who left more history behind than most.

That Ursula was ready to share her voice with the world again gave me hope that she was still capable of learning these lessons, too.

"All set?" Dante asked, stopping beside me. I nodded, and he opened his free arm, gesturing toward the open SUV door, keeping his other wrapped around Alexander's urn. "After you, Mrs. Lilosa."

We climbed onto the bench seat behind Murphy and Mandy and buckled up. It was a long drive to the cave, but with Dante's fingers laced with mine, and our family finally reunited, it could have taken all night, and I wouldn't have cared.

This was exactly where I belonged. Where every decision

I'd ever made had been leading. Call it rags to riches—or penal to regal—no matter how you sliced it, I was a kickass vampire princess who was here to stay.

There would be more criminals and bureaucrats seeking to overthrow House Lilith. More problems needing to be solved, and battles needing to be won. Of that, I was certain.

But for once, I could finally trust that everything was unfolding as it should.

The blood will run again in…

BLOOD SHOTS

A BLOOD VICE SHORT STORY COLLECTION

Coming Soon

Missing Jenna and the House Lilith gang?
Sate your lingering bloodlust with this collection of
bite-sized shorts from the world of Blood Vice!

Including:
Blood and Honey
(a Mandy and Cable spin-off short)
Bloodnog and Mistletoe
(Vampy Holidays from House Lilith)
Mother of Eternal Blood
(Lilith comes to America)
Bloodhound
(another Mandy and Cable adventure)
Lifeblood
(Imbolc at House Lilith in 2120)
The Blood Will Run
(mythic vampire poetry)

ACKNOWLEDGMENTS

I'm sure I sound like a broken record on this page, always thanking the same people. What can I say? When I find a solid team, I stick to them like glue. So, at the risk of repeating myself for the 8th and final book in the Blood Vice series, here are the amazing people who helped make this book and so many others possible: my sweet husband, Paul, who is my number one proofreader and sounding board that I bounce all my ideas off; my loveable kiddo, Xavier, who fills my writing breaks with hugs and smooches and previews of his written masterpieces; Chelle Olson, my incredibly patient and much appreciated editor, who polishes my prose and makes it shine; Rebecca Frank, my wonderful cover designer, whose work is always spot-on and dazzling; my gorgeous sister, Justina, who was the cover model for the Blood Vice series; Hollie Jackson, whose lovely voice brings Lana to life in the audiobooks; THE professor, George Shelley, who is always eager and willing to proofread my work and offers excellent feedback and encouragement; the Four Horsemen of the Bookocalypse, my awesome critique group that I consider as much family as colleagues; the Grim Readers gang on Facebook, who share my macabre sense of humor and offer inspiration and camaraderie; and, last but certainly not least, YOU, dear reader.

Thank you for spending your valuable time in my little world of make believe. I hope you enjoyed Jenna's adventures. She and the gang will return briefly in *Blood Shots* (The Blood Vice Short Story Collection), and then I'll be traveling back in time to a new world, the city of Late Boston, for a steampunk trilogy that begins with *Cursed Cogs*. I hope to see you there!

ABOUT THE AUTHOR

USA Today bestselling fantasy author **Angela Roquet** is a great big weirdo. She lives in Missouri with her husband and son in a house stuffed with books, toys, skulls, owls, and glitter-speckled craft supplies. She's a member of SFWA and HWA, as well as the Four Horsemen of the Bookocalypse, her epic book critique group, where she's known as Death. When not swearing at the keyboard, she enjoys boating with her family at Lake of the Ozarks and reading books that raise eyebrows. You can find Angela online at
www.angelaroquet.com

If you enjoyed this book, please leave a review.
Your support and feedback are greatly appreciated!